u n b a b b l i n g

reyoung
unbabbling

Dalkey Archive Press

Library of Congress Cataloging-in-Publication Data
    ReYoung, 1950-
        Unbabbling / ReYoung. — 1st ed.
            p.   cm.
        ISBN 1-56478-164-X (pbk. : alk. paper)
        I. Title
    PS3568.E94U5   1997   813'.54—dc21   97-23672

This publication is partially supported by a grant from the
Illinois Arts Council, a state agency.

Dalkey Archive Press
Illinois State University
Campus Box 4241
Normal, IL 61790-4241

to adria

this is sgrizzi's book

who are you talking to?

I

unbabbling

/ /
I knew I shouldn't have gone to that goddamn party, but I
was feeling cocky, confident, sure of myself and my success.
With a drink in my hand and the stars just beginning to
show in the night I strolled among the concrete pillars and
iron beams, watching the others watch me, watching their
eyes, their mouths, the gestures they made, watching to
see how much they knew, how much they might have
guessed. That damned Lenore. She was so cool, so smart,
she had it all figured out. What a fucking stroke of genius
to have the dinner at an actual construction site, to create
that image in everyone's mind, so they'd associate me, my
name, with all that work going on.

There's only one thing, Harry. You've got to start building up some kind of pedigree. You can't just tell people you
started at the bottom like some clown off the street. They'll
want to know where that bottom is. They'll want to know
where you went to school, who you know, all your friends,
family. They'll want to know what kind of trouble you've
been in, how you got out. That's why you have to tell me
now, Harry, so I can help you later. Where is that bottom?
How far down do we have to go? /
/ /
A few weeks earlier I stood at the window in Lenore's

office, watching the cars moving in the street a hundred stories below, watching the steady trickle of pedestrians on the sidewalk, all so tiny, so small and far away, all going about their business, going to work, going home, going to eat lunch in some toxic little dive, going to some squalid little slab to fuck and empty themselves of their loneliness and despair, going to see the doctor, to the hospital, to die.

Lenore sat at her desk, the smoke from her cigarette drifting in a slant of sunlight, her eyes bright, green, those sudden hot slices of lime that made me blink, look away, look for a place to hide. Yeah, sure, I could have excused myself, gone to the bathroom and splashed cold water on my face, combed my hair and straightened my tie. She'd know I was stalling for time, trying to come up with some lie. Of course I was going to lie. What else could I do but lie? Even if it was God, I'd lie. Don't overdo it, that's all. She wasn't asking for my whole goddamn life story. Just a plausible chain of events to explain what the hell I was doing here now. /// /// C'mon, Harry, wake up! The torch sputtered and flared next to my face. The guy above me grunted, heaved a stone into my arms, I turned, heaved it into the arms of the man below me, some sick, scrawny little fuck with a scraggly beard and a hard little pot belly swelling out of bare, bony ribs. The weight was too much for him, it almost bent him double. I heard him gasp, groan, knew he'd torn something inside, another wound that wouldn't heal, another poisonous little wellspring leaking pus and blood. I took another stone, passed it down, the little guy gasped, staggered, dumped the stone at the feet of the guy below him. Poor fuck, he wasn't going to last the week. He'd crawl off in some corner and die and that'd be the last anyone ever heard of him. You've gotta be strong, you've gotta be quick,

you've gotta watch out for yourself. I liked the weight and the heft of the stone. I liked to hold it in my arms. I liked to feel its rough edges lacerating my naked skin. It made the stone real. It reminded me of where I was and how much I wanted to get out of there. I looked down at the bright red trickle of blood drying in the limestone dust on my stomach and I laughed. I felt tough, I felt strong, I felt like I could endure this as long as I had to. On the wall next to my face the torch flared again, smoked and sputtered. I turned, reached for another stone, passed it down, I was already thinking how goddamn good that beer was gonna taste when I got off work at night. //////////////////////////
///
God, that first cold beer, you can already taste it going down, you can feel that cold slug in your belly. Just the thought of it's like an ice-cold shot of morphine hitting your vein. All your joints, all your tired and aching muscles begin to relax and sag in a great big sigh of relief, in a pronouncement of faith in God and existence. Jesus Fucking Christ In Heaven, It's Friday! Even if you have to work tomorrow, even if you haven't had a Saturday off in six months, right now it's Friday and Friday isn't a day for working, it's a day for goofing off, for laughing and getting drunk with your friends. And oh God! Oh Man! That beer's gonna taste so good! Everybody's talking about it up and down the line, they're starting to loosen up and get in the mood, they're pushing and shoving each other like a bunch of kids, they're tossing around blocks of stone like beach balls. Even the foreman's looking at his watch. He's a big, mean son-of-a-bitch with hairy arms and a rock jaw, and he's got a shitload of things on his mind, deadlines, payrolls, a shipment of stone that's two days behind. He's growling and muttering to himself and everybody around, fucking management doesn't know a goddamn thing about

efficiency and getting the job done. Yeah, sure, if he had a couple more guys like Harry. But ol' Harry's one of a kind.

Alright you fuck-ups! he hollers in a voice worn with whiskey, tobacco, years of cursing the boss above and the man below. But you better get some sleep tonight because tomorrow I'm gonna bust your fucking ass! And boom! Just like that! Everybody's laughing and shouting and slapping each other on the back. Yayyyy, it's Fridayyyy! Let's go, buddy! C'mon pal! Hey Charlie, y'hear? Harry's buying! Yayyyy, Harry! And man oh man! That first beer is going to taste so goddamn good! That first cold beer! Even after the waitress clunks that big sweaty mug of golden frothy brew down on the table in front of you and you wrap your rough, worn hand around the ice-cold glass and raise it up to your mouth and swallow and swallow and swallow that cold carbonated salty sea down your throat and into your stomach and come up gasping for air, Oh God! Oh Man! That's so good! I can't breathe! Hey! Mabel! Bring us another round! And you're talking about work and the job and Jesus Fucking Christ! This fucking red-hot little babe who just this minute waltzed into the bar in this tiny fucking red outfit with her tits and ass busting out everywhere. Geez, Harry, look! look! look! What the hell's she got under there, fucking water balloons? And you're staring at this chick and still shaking your head over how good that first beer tasted, even now, this very moment you're knocking down the second and calling for a third. Yeah! Over here! Another round! And a bag of peanuts! And some chips! And turn up the TV! So goddamn loud in here I can't hear myself drink! And oh my God, lookit that! Now the chick in the little red outfit's dancing on the fucking tabletop, you can see her goddamn cunt hairs curling out of her panties, her top's soaked with sweat and spilled beer, her nipples are erect. Whooee! Man! This is what it's all about, guys! Right

here! Right now! Me and you and Harry! Busting our ass
all day, getting the job done. An' you think they notice up in
the front office? Fuck no, they don't notice, they don't give a
fucking goddamn if we rot in hell s'long's they get their
goddamn money. Ah, fuck 'em, right Harry? What the hell's
it matter? S'right here! S'right now! S'life an' work an'
friends! And you're shaking your head, yesh, yesh, yesh,
and dumping money on the table for 'nother round. An' a
coupla shots of whishkey this time! By now everybody'sh
drunk on their ash, everybody'sh tired and red-eyed and
the first beer'sh so long gone you can't even begin to remember how many or how long. And the chick in the little
red outfit's sloppy and laughing between a coupla big goons
at the bar, only now her mouth looks too wide and her
nose's too big and she's got mascara and grease paint
smeared all over her face like a fucking clown. And the
bottles and glasses in front of you are swimming with
burnt matches, cigarette butts and gobs of phlegm. And
you're thinking maybe you oughta get going soon. But the
waitress is setting down another cold one, and it feels so
good, so cold, it's the cold you want. You press the cold per-
spiring bottle against your forehead, your temple, your
cheek. Suddenly you realize you're past your limit, you're
going to be sick, you've gotta get out of here right now,
you've gotta go home and get some sleep. But it isn't sleep,
it's right now, it's this moment and these friends. C'mon,
Harry, don't be such a goddamn pussy. Ha ha, Harry's a
pussy. They're all giving you a hard time, they don't want
you to leave, they're trying to hold you back. And you know
something's going to give, something's going to let go. But
it isn't you or your buddies, it's the table behind you that
explodes, knocking over chairs, smashing bottles and
glasses. You turn around just in time to see a big knuckly
fist smack into a fat drunken face, noses and mouths are

getting twisted up like silly putty, foreheads and cheeks split open, revealing smears of ketchup and hard white plastic underneath. //////////////////////////////// /// That doesn't sound like any fun, Harry. The girl's voice closed around me like a soft warm bath, her face an amorphous blob of flesh floating in a halo of candlelight. I raised the coffee to my mouth. It was bitter, cold. Then I remembered. I was staggering down the street, knocking into people, peering into shop windows, restaurants, all-night diners and cafes. There was an open door, I smelled incense, spice. It was dark, quiet. I lurched inside, collapsed in an empty booth. Then the girl was standing over me with a cup in her hand. You look like you need this, she said. I thought she was the waitress, I was expecting her to pull out a pad and pencil. Do you mind if I sit down? she said. I nodded at the other seat, Yeah, sure, sit down, not really wanting her to, wanting to be alone, miserable, any other time maybe, but not tonight.

Her name was Cassa. I saw you when you came in, she said. You looked like a monster. I like monsters. What's your name, monster? I told her my name. Ha, Harry! she laughed. That's no name for a monster. I don't think you are a monster. I liked that right away, the way she kept calling me monster in that kind of tough, teasing voice. I liked the way she looked too, not just the leather jacket and torn jeans, but the coarse black hair cropped close to her skull like a cowl. It made her face and her features larger, eminent, gleaming, like a prisoner of war, like a refugee. Yeah, sure, a refugee from what? Too much money? Class? The suffocating little mausoleum she shared with mummy and daddy in some upscale bullshit high-rise in the Heights? I tried to get a better look at her eyes, her mouth, tried to imagine what it'd be like to kiss her lips, her breasts, to lie down in bed with her and make her moan. Make myself moan more likely. I felt the nausea rising again in my stomach, groaned.

Ooo, she mocked me. You do sound like a monster.

Yeah, sure, I'm a monster, I said. At the moment I just wanted to drop my head back on the table and die. But she wouldn't allow that, would she? She wanted me to keep talking, tell her about myself.

Like what? I said.

I don't know what, Harry. The usual, like how's a monster live? In a cave? In a hole in the ground?

Something like that, I said, struggling with another wave of nausea. I was starting to feel sober now but my head was pounding like a fucking jack hammer and some kind of chemical reaction was taking place in my stomach. I picked up my coffee, examined the oil slick floating on top, set it back on the table. ///////////////////////////////// /// You don't think in terms of day or night. It's always dark. Not a healthy dark, not a dark like the night, but a poisonous dark, a dark suffused with glowing clouds of nitrogen and sulfur. The torches smoke and sputter in your face. The air is thick, heavy, hot. Your breath burns in your lungs. The sweat pours down your back, your chest. You're worn out, filthy. All you wanta do is lie down and die where you fall, but there aren't any coffee breaks, no union stewards, time and a half, health benefits, retirement fund. Only now and then something happens up the line, a wall collapses, there's an accident. For a while the whole line comes to a standstill, the men sway and rock on their feet, their eyes glazed, their bodies white with lime, chunks of stone still clutched in the thick, rough hands hanging at their sides, everybody worn out, weary, beat to death, wondering how much longer this little respite is going to last. Then the foreman's at your side, screaming, furious, red in the face, You fucking assholes! Get back to work! Now!

At night you go home to your slab, your coffin in the wall, just yank another brick out of the stack, stick in hot water, electricity and a piece of glass so you can stare into the soup. Occasionally the sun glows behind the clouds like a dirty, fly-specked lightbulb. Who knows, maybe you even try to brighten the place up a little, buy a plant, one of those dark green, bitter things that cling to walls, cliffs, thriving on chemicals, the smothering red and yellow clouds of pollution pouring out of the smokestacks and chimneys. A week later it turns yellow and collapses like a poor little canary sent down into the mines to sip the poison air from the broken earth and chirp a final warning to the men working near. If you open the window the noise from the street's too loud, the apartment fills with exhaust fumes, it makes you sick, you go to bed with a headache, feeling nauseous, lie in the dark waiting for the lights to go down and the movie to start. All you get is static, shadowy faces moving in a crackly blue and white background, like the sound of the rain falling down the ventilator shaft. Maybe you roll a joint, pour a drink, light up a cigarette, jerk off to a skin magazine. Maybe you sit up all night and drink and smoke and stare into the dark until you're so fucked up you can finally pass out, fall asleep. Who knows, maybe you even have a secret life, ambition, every night after work you pick up a pencil, pen, furiously scribble notes, ideas, scraps of dreams. If only you had the opportunity you could do something great with your life, you could be somebody. At some point you wake up on the line again, passing stones down the soot-blackened lacework of archways, buttresses and columns that open onto and abut nothing but darkness and night. The scaffolding's old, rotten, it creaks beneath your weight. Every time you hear a

crash or an explosion there's a moment of horror while your brain frantically sorts through all the possible or rather impossible scenarios, is it me? am I the one? am I falling? Then you hear the scream, like a hot spindle of glass stretching out across the night before it cools and snaps and the sound disappears altogether. For a moment there's nothing, not even silence. And then the noise begins again, somebody bangs an empty bucket on the ground, somebody coughs, somebody takes a final drag on his cigarette, somebody else grunts, shoulders a stone. Maybe a week later somebody says, Poor Joe, and somebody else says, Yeah, poor Joe. And maybe a month later somebody else says, Hey, remember that guy Joe? Whatever happened to Joe? After that nobody says anything. You just cinch up your asshole, grab another stone, try to forget about what lies out there beyond the torchlight, beyond the last particles of light, when the darkness opens its jaws and roars. ///
///
I stopped talking, horrified at myself and my words and afraid to look into Cassa's eyes, to see there her revulsion, disgust. What is this guy, some low-life creep off the street? But it wasn't true, she didn't despise me. She turned in bed, her eyes damp with salt water, tears, maybe even love, was it possible, already love? Poor monster, she said, putting her arms around me, closing me in the warmth and smell of her breasts. /////////////////////////////////////
///
Yeah, but that wasn't the first night, was it? Because the first night we just met and I was feeling so bad. I remember we took a cab, and the wet streets, and the cold leather seats—that smell of mildew, puke, cheap perfume, the residual bouquet of the cabbie's past fares. Then we were going up the stairs, I was fumbling with the key, the lock, oh

yeah, right, right, right, that's right, we did go back to my place that night. Although how the hell I managed. I remember I tried to make some excuse, I didn't feel good, the place was a mess, maybe we should make it some other time. But she wasn't buying it. She said, What's the matter, Harry? You afraid of catching a disease? You have somebody waiting for you in there? A girlfriend? A guy with a gun?

I felt something hot and heavy slide through my bowels. What if she was one of those crazy chicks in the paper, they pick up guys, drug them, subject them to all kinds of humiliation, torture, shit and piss on your face, slice you up with a razor blade, cut off your dick, then leave you hogtied and howling with pain, horror, that still prescient grief when you began to regain consciousness, realize what'd been done to you—even then that little bit of comic relief playing in your brain, they can't fix it, can they? make it better again?—all to avenge some old slight or suffering, some stepbrother, uncle, even Daddy creeping into the bedroom at night, fucking her in the ass, the mouth, calling her names, you little bitch, you whore, then pleading with, wheedling, threatening her, please don't tell anyone baby, you little slut, I'll kill you if you tell anyone. But that was nuts, wasn't it? Just my own paranoia. She was just a normal girl with normal urges like anybody else. She pushed open the door, turned on the light, laid bare my cave, my dragon's den. Yeah, sure, let's get carried away again. It was just a lousy dump like anywhere else.

Ooo, the monster's lair, she purred in an absurd puppet's voice, picking at things like a prissy interior decorator, shuffling through a pile of papers on the kitchen table, the only table. What is this stuff, Harry? Bills? Advertisements? You gonna make paper airplanes? She picked up a page, started to read aloud. /////////////////////////

///
We stood in the tall grass, and we listened and we watched
and we waited, and we knew where everyone was, and we
knew what they were doing. We knew all the sounds, and
we knew all the signals. We knew the grasshopper's wings
winding and unwinding in the grass, and we knew the column of ants moving in the grass. We knew the steady trickling sound that follows death and the smell of death, and
we knew the trickling and carrying away of the parts and
the remains of death. Even in the middle of the day when it
was the hottest, when the dust settled to the earth and the
sun sizzled in the trees and in the grass, in the middle of
the day when our eyes began to close and we relaxed a
little and thought about sleep, even then we listened and
we watched and we waited. And we always knew where
everyone was. And we always knew what they were doing.
No one ever said, Hey, where's the elephant? Or, What are
the flamingos up to? Because we all knew, without opening
our eyes or looking in their direction. We could feel their
presence and the void their presence filled. As if something
wanted the elephant there, beneath the ancient baobab
tree, fanning itself with its great leafy ears, tracing butter-
flies in the thick floury dust at its feet with the tip of its
great trunk. Or over there, at the edge of the marsh, the
vast and unimaginable flocks of flamingos perched like
pink satin pillows on bamboo reeds, the vast and unimaginable ballet of flamingos with necks crossing and uncross-
ing in an endlessly replicated entrechat. Or there, rumi-
nating in the louvered sunlight of the dried cane, the
zebras, as if the whole concept of duplicity and opposing
forces, of chiaroscuro, good and evil, even the ragged tearing apart of night from day could not exist without their
striped hides. And there, over there, lying in the shade of
the acacia, there, mindlessly gorging itself on a bloody

brown sack of bones beneath the sweet yellow fragrance and the thorns of the acacia, there, over there, watching you and watching nothing from the shadows of the acacia /
//
Yeah, I know, you've heard this story a hundred times before, the lion, of course it's the lion. But I was enthralled, the sound of Cassa's voice lulled me further into my drunken stupor. The tough talk and hard edge had softened in her throat, she breathed into the words and made them her own. Hey! That's private! I cried, rousing myself from my daze, tearing the page from her hand, putting on a little melodrama of my own. But she just laughed at me, bared her perfect teeth, I told you monsters were more interesting, Harry.

Suddenly my name sounded funny in her voice, simultaneously full and hungry. She pressed her body against mine, raised her mouth to be kissed. I don't know if I can do this, I said. I haven't even taken a shower. Then she was pulling up her t-shirt, unbuttoning her jeans. I was instantly hard, aching to be inside her, she was already wet, gushing around my finger, then my cock, we were on the bed, fucking, and it felt so good, I wanted to make it last, but my head was starting to pound again, the blood was slamming in my brain, then I was coming, I heard her moan, laugh, her teeth bared, her eyes bright, shining, like someone high on cocaine, like someone lying, I didn't think I was going to come, she gasped, and then, when you were, I was too.

I wanted to say something, tell her she was full of shit, that I didn't trust her. I wanted to tell her how grateful I was, that I wanted to believe in and love her. But I felt so tired, all I could do was lie next to her and stare at her mouth, her breasts, while she played with my hair, the amulet at my neck. She ran her hand over my stomach,

chest, fingering my scars. What are these, Harry? More
monster work? In the dark? In the night? When nobody can
see? Something like that, I mumbled, my voice slurred, my
thoughts beginning to tumble and blur, my mind disintegrating into sleep, oblivion, work only two-three hours
away. Then she was out of bed and getting dressed while I
watched, dazed, trying to fix in my brain the back of her
neck, her bare shoulders, the knobs of her spine, that last
little wiggle of her ass when she pulled up her pants, because I was absolutely certain I'd never see her again, even
when she turned to zip her jacket and said, Tomorrow
night, tonight I mean, if you want you can come by my
place. ///
///
Cassa lived on the top floor of Occidental Towers, a dark,
brooding colossus that had erupted out of the university
district during the neo-gothic boom. After work I got
cleaned up, took the C-train up out of the early darkness
and night that settled over the Foundation in a blanket of
smog and into the last gleaming light of evening streaming
through the iron girders of the old Billingham Station.
Then the elevated, rattling through the once aristocratic
and now almost burlesque clutter of brownstones and
Victorian manors that lined the streets like dilapidated
whores covered with endless coats of house paint to hide
the crumbling bricks and sagging eaves. Past the dark
little shops and bars with their names announced in pathetic flourishes and scrolls. Then the goddamn elevator
was out of order. I had to take the stairs. By the time I
reached Cassa's floor I was gasping, out of breath. I rang
the bell several times, then turned to leave, instantly
pissed, the fucking bitch, she was just playing with me,
stringing me along, she never intended to see me again. At
that moment Cassa answered the door, startling me, her

close-cropped skull made her face and her eyes suddenly too bright, too wide, like the faces pressing out of concentration camps, everything, her black t-shirt, torn jeans, bare arms, feet were spattered with paint. She looked annoyed, distracted.

I didn't hear it, she said.

For a moment I thought she wasn't going to let me in, send me away like a stray dog, errant delivery boy. Then she relented, motioned me inside. I followed her down the hall, staring at the back of her neck, her shoulders, ass. For one ridiculous moment I even envisioned a reprise of last night, she was leading me to her bedroom and in another minute we were going to be back in the sack, making love, fucking, only this time in a big flouncy bed with satin sheets and mirrors, maybe even music, colored lights. But that really was ridiculous, she wasn't thinking about last night or me either.

This is where I work, she said, her voice flat, dispassionate, like she was showing a repairman the broken TV. There was a mattress on the floor, a couch in front of the plate glass window, a rack of clothes standing incongruously in the middle of the room. Everything else was paint, canvases, the brain-numbing smell of oils, thinners, the walls, floor, the cathedral ceiling splashed, spilled, stacked with paint, pots of paint, brushes, drop cloths draped over wooden ladders, easels. I guess I thought she was going to play tour guide, museum curator, show me some of her sketches. I thought wrong. She'd already forgotten about me. She was working her brush into the ochre sludge on her palette, approaching the canvas. For the next hour and a half she shut me out altogether, pushed the thick furrows of pigment and oil into ever-widening circles of hot yellow sun, burnt brown fields, seared farms, grasslands, cattle with wormy hides stretched over bony ribs, everything heat, barrenness, the sun become a white hot furnace blasting the plains, striking man and beast, flaring up on primitive lodges built out of sod, bark, skin, igniting gnarled and twisted tree trunks, drying up water holes, a pastoral, in other words, in hell.

I sat on the couch, breathing paint fumes and thinner, chain-smoking one cigarette after another, trying not to stare at her face, her ass, the determination with which she worked, trying not to give her that satisfaction. I uncorked a pint of whiskey I carried in my jacket, stared out the window, out over the gray slate and red-tiled roofs bristling with a thicket of gleaming TV antennas, pipes, clotheslines and chimneys. And then beyond the city and the last buildings of the city, the broad brown stretch of plains where the sun was just beginning to collapse on the horizon like a red silk lantern. And then the sky faded into ivory and twilight and the first stars twinkled and glowed in the deep black canopy of night and the lights came on in the buildings, slowly at first and then all at once. It was like a switch thrown, a button pressed, the night made suddenly apparent and real, the night that finally drew Cassa out of her world and back into mine, Talk to me, Harry, remind me you're still there. She was half-facing the canvas, staring at it, her eyes bright, blinking, hands trembling with excess energy.

Talk about what? I said. I felt hurt, resentful. The fucking bitch ignores me all evening, now she wants me to talk. Maybe I just couldn't reconcile the way she was now, tonight, suddenly so dark, subdued, sober, with the way she was last night, this morning, whenever it was we lay down in bed together and fucked, struggled, maybe even, for a minute, thought about love.

Cassa shrugged. I don't know what, Harry, how about the war. You know something about that, right? Suddenly my heart began to bang and pound in my chest, my breathing came in gasps. Here it comes, I thought, the guilt, the accusations and interrogations, how could you? and how could you not? I was stammering, stuttering, trying to come up with an answer. But I didn't have to say anything. Cassa had it all figured out, the scars on my body, the lion's tooth amulet—Remember, Harry, you told me last night?

How the hell am I supposed to remember last night, I growled. I can't even remember five minutes ago. But Cassa only shrugged again, came over, took a drag off my cigarette, reached for the whiskey, staring at the label before she took a long, deliberate swallow. Who knows, maybe she thought I was repressing a bad experience, maybe she thought I needed her to nag, wheedle and beg me, come on, Harry, please? You can tell me. But that wasn't her game.

Hey, she said, don't get so uptight. You don't have to tell me if you don't want to. I just thought it might help if you talked about it. She handed the bottle back to me, played with my hair, ran her fingers over my face, neck. I liked it when she touched me like that. It made me feel warm inside, made me feel like I could trust her again. Then we were pulling off our clothes, we were rolling onto the mattress, the floor./////////////////////////////////////
///
Everything changed at night. We stood in the tall grass and we listened and we watched and we waited, and the yellow cellophane light washed over us and paralyzed us so that we couldn't move. And on the horizon the tall blades of grass turned black against the red sky and our eyes filled with the red light. And then the shadows crept among us and the crickets began to chirr in the grass and the air began to cool, and we felt the velvet membrane of night slip over our heads. And far away, very far away in the distance, we saw the fires begin to flicker and glow on the side of the

mountain. And some said the fires could teach us things, that we could learn from those fires, that they were the voices of our ancestors calling to us across time. And some were afraid and said the fires were sent down from heaven to destroy the earth. Listen! they cried. And when we listened we heard people shouting, we heard horns honking and breaking glass. Then the night was filled with screams, they rushed over us like a hot wind, like a nation of souls dying in flames. And we all knew what we were thinking, and we were all thinking the same thing, and it was sudden and violent and hot. And we listened as hard as we could. We listened harder than we'd ever listened before. And we watched the fires on the side of the mountain, and we waited. And each night the wind blew, and the fires flickered on the side of the mountain. And those fires were like red-hot metal beads being drawn through our brains. And we wanted to know what those fires were, we wanted to understand those fires. But they were so far away, we couldn't see what they were. Unless, of course, you had a telescope, and if anyone did it would have been me. But then the others would realize I was different from them, they'd run away and hide or even try to kill me. ////
///
Wait a second, Harry, I don't understand. Which were you now, a man or an animal? Cassa was mixing paints, cleaning her brushes, approaching the canvas again. I started to get pissed, I thought she was ignoring me again, but she said, C'mon, Harry, keep talking, I want to hear more of your story. She said she liked me to talk, she liked to hear my voice while she painted, she said it reminded her of where she was when she got out there too far, it reminded her how to get back. Of course I knew what she was doing, digging, searching for clues, keys to my private life. Like I was some kind of fool, like I was going to open up, spill my

guts that easily. I'd light another cigarette, pour another drink, pick up the story again. I made it up as I went along out of dreams, nightmares, even pieces of the truth, it didn't matter how much truth, she wasn't paying attention, it was just more noise, like the TV crackling in the background, like the gun shots and sirens in the street. Although now that I think of it, it couldn't possibly have been that same night, but rather that night and then weeks and months of nights, until the talking and telling had disintegrated into one long night. /////////////////// /// It was a marriage of sorts. My stuff began to accumulate at Cassa's place, I thrust my discord into her disorder. Together we created a plaster and fabric collage of sweat and paint-crusted t-shirts, socks, underwear, jeans, the focal point my muddy work boots staggered together like drunken soldiers in the middle of overflowing ashtrays and empty bottles. All she had to do was put a frame around it and call it a still life, low life. I'd come home—when did I start thinking of it as home?—from work, worn out, filthy, half the time drunk, sucking down quarts of beer on the uptown train, grinding out cigarette butts in the aisle, putting my muddy boots up on the seat. It was my magic circle, my ring of fire, I used it to keep away the suits and ties, keep away their cowardice, their fear, the horror rising on their faces as the train rose uptown and they began to realize that I, the sole barbarian, still remained among them, huddled on my own little island of fear. I wanted to shout at them, What the fuck are you staring at? You think I'm the fucking monster? Fucking assholes, I growled, lurching off the train. I'd stagger up the sidewalk, knocking into people, elbowing my way through the crowded cafes jammed beneath the dark, smokey little gallerias, the students drunk, laughing and shouting across their tables.

I hated them, hated and envied them, their money, their privilege. I felt like a fucking animal in their midst. I was ashamed of my sweat and filth. I couldn't wait to get home, get fucked up, sit in front of my window and watch the red sun going down over the plains. //////////////////////// /// But it was Saturday night, suddenly Cassa had to go out, she wanted to take me to a club down the street where her artist friends hung out, some smokey, neon-lit little pit seething with black leather and dark glasses. Her friends waved their cigarettes in the air, tossed back mops of purple and black hair, their ears and eyelids, noses, mouths and fingers studded and pierced with gleaming rings, tacks and gold-plated razorblades. I could never connect the names with the faces, Mildred and Madge, Peter, Paul and—Freddy?—the token queen, speaking to me in that grotesque parody of a female voice, smothering me in waves of sickening perfume, We've heard so much about you, Harry, you're one of those suicidal edgers, aren't you? What's it like working on the edge, Harry? Do you wear a parachute? A safety harness? What do you think, ladies and gentlemen? A tragic end to a burgeoning romance? At least you've had plenty of experience in black, Cassa. The veil will become you. Don't you think, Harry? All because Cassa was telling everybody I was some kind of poet, writer, hero of the working class, like it was so goddamned noble to sweat all day and bust your ass. I flinched when she said war vet, but her friends didn't give a shit. Only Freddy raised his fingers like claws and purred, grrr. But even that was part of the plot, wasn't it? To weave me, the brute, inarticulate beast in my rags and skins into their gilded tapestry. Make me, the terrifying and unknown, suddenly known, familiar, no longer something to be feared but to push out in front of the crowd like a totem, a trained

circus bear, get back! The monster's on our side! When all
that time it was me, I was the one who wanted to run away,
hide. But Cassa, that bitch, she wasn't even there to protect me. She was at the bar getting a drink, she was in the
restroom putting some kind of powder up her nose, she was
out on the dance floor, drunk, crazy, laughing and shouting
and flirting with every asshole in the place. By then I was
beginning to figure out her own particular manias. Party
and paint, paint and party. She worked herself into a static
frenzy in front of the canvas, then let it all out, released it
in a social fury. Somehow we ended up arguing. She called
me a jealous asshole. I called her a bitch. Then we were
spitting at each other across the table, her friends' faces a
blur of drunken, amused spectators. By the time we staggered into the street we were yelling at each other, knocking into people. At the next corner Cassa darted down the
steps to the metro, boarded the final train downtown with
me behind her. Then we were glaring at each other from
opposite ends of the car with some poor, bespectacled creep
sitting terrified between us.

Half an hour later we got off at Foundation Square,
still not speaking, wandering the streets together and
apart with cats howling and the stink of garbage infusing
the neon fog. It was late, almost morning, the first gray
light of morning. We were in the strip district. I was worn
out, beat. Cassa looked completely wired, tuned, her eyes
like camera apertures, sucking in light, color, movement,
the dirty pavement a dull mosaic of broken glass, rotting
fruit, the silvery scales of fish flopped in piles of crushed
ice, pigeon shit, massive green gobs of phlegm and soggy
wads of tobacco expectorated from the beard-stubbled
sumps of grunting neanderthals, dark men in steaming
wool sweaters who stopped unloading the sagging trucks
and wagons long enough to leer at Cassa, sneer at me, my

glaring impotence, laughing, mocking us in a raw plains dialect, like the whine of a ripsaw through a fresh plank of pine. I started to get pissed but Cassa wasn't fazed. I saw her mouthing the words, repeating them to herself, searching among them for what—authenticity? The exact sound and smell of the plains, of sweat and labor? So she could take it back with her to the studio, work it into her paint? Or was it something else altogether? Origins? Beginnings? The other half of her life? Existence? Extracting from the nasal keen and drone of those harsh male voices traces not only of the plains, but her mother's voice? ////////////// // Cassa stood in front of the canvas, her face a frown of concentration, her thoughts and her mind still buried deep in the layers of pigment and oil. At first I thought it was a self-portrait, but different somehow, older, wiser, already creased and lined from a lifetime of sun and wind blown across infinite stretches of veldt and savannah. Her mother, of course. And her mother's eyes, old and weary and full of pain, that tore themselves from the canvas, met mine.

Everything I know about her, everything I put on these canvases, is an illusion, made up, I only know it from books, movies, imagination, the stories my father tells me. He met her out there, you know, on the plains. I think you'd like my father, Harry. Maybe I'll invite him for dinner sometime. /////////////////////////////////////// // One night Cassa and I were sprawled on the mattress, naked, in the middle of making love, when I still knew how to make love or was first learning how to make love, and something, a shadow or a noise, made me look up and I saw a face in the doorway, an older man, her father of course. Even in the dim light I could see the pale blue eyes gleaming, watching us, observing us as if we were a pair of interesting bugs. He didn't say anything, denounce Cassa, call her slut, whore, order me out of the apartment, threaten to call the police. He just turned, went out to the kitchen, a minute later I heard ice clinking in a glass. Dad's here, Cassa said, opening her eyes into mine, returning from some journey of her own.

That was our ceremony, our wedding bells, our sanctum and benedictus, witnessed and celebrated by her father's indifference, tacit approval. For a while I even had this crazy idea he'd encouraged Cassa to lure me up there to her apartment for some kinky thing of his own, who knows what, voyeurism, an incestuous menage a trois, something sick like that. Then I decided he was just trying to be cool, hip, the dispassionate scientist, observer. Which means what? That he really was sick, just as fucked up as everybody else, the enlightened professor having a wet dream because his daughter's shacked up with some low-life scum?

Cassa! Harry! he cried, dumping sacks of groceries on the kitchen table, crushing us in his embrace, in the smokey woolen smells of flannel and tweed. Not some timid little college professor blinking up at me through coke bottles, but a big, strong guy, maybe fifty, sixty. He looked like he'd been humping stone all his life, his face rugged, permanently tanned, his hair an anarchic mix of snow and sand, his eyes pale, blue, like patches of winter sky. While I crouched over the kitchen counter, chainsmoking and swallowing hot black coffee, Cassa moved back and forth between the stove and the sink in a neurotic flurry of cutting and chopping, stirring and frying, her father hovering around her, gesturing, talking, meetings, organizations, all this university stuff. ///////////////////
//

Of course that's more bullshit, my defective memory. Cassa never cooked anything in her life. We probably just sent down for pizza, Chinese. Who knows, maybe her old man even played chef, whipped us up something to eat, treated us to one of his famous culinary fetes. After dinner he brought out a bottle of scotch, stuck a cigar in my pocket, Hand-rolled, Harry—from the plains, not like this domestic shit. And why should I object? It was Cassa who protested. Dad, no, it's too much, Harry's gotta work tomorrow. But her father only laughed. Nonsense, Harry's young, he's tough, he can handle it. By now we were on a first name basis, her father was Frank, I was Harry, it was the Frank and Harry show. We ended up killing the bottle, staying up late, drinking, talking, work, the economy, the war. He clasped my shoulder in his big, thick hand, But you know what I'm talking about, Harry.

I felt my heart seize, my lungs compress, I blinked, looked away, caught Cassa's eye. Of course it was her, the fucking bitch. Yeah, I know, she was only trying to help me, get me on his good side, she didn't mean to subject me to the prying, the probing and interrogations, what year and what company and what outfit? But I was wrong again. Her old man, Frank, wasn't interested in me. He was just like everyone else, he just wanted someone to tell his own story to, what it was like for him, when he was still a young man just out of college and too full of life and breath to sit still and suffocate in some dreary desk job. He poured more scotch, packed and tamped a gnarled tobacco pipe, clenched it between his teeth, struck a match, sent an orange flame up through a cloud of aromatic blue smoke. / / /
/ /
Of course, times were different then, the military was still a fashionable option. They commissioned him second lieutenant, sent him along with the surveying team to study

the wildlife, to catalogue birds, plants and animals. At the time it seemed like a great adventure. He rode horseback across a vast arena of sand and wind and nomadic wetlands, the birds, grasses, roaming cattle all dependent upon the infrequent rains, broad gleaming sheets of water that appeared and disappeared again like mirages, leaving behind blinding deserts where the grains of sand gleamed like millions of unstrung beads and horned and scaled and fanged creatures watched them pass from every crevice and reservoir of shade. They splashed through waterways and bayous, picking leeches from their thighs, swatting at horseflies and mosquitoes, wearing pistols on their hips against the crocodiles and poisonous snakes sliding through the reeds. He didn't realize it then but he was riding on the very cusp of the storm. Behind them a great wind of building and construction was beginning to blow, never deviating from its path, destroying itinerant waterholes and oases, growling across rivers and swamps, crushing beneath its heavy tread speckled blue eggs laid in nests intricately woven of sticks and reeds, grinding up wings and feathers, claws and scales and mewling little balls of fur.

Frank drew on his pipe, stared at a spot over my head, his eyes filled with sky and heaven and a vast stretch of eternity beyond. All that time he thought they were building roads to carry civilization into the wilderness. Instead they were building highways to cart back the plunder of the earth. The lines of men went on for miles, passing the stones before them, setting them in place, tapping and aligning them with crowbars and wooden mallets.

Frank's eyes flickered. Poor devils. We called them conscripts, but they were really slave labor. We worked them from sunup to sundown, all of us choking on our own dust, cursing the heat, the sun beating down on our backs. It went on and on, the terrible heat, everything so dry, so unbearably hot. You couldn't touch any metal surfaces, the jeeps, fuel tanks, even the barrel of your rifle. Of course they had those old Brenfelds then, with all that bare metal. But they were still pretty good protection against spears. Bandits, you know. Marauders, renegade tribesmen, displaced by the encroachment upon their territory, by the worsening drought. Everything was dying, the trees, cattle. Whatever shade there was you created yourself. You learned to walk in your own shadow. Every breath was painful. Every step. Even eating, because it was so hard to swallow, because your mouth was so dry and you didn't have anything to wash it down.

They looked like skeletons, wraiths, their uniforms flapped in the hot wind, there was sand in the hollows of their eyes, in the crevices of their skin. At least that's the way Cassa's mother saw him when his convoy entered her village, not as a noble liberator, but a ghost in rags. Of course, she'd seen so much worse by then. The drought, famine, slaughter, the mass migration of tribes, peoples, an entire nation and race on foot.

He started to re-light his pipe, let the match die. She was almost ten years younger than him. Educated—taught how to scrawl her name on paper and perform basic math —in a sod and pine shack by some poor, deluded scholar sent out to that hell on a government program. But still so much older and wiser than him in so many ways. She taught him everything, about the plants and animals, how to survive, how to love that life, as harsh as it was. She showed him what they were doing to the land, raping it, pillaging it, destroying all its subtle and intricate systems of survival developed over thousands and millions of years. And that's what he took Cassa's mother away from, her homeland, her roots, everything she ever knew and loved

in her life. ///
///
The pipe'd gone out in his hand. His eyes were moist, shining, seeking further still the bounds of eternity. I felt a tiny
mechanism of doubt begin to whir and grind in my brain.
Yes, of course I can see it now, another snare being set, the
sympathetic moment, baited with a tidbit, morsel, the
loved and lost, the sainted and martyred holy mother and
wife, that young and feral wife he brought into the city like
some strange and soon to be extinct animal in a cage. But
then, I was feeling drunk, sentimental, I enjoyed listening
to his nonsense, I thought I might even learn something
useful. //
///
Of course he was on a mission by then. Stop the destruction, the madness. He got into politics, took every opportunity to declaim against the war he felt even then to be inevitable. And, of course, he made enemies. Because that's
where the money came from, the war build-up, research
and development. And he was trying to stop it. For his ac-
tivities he was refused a visa, they were no longer allowed
to travel on the plain. Then Cassie's mother died, cancer,
the disease of civilization—his words. He was devastated,
he blamed himself, because he brought her to this place,
subjected her to this madness. On top of that the war happened anyway. He got out of the public eye altogether, took
a position at the university, tried to restrain his anger in
his classes, ranted and raved when he found somebody
who'd listen.

I felt the thick heavy hand squeezing my neck, my
shoulder, testing muscle and bone and resistance to pain,
the pale blue eyes penetrated mine, searching for something deeper, a weakness, a flaw, a trigger mechanism. But
it was just parental concern, wasn't it, Doc? A father's love

for his daughter? Is this guy OK? Is he going to work hard and bust his ass and take care of Cassie and the grandchildren? He splashed more scotch in my glass, held a match to my cigar, Cassie tells me you're a writer, Harry. I'd like to see some of your work.

No, not a writer, I pontificated, gulping scotch, puffing on the stogie, beginning to enjoy the persona Cassa was establishing for me. I just scribble things down when I have time. I knew I should slow down, take it easy, but I was enjoying the flush of alcohol in my brain, enjoying the rich, narcotic aroma of tobacco in my nostrils. Suddenly I could see it all, I was going to be big, very big, soon everybody was going to see how big, I was going to do great things. I was raving, spouting all kinds of drunken, deranged nonsense. At the time I believed it entirely, implicitly. Everything I said was divinely inspired, it came from my guts, soul. I never imagined Frank might think otherwise, that he might perceive me as an idiot, fool. He leaned closer, his eyes gleaming, that blue winter sky so deceptively limpid and clean. What sort of things, Harry? /////////////////
///
But now I'm getting confused, I'm not sure anymore if it was that same night or another. Because at some point I realized he was holding a tape recorder in his hand, maybe he'd been toying with it all along, starting and stopping it, fast forwarding and rewinding. Suddenly I was stammering, tongue-tied, what if he'd been taping this all along? And me, so stupid, divulging myself on record like that, giving him that power over me. But Frank was cleverer than that. At the end of the night he handed me the tape recorder. Take it with you, Harry, talk into it, make it your friend. Don't think about what you're saying. Don't censor yourself. Let everything out, all your hatred, your anger. Later, if you like, we can listen to it together. We can talk

about it, try to figure it out. It's a good exercise for writers.
///
Yeah, sure, figure it out. When I still couldn't figure out
what the fuck I was doing in that lousy slab. I felt like an
impostor, thief. Then I'd think, wait a second, Harry, that's
exactly what he wants you to think, you aren't good
enough, you don't belong here. Because then I'd feel like I
had to prove myself, like I had to grovel and beg for Frank's
hand outs. Sure, maybe I was taking advantage of a good
thing. Not just Cassa, but the rent-free slab, additionally
provendered with the bottles of wine, the loaves of bread
and rounds of cheese, the tins of olives, artichokes and
palm hearts, all those treasures, those delicacies of the
plains that Frank, her father, thrust into our arms when
he came to visit, for dinner, for the company of young lives.
Because that was it, wasn't it? Not that Frank was some
drooling old gargoyle clutching a spurting, desiccated slab
of meat in his hand. But that he was lonely. He missed the
life and laughter and camaraderie of his youth, his friends.
Besides, even Cassa thought the goddamn tape recorder
was a good idea, it'd help me with my work, my writing, the
great epic I spun out of that oracular stupor I put myself in
night after night, after the last red sliver of the sun had
slipped below the horizon and the first stars appeared in
the sky. Then I'd light a joint, a cigarette, pour myself a
drink, turn on the machine. ///////////////////////////
///
I'm sorry, what were you saying about the stars? Cassa
sounded annoyed, distracted, like I was the one interrupting her.

No, not the stars. It was the fires, on the mountain. I
lay on the couch, my arm across my forehead, a cigarette
smoldering between my fingers, watching her squeeze a
thick white worm of cadmium onto her palette. But she

wasn't listening anymore, she was already back at the canvas while I went on talking into the night, into the void, into whatever existed beyond that cold black plate of glass.
///
In the morning the stars faded into the pale blue wash of sky and the fires on the mountain disappeared into the brown haze that surrounded it and we forgot all our fears of the night before. But then the haze began to spread outward from the horizon. It's locusts! somebody cried. They'll eat everything in sight! They'll leave us in famine! Someone else said it was a great cloud of dust, that it bore with it the drought. We'll die of thirst! It's swollen tongues and creaking bones! No! others cried. It's a fire! It's burning up the plains! It'll scorch our flesh, sear our lungs!

Still the haze came closer. We felt a tickling in our throats, our eyes burned, our nostrils filled with the smell of diesel fuel, hot oil and gasoline. Through the haze we saw strange machines driven by madmen. Furious, sweating, their bodies bound in leather and brass, they whipped and drove before them wild-eyed beasts and even other men stripped naked and chained to the beasts. We could see the terror in their eyes and in the eyes of the men they sent ahead to scout and forage for food. Sometimes we caught them, dragged them into the brush and ate up their screams and their protests along with their sweet succulent flesh. ///
///
You were a cannibal, Harry. Wherever Cassa was in her own world resolved itself and for a moment she was back in mine, just long enough to light a cigarette, take a hit off my whiskey, the joint. Yeah, I was a cannibal alright. ////////
///
But then more men came. The sunlight gleamed in their eyes, and on their guns and spears. They sent out patrols

on horseback. They drove after us in machines that roared over the earth. They ran us down and butchered us from behind, they didn't hunt out the murderers among us, they slaughtered us indiscriminately, hacked up the bodies of those who fell for meat. At night we smelled the flesh of our own kind roasting over their fires, and we were sickened because it was a good smell. Then our terror overwhelmed us. We tried to run away but we didn't know where we were going. We called out to each other for help but we couldn't understand anything anymore because our minds were filled with screaming. It drove us mad. We attacked and killed each other. We destroyed our homes. If we stopped to rest, to catch our breath, the screaming drove us mad again. At night we gathered together in small groups. We made truces, alliances, then murdered our allies in their sleep. // // Civilization, I guess you call it. Frank clenched the gnarled briar tobacco pipe between his teeth, leaned back in the deep leather chair, his hands clasped together behind his head, his eyes fixed on the ceiling where an aromatic cloud of tobacco smoke drifted and gathered, the lion at home, in his office, his professorial lair. On the wall behind him the shelves were packed with journals, papers, books, MAN'S DOMAIN, LAW AND CIVILIZATION, ARGUMENTS AGAINST INSANITY.//////////////////////////////// // Insanity is an abdication of the responsible I-throne in favor of the obsessed I, the I addicted to itself and its imagined control or lack of control over the world around it (p. 376). // // All those books with Frank's name on them, books that explained in rational terms the terror of the unknown, the terror carved into the wood and stone masks cluttering the walls, the floor, even the ceiling. The souvenirs Frank'd brought back with him from his younger days on the plains —against his wife's advice, he once said—with deep, cruel slashes of chisel and machete for ears, eyes, nose and mouth. The gods and deities the various tribes put forth to terrorize, frighten away the objects of their own fear, the yelp and howl of jackals, hyenas, the monsters and beasts and even other men circling their little periphery of fire-light and fear. Fear, that was the word Frank kept return-ing to, pushing it in my face. You can only hide in fantasy for so long, Harry. At some point you have to confront the truth. He clenched the pipe between his teeth again, reached for the tape recorder sitting on his desk. Suddenly I felt like a child in the principal's office, waiting for his dismissal, approval. I squirmed in my seat, looked for somewhere to run, hide. //////////////////////////// // You can't imagine what it was like. I lived in constant fear. I never closed my eyes, never slept, hoping I'd survive, live long enough to escape. I didn't want the others to see I was so afraid. It was like one of those horrible nightmares, my fear attracted their attention, I could feel their thoughts bending toward me, feel the weight of all those eyes upon me and the questions they were asking me. I wanted to run, hide, but if I tried I'd give myself away, they'd know I was thinking of escape, that I wasn't one of them, maybe they'd even try to kill me. And even if I did get away, then what? Try to reach the mountain where the fires burned? Would the men who lived there recognize me as one of them? A straggler, even a deserter, dragging himself in off the plain? Or would they cry out Monster! Shoot me dead without a word to explain?

One night I finally managed to sneak away. It wasn't

even night anymore, but that in between time when everyone still drowsed in the numb gray fog of too much watching, too much waiting, when they were just beginning to re-
ceive the signals that told them they had survived another
night and now it was time to wake, to begin watching and
waiting again. By then I was far out on the plain, fleeing
toward those distant points of light flickering and dying in
the brown and gray swirl where the mountain rose. I
wanted peace of mind, I wanted security, I wanted a place
with rules and regulations where I didn't have to watch all
the time, where I didn't have to be afraid. I wanted civilization. ///
///
Then I was jerking awake at six a.m., my face smashed
against the window of the downtown express, watching the
iron girders and masses of concrete flash past, the sudden
fluorescent glare and crowd of faces at the next stop.
Jerked awake again half an hour later crunched up in the
cold plastic seat of the Grubb Street trolley, got off at the
job site, my head aching, my neck sore, my mind a wad of
cotton gauze. Yeah, sure, a coupla cups of burnt coffee and
some kind of syrupy sweet pastry sludge from the kiosk on
the corner, and an hour or two on the job, I'd really start to
wake up, get back in the rhythm, I'd be sweating and moving stone and swinging the pick, my mind'd start working
again, I'd start getting ideas, images, the torch burning
next to my face, the long lines of men stretching up and
down the walls, but it was already mutating in my mind, it
was swelling into something epic, huge, I could see a great
citadel rising from the rubble, a gleaming glass and steel
metropolis penetrating the clouds. I couldn't wait until I
got off work, I was gonna go home, write it down, play with
it a while. And somebody was passing a joint up the line,
and somebody else was passing a bottle down, and we were

bullshitting and getting into the work thing, the mindless
donkey labor thing. By the time I got home at night I was
worn out, beat, so fucked up I couldn't even remember
where my own asshole was when I sat down on the toilet to
take a shit. I'd stand under the shower for half an hour,
rocking on my heels, the hot stream beating my aches and
bruises, breathing steam and sulfur fumes, trying to wake
up, clear my head. Then I'd stretch out on the couch, telling
myself I'm just gonna relax a little, then I'm gonna sit
down and work on that idea I had today and I'm not gonna
let Cassa or anything distract me. But the only thing was,
that red sliver of sun was just slipping beneath the skyline
and I could feel that old dread coming on, work, the job, tomorrow and the next day and the rest of my life. And then
I didn't feel like doing anything, I just wanted to lie there
and die, try not to think how I was wasting my life. I'd fire
up a joint, take the cap off the whiskey, light a cigarette,
stare into the darkness gathering outside the window. ////
//
Harry? At some point Cassa'd startle me, yank me out of
the narcotic bath of oils and paint thinner. Come on, Harry,
don't fade on me yet. She'd made a pot of coffee, something
to eat—opened a can of soup anyway, getting herself wired,
ready for another round with the canvas. She wanted me to
stay up, keep talking, tell her more of the goddamn story,
because that's all she ever wanted from me, the story, the
words, the inspiration, she didn't give a shit about me, my
life, when all she had to do was get up at one or two in the
afternoon and play artist while I dragged my sorry ass
through another day, swearing that tonight, tomorrow
night, this weekend, goddamn it, I'm really going to do
something with my life. ////////////////////////////////
//
I ran night and day, lapping water out of the brackish pools

left standing from long past rains, chewing the seedheads of the tough brown grass that scratched and burned my bare legs. I was worn out, exhausted, but I continued to run, my heart pounding in my chest, my ears filled with the sound of my feet striking the earth, every step another beat, until my thoughts and my mind were filled with a solemn, steady drumming, boomp, boomp, boomp, thumpa-boomp, thumpa-boomp, boomp, boomp. But it wasn't the sound of my heart failing, was it? It was the sound of another set of feet striking the ground somewhere behind me, matching me step for step, then occasionally slipping behind a beat. When I stopped to listen the pounding stopped. When I looked back over my shoulder I couldn't see anyone, my pursuer must have ducked down in the grass. Suddenly my heart beat wildly, I started to run again but I could barely move, I was struggling in a molasses dreamslur of trying to run, trying to flee, escape some unseen horror. At last I forced myself to break free, run harder, faster. I ran faster than I'd ever run in my life, I ran impossibly fast, my arms and legs a blur, sweat pouring down my face and chest. Finally I couldn't run anymore, I fell to the ground, exhausted, gasping for breath, my eyes burning, the smell of dried grass filling my nostrils, watching a line of ants trickling past my nose, feeling the bright hot sun lying across my back, expecting death at any second, the claws raking my spine, the snarling fangs and snout buried in the hot black pudding of my still functioning guts. // // Yeah, sure, in the beginning it was just fairy tales, bedtime stories. And then there was that unconscious leap, I could feel my face twisting up into one of those horrible rubber Halloween masks, and then I was vomiting up all this terrible shit about fighting and killing, torture, blown-up bodies, it was like some kind of disease, dysentery, I couldn't stop myself, it just kept running out of me, foul and stinking of shit, decay, until I realized what I was doing, stopped cold, trembling, soaked with sweat, afraid to look at Cassa, to see in her face the recognition, that I really was a monster. But she never blinked, never said a word, she continued to work at the canvas, her face dark, her hands driven with suppressed fury, making sudden bloody gashes in the thick layers of paint.

You aren't listening to me! I yelled, drunk, enraged, my voice thick, slurred, impotent, my face screwed up like a baby's. Then she'd step away from the easel to change brushes, squeeze more paint onto her palette, and it was all there, everything I told—shouted at her—slapped and slashed across the canvas in that oozing eel sludge of pigment and oil, the arid and desiccated pastoral scenes exploded, transformed into something apocalyptic, disturbing, like evolution run backwards, pieces of men and beasts, hoof and tail, arms, legs, heads and snouts blown all over the place, buildings exploding, palm trees in flames above burning black pools of blood and oil.

Until even Cassa couldn't stand it, she'd back away from the canvas, staring at it, hating it, her eyes burning, body trembling, hands twitching. She'd wander around the studio, looking lost, disheveled, in shock, like she'd wandered in off a battlefield. Drop down on the couch next to me, light a cigarette, sip whiskey, leaning her head against my shoulder, depending on me of all people in her moment of weakness, finally falling asleep like that while I sat up, sometimes all night, a cold hard presence at her side, staring at her face, the slow rise and fall of her breasts, smoking one cigarette after another, sipping whiskey, just me and the machine, Frank's tape recorder, talking to it, whispering into it, enjoying in some perverse way the rasping of

my beard stubble against its shiny, metallic surface. Until
I couldn't talk anymore, until my brain went numb and the
words disintegrated into useless chunks of sound wound
up on a tiny spool that gleamed in the dark like a vial of
poison. ///
///
We fed off each other's neuroses, turned the studio into a
slaughterhouse, bombed-out field hospital. I'd stagger
through another day, worn out with booze and drugs and
lack of sleep, come home and find Cassa completely naked
in front of the canvas, her skull bristling, water trickling
down the bony knobs of her spine, her ass wet and shining,
a puddle of water at her feet, pulled out of the shower by
some urgency to paint, burn off excess energy, expunge the
accumulated detritus of her soul, exorcise her own demons.
She didn't hear me come in, she was completely absorbed
in her work, she made violent, arcing slashes with her palette knife, trying to force the storm in her head onto the
canvas. Her painting was brutal now, primitive, she
dragged her brush across the canvas like she was mopping
up an operating room, her face contorted by an internal
conversation, an argument of angry contradictions, self-ac-
cusation, like a penitent, nun, prisoner of war, of hatred, of
somebody else's crimes. While she painted I lay on the
couch in a narcotic haze, sucking on a cigarette, a joint, a
glass of whiskey, staring at her shoulders, her bare ass,
thinking about fucking her from behind, about jerking off,
about eating a bunch of pills and stepping off the edge tomorrow. I felt so goddamned tired, depressed. I was beat,
filthy, too exhausted to think, move, get up and take a
shower. My mind was completely eaten up with paranoia,
doubts. I was convinced that her silence, the silence of the
night, the silence she invoked, not by anything she said,
but the intensity with which she worked, equaled betrayal,

that there was some kind of conspiracy. That old idea again, that she was sent down below to find me in particular, to locate me, drag me up there to her apartment on her gossamer tether. Yeah, sure, sent down by whom? Her father of course, the organizer, commander-in-chief of some secret movement, willing even to use his own daughter. But now I was talking to myself again, talking to the machine, talking incoherently, babbling all kinds of toxic bullshit into the atmosphere, I was actually shouting this insane crap into her father—alright, Frank, Frank—into Frank's face. Of course, she isn't your daughter at all, is she, Frank? She's just another stooge, operative, out on assignment, she fucks me, humors me, does whatever you tell her to do. And all this time I thought you were just a normal pervert.

My heart pounded in my chest, I was horrified at myself, my words. What the fuck was I saying? They were going to be banging on the door at any second, drag me into the street kicking and screaming. But Cassa just laughed at me, she thought it was a joke. She grabbed the tape recorder from my hand, spoke directly into the microphone, Did you hear that, Dad? Did you hear what Harry's saying? Is this what you wanted? C'mon, Harry, say something else for Dad. Spill your guts, tell him your whole life story. Afterwards you can stick in a few commas, periods, sell it as a book. The fucking bitch, I was so pissed I couldn't hear the sarcasm in her voice. What if you had to work a real job for once in your fucking life? I shouted. That's what I've been trying to tell you, Harry! she screamed back. You don't have to stay in that stupid job. Dad can help you find something better, maybe you can go back to school, do something with your life. C'mon, Harry, don't be angry with me, it's just an idea. Somehow we both ended up naked, making love, war, fucking violently, knocking over easels, paintings, crashing to the floor, the mattress, everything trashed out, the sheets soaked with sweat, juices, sex, love, whatever it was, become something strange, necessary, like turning on the faucet for water, eating bread to still the hunger, an almost painful interlude between sleep and the job. By then I was a total wreck, on the verge of tears, begging her, please, just tell me what the fuck I'm supposed to do? She'd reach out, pull me into her arms, It's alright, Harry, it's OK. In the end we'd both be crying and holding each other. Then the paranoia'd start again. She was manipulating me, it was just a mechanism for compassion she'd learned in some espionage school, at her mother's breasts, in her female genes. I'd get angry again, push her away, I wouldn't let her touch me, she was smothering me. It reminded me of my mother when I was a kid, the way she used to hold me in her arms, rocking me and telling me, It's alright, Harry, it's OK, when I knew it wasn't alright, it'd never be OK, the fucking bitch was lying to me, trying to reassure herself. / That's what I fucking mean, Harry, that's the way it was with fucking Liz, man. I'd fucking tell her and tell her but she didn't fucking understand, man. It's like the fucking war didn't even fucking happen for her, man. Like the war was some kind of fucking game on TV, man. Like, honey, can you change the fucking channel now, I'm tired of this shit, man. Like, you can just push the fucking button and turn the fucking war off now, man. You know what I mean, man? The fucking bitch never understood. The fucking war isn't only on the weekends, it's all the fucking time, once it fucking starts it never fucking stops. You know what I'm talking about, Harry. You went through that shit, you were fucking there, man, you made it back, they should've made you a fucking hero, man, you should've got a fucking

medal, man. ///////////////////////////////////////
//
When it got to be too much, when things between Cassa
and me had disintegrated into fighting and craziness all
the time, I had to get away, go back downtown, talk some
shit with my buddy Al, another loser vet I met at work, and
a redneck bigot asshole on top of that, but also a real good
guy because he went through that shit, he knew what it
was like. That's right, Harry, that's right, man, that's right,
that's right, that's right, that's exactly what the fuck I'm
talking about. We'd get completely trashed, passing a
bottle of cheap-ass booze back and forth, filling ashtrays
with cigarette butts, roaches and bottle caps, tapping out
lines of speed and cocaine and anything else we could find
to blow up our noses while the TV screen flickered and the
stereo blasted some kind of insane fucking noise that made
no fucking sense at all here but plenty of fucking sense
over there. In the end we were both shouting, insane,
trashed out of our fucking minds. I knew I should go home,
get my ass out of there, Cassa was probably wondering
what the fuck'd happened to me. Although by now she
knew very well what had happened, I was somewhere getting drunk, fucked up, another lost night, weekend, with
one of my loser buddies. Yeah, sure, if I had someone else to
talk to, someone a little sharper, smarter, a little more ar-
ticulate, who understood what it was like out there, who
could explain it to you in words that actually made sense.
Yeah, I know, her old man. You were out there, weren't you,
Frank, you know what it was like. But that was a long
fucking time ago, motherfucker, under mighty fucking different circumstances. Yeah, sure, the tape recorder again,
that clean, efficient little machine jammed in the middle of
pizza cartons, crushed beer cans, drugs, paraphernalia,
and my voice, yelling over the noise of the stereo and the

TV, You've got half my fucking life on tape, don't you Frank? Whatayou think about this shit? The next day, half-way sober, hung-over, I'd think, oh man, you can't let him hear that shit. He'll have you locked up, thrown in some hole you'll never get out of. But that was just more para-noid bullshit. Frank didn't give a shit about me, my life. It was just research, just more material for one of his god-damn books. Besides, he could play the fucking tape back-ward and forward a hundred times and never figure it out. You had to be there, you had to go through that shit. / Shit, Al, Cassa's alright, she loves me, she tries to under-stand, it's not her, it's me, it's what I did. How the fuck's she supposed to understand? If I told her the real truth she'd think I was a fucking monster. If I could just wish it away, make it untrue, if somebody'd say to me, It's alright, Harry, it was just a bad dream, you fell asleep watching the news on TV. I was such a fucking idiot. I didn't know any-thing when I went in, I was just another dumb-ass kid off the street. Nobody warned us, Al, we didn't know it was going to be so fucking bad. We didn't know we were going to get killed or that dying was so bad. No heroes, no fucking little tin soldiers lined up in their fucking neat little coffins in their fucking starched uniforms with fucking rows of medals on their fucking chests and that handsome face and that strong jaw stilled in the rage and joy of life. You get blown to bits, a hand or a foot or a pile of guts sent home in a plastic bag with a few broken teeth and a set of dogtags, dear mom and dad, here's your boy. Who the fuck knows how many people you killed, whether it was even the enemy or your own fucking men, you just pointed your goddamn gun and hoped to God it went off. You know what I'm talking about, right, Al? /

You have to understand, this is a normal response, Harry. Resentment. Anger. Denial. Your brain cannot accept that you took part in the killing, especially when you were taught all your life that it was wrong. And suddenly you had this discrepancy, it was alright in certain circumstances. Of course you were afraid. Everybody was afraid. And then, on top of that, you got out of there, you made it home alive, and you felt guilty because you left the others behind, because you were living a normal life when you knew they were still out there dying. ////////////////// // Listening to the tapes with Cassa's father was an act of humiliation, self-abasement, even bravado. I can still hear my voice, thick, slurred, fucked up, trying to sound tough, trying to sound stoic, angry, defiant. But Frank was tough too, he was smart, he was unrelenting, he looked me straight in the eye, forced me to stare into that vast open sky. C'mon, Harry, don't give me any more of that bullshit. I wanta know what really happened, I wanta know about you, how you feel inside.

I knew what he wanted, he wanted me to break down, bawl like a baby. One night he must have punched the right button. Suddenly I was sobbing, my face was hot and wet with tears, I was blubbering all this nonsense about some guys in my squad who got blown away. But that still wasn't enough, was it? Frank still wasn't satisfied, he wanted more, not just the crying and the tears and the confession of terrible secrets. But the collapse, the total capitulation of the man, person, thing, until there was nothing left but a quivering lump waiting for the thumbprint of God, Now listen, Harry, here's what you do.

Frank stared at me a long time, carefully packing and tamping his pipe before he struck a match, sent up a cloud of smoke and flame. It's not that easy, Harry. You'll have to

work harder than you've ever worked in your life. You'll
have to clean up your act, take responsibility for yourself. I
have a friend in Public Works. There's a certain job avail-
able, you have the experience, the right credentials. I'll tell
you right now, Harry, you won't like it, you won't like the
people you work with. But it'll get you into the system, it'll
teach you things you can use later. Of course you'll have to
go back to school, finish your degree. I can help you with
that. It's up to you, Harry, take it or leave it. / / / / / / / / / / /
/ /
Harry? Are you alright? Cassa's voice filtered down
through a warm red light. Suddenly I was grabbing for the
alarm clock, my pants, I gotta get up, get going, I'm late for
work. But it was nothing, just a momentary rush of panic,
just Cassa wiping my forehead with a damp cloth. It's
alright, Harry, the job doesn't matter anymore, remember?
But I couldn't remember. What the fuck was she talking
about? Had we come to a decision? Something to do with
Frank? Then I'd fall asleep again, after a lifetime without
sleep I slept on and on, my whole reason for being sleep
and the act of sleeping, wake two or three hours later,
soaked with sweat, trembling, extracting myself from another nightmare, dream. /
/ /
I felt sick, feverish, my entire body ached, I just wanted to
lie back down, sink into oblivion. But I made myself get up,
start running again. The pounding in my temples grew
worse as I ran on, trying to ignore the cramps in my side,
the pain in my ankles. The tall grass sliced and burned my
bare legs. I felt numb, rubbery. I was half-wading, half-
swimming through the grass, only it wasn't grass anymore,
but thick green waves of house paint. Then I was standing
on the bridge of a ship, I could feel the salt spray in my
face, the great engines pounding below deck. Thick black

smoke poured back from the ship's twin stacks, darkening the horizon. Then it was night, not a night of stars, of moonlight and dreamy young lovers kissing in parked cars, oh my darling, my dearest, I'll love you forever, I'll never leave you, but a night sick and glowing with the flaming farts of factories and mills, a night stinking of sulfur, the sour rotten smell of molten steel. On my face I could feel the heat and blast of a great furnace where soldiers of labor worked endlessly, heroically, to build and forge a city out of steel, to anchor it in concrete, to heat and illuminate it with ten billion trillion volts of electricity generated by hydroelectric plants and coal furnaces, not just a city but a blazing cathedral, a tabernacle of light rising up out of the iron girders and beams. Welcome to the new world, Brother Harry! Go down to the mess and get yerself some grub, then report back here in uniform at oh eight hundred and we'll put you to work! /////////////////////////////////// /// **And Now! Headlines From Previous Wars! Troops Come Home! Heroes Welcomed! Ticker Tape! Parades! Prez Sez Time To Put War Behind Us! Yes, Ladies And Gentlemen, It's Back To Work For Our Boys In Uniform! Peacetime Economy! Blah! Blah! Blah!** // /// Frank stood behind Cassa, drawing on his pipe. The eyes are good. I think she's captured the eyes, don't you, Harry? I sat on the couch, my head slumped against the cold glass, squinting myopically, thinking to myself, what fucking eyes? I don't see any eyes. Finally I began to see the eyes staring back at me, the shadowy figure of a man evolving out of the tall grass. I squirmed on the couch, wished I had a drink, wished I could just get fucked up again, forget the whole goddamn thing. But that wasn't possible, was it? We made a deal. No more booze, drugs, not even a fucking glass of wine. Because of the fucking kid, Cassa said. Because she didn't want to have some kind of fucking freak, she wanted it to be normal, have a chance in the world. She'd shuffle around the apartment with one hand on her belly, the other supporting her back, like one of those skeletal apparitions she was painting now, the wandering tribesmen, the widowed and orphaned women and children, suffering from hunger, malnutrition, the collapse of their societies. Even now, when she had an excuse not to, she stood at the easel for hours, barefoot, on the cold cement floor, in a daze, her voice when she spoke distant, detached, as if she were beginning to become interested in this thing filling up her belly, womb, that empty black universe she bore inside her body. /////////////////////////// /// One night she woke me out of a dream hissing, Harry, look, it's the moon. I pried open my eyes and there it was, framed in the black square of the window, the moon. I kept saying moon, moon, moon, over and over again until that cold, white thing filling the sky fit inside that word and that sound, moon. And then I remembered the moon. The powdery white light lay on the grass and the points of steel gleaming in the grass, and we watched, and we waited, and we could hear the sound of the insects trickling and streaming in the grass, the sound climbed and rose until it had reached an incessant scream, until you couldn't stand it anymore, you felt like you'd go mad if somebody didn't just shoot or drop a mortar and the hell with what happened next, if you lived or died. Then I lay awake the rest of the night with that vague, itinerant fear hovering in the periphery of my brain, telling myself over and over again, that was then, Harry, and this is now, so close your eyes and go back to sleep. /////////////////////////////// ///

In the morning I took the train down to Grubb Station. Just when I thought I'd finally made it out of that squalor, Frank was pushing me back down with this stupid job. Yeah, sure, at first I thought it was so goddamn great, no more pick and shovel, I made a helluva lot more money, people treated me differently in a suit and tie. That was before I realized it made me a target, an enemy of my own people, the people I used to live among.

I used to pass this little family scene outside the station, the woman sat cross-legged on the sidewalk, holding out a tin cup for the coins, the scraps of dirty paper and bits of dross to come raining down from the hands of the gods, she's rocking a mewling bundle in her arm, reaching out a thin, consumptive hand to yank a pot-bellied male child out of the street by the waist band of his tattered red shorts, draw him back into the brood, a nest of sick, scraggly chicks with large damaged eyes, they're huddled around a smoky cooking fire of newspapers, oil-soaked rags, a hasty soup of shoe laces, soles, tongues and toes bubbling away in a five gallon insecticide can, the soot-blackened patch of concrete their kitchen, bedroom and bath. /// /// Hi, are you the lady of the house? My name's Harry and I'm here today to tell you about the marvelous Hovermatic vacuum cleaner and portable TV, you'll breeze through those pesky household chores in minutes while you keep up with your favorite daytime dramas. ////////////////// /// One day a small dead bundle gets pushed out in the gutter, picked up by the big stiff brushes of the street cleaning machine and batted down the street. The next day another bundle appears in the woman's arms. Sometimes I'd see a man hunkered down next to her, drawing on a hand-rolled

cigarette, his brown face creased and lined liked dried tobacco leaves, his eyes tiny flames flickering in cavernous
recesses, staring out into the street, contemplating another day of putting in resumes, looking for odd jobs, scav-
enging in subways, garbage cans, alleys, lying drunk in
gutters, doorsteps, every two or three days he finds his way
back to this little sidewalk homestead, to this woman and
these children. Daddy! It's Daddy! Daddy's home! Yeah, I
know, you don't think people like that feel the cold, you
don't think they feel the hunger, you don't think they have
eyes, you think they don't see you, you think they won't
remember you, won't try to get even with you, you think
you won't be the one to ignite the hatred smoldering in
their eyes. ///
///
I started walking up the street, I could feel the venomous
red eyes watching me out of the dark alleys like tiny flames
flickering in the recesses of caves. I heard pounding all
around me, boom boxes, hands, fists, drumsticks beating on
garbage cans, beer cans, railings and light poles, I was really starting to feel scared now, it was like a dream, I was
flying up the sidewalk, my arms and legs flailing, my briefcase banging against my leg. At the next corner I stopped,
my face damp with sweat, my heart pounding, trying to
catch my breath. What the hell was I running for? These
were my people, this was my territory, home turf, the place
I grew up. I can still remember certain details, the steam
radiator in the hall, drawing faces in the grime of the
kitchen window, going down the stairs in the morning,
peeling wallpaper, piles of trash, shit, human shit, in the
corners. It was always dark, scary, hands moved in and out
of the shadows like puppets, passing drugs, money, in the
flare of a match and the smell of tobacco I saw a woman
kneeling on the dirty parquet floor, her face pressed into a

man's crotch. I can still hear myself trying to explain to my
mother in my little voice, It was just like the ladies in
church, ma, the way they kneel on the stones with their
faces pressed against the marble skirts of the saints.
Smack! Don't you go talking like that! Sometimes it was
just a bum trying to get in from the cold, a junky nodding
off. One morning I stepped over a body lying like a charred
store mannequin in a foul smelling pool of liquid that
smelled of puke, stale piss, rotten meat. You wouldn't think
a smell like that could become something good in your
memory, like standing outside a bakery and inhaling the
warm sweet smells of bread and cakes, pies, pastries and
jelly-filled donuts. Because it's something real, like a tree
or a rock you can grab onto in a flood of memories, because
it establishes you in a past, it confirms that you were there,
which in turn confirms that you are here now. But the
smell is always better than the thing itself, like tobacco or
coffee or scotch. If you eat the substance, the stuff, it's
never as good, it sits in your stomach and rots, it gives you
indigestion. Of course, these are my thoughts now. You
don't think those things when you're hungry, you don't
have the perspective to think those things. You're too busy
watching and waiting, your whole life is a watching and
waiting for something to happen, something to come along,
free you, allow you to escape that existence. ///////////
///
And you put up with that lousy half-life in that lousy rotting hive until you're old enough, not according to the law,
which requires that you spend eighteen years in that
prison, seventeen with parents consent—What parents,
sir? I am my own parents. Don't get smart with me, sol-
dier!—but old enough anyway to lie, to swear, to growl at
the recruiting officer, Yeah, I'm old enough, your face already gaunt and hard with just enough beard stubble at

the age of fifteen to be convincing, beard stubble forced by long cold nights in the streets, forced by the rush of hormones and adrenaline flushing through your veins, those alternate rushes of fear and exhilaration when you ran down some dark, stinking alley with gunfire echoing all around you, maybe it's not even the cops, maybe it's just another gang loaded down with shotguns, machine pistols, they wanta cut you up, bash your fucking head in for messing in their territory—all that you left behind when you signed up, when you dropped out of that world, went out on the plains with thousands of other eager, nervous, frightened young men to push the arms of civilization farther into the darkness, and suddenly you had everybody together, raw-boned, freckle-faced crackers and big fucking spades and tough little beaners from the east side, who knows, maybe even some crazy howling ragheads from the desert, inscrutable yellow and red skins with slanted and almond and olive eyes. It didn't matter where you came from, everybody was together, you were all crazed, laughing and shouting all this bullshit jive with reefer and booze and crystal methedrine in your veins and Independence Day going off over your head. And then a shell lands right in the middle and suddenly you're sitting in a pile of smashed cherry pie and scattered limbs screaming AAAA-HHHHH! AAAAHHHHH! AAAAHHHHH! over and over again because you alone were untouched, because all those other lives and all those other voices that were laughing and shouting around you a second ago stopped, and were gone forever, and you alone kept talking into the void. But you said you weren't going to think about that stuff anymore, Harry. You have to stop thinking about that stuff. / / /
/ /
I'd started walking again, shedding memories behind me, it doesn't matter whose memories, they belonged to some-

body, that's all that counts. At the next street I stopped in front of a rotting tenement, checked my address book. One time a guy in the agency got the wrong number, they bulldozed an entire block before anyone could convince the authorities they'd fucked up. It was a real circus, people wandering the streets in their underwear, dazed, crying, hysterical, clutching pillows, phone books, teddy bears. / / /
/ /
Headlines: Out With The Old. In With The New. Economy Booming. City Embarks On Urban Renewal. /
/ /
Of course they blamed it on terrorists, mad bombers. I remember Frank only laughed, clenched his pipe between his teeth, his jaw hardening into a knot. Yeah, sure, he could laugh. What did it matter to him whether it was bombs or bureaucratic fuck-ups, they both served the same purpose. Which was what? To disrupt and ruin the lives of those wretches, until they had no choice but to lie down and die, or else join the growing population of hungry and enraged in the streets, the pregnancy of a revolution. And all that time I was doing the dirty work, I was Frank's fucking pawn, the executor of his will.

Yeah, I know, you're thinking, whoa, all this is happening because of one man? But then, when I started to doubt myself, when I thought I really was going crazy, I'd think, yeah, but why not, Harry? He has the perfect job, he's in touch with hundreds of people every day, the kind of people who might sympathize with his way of thinking, students, other professors. Besides, what if Frank was only one such organizer, what if Cassa and I only one cell? But that was none of my business. By then I'd learned the rules of the game, shut up, do your job, like anywhere else. I went up a couple flights of stairs, pounded on the door. Bang! Bang!

Bang! Open up, it's the Building Inspector! Inside you hear
a voice, Alright! Alright! I'm coming! I'd gotten used to inviting myself into peoples' homes. No, not homes, let's call
them hovels, dens, the filthy caves they live in. In the beginning I was apologetic, almost deferential, I hated doing
my job. I'd think, how can you do this to these people,
Harry? You used to live among them, they're just like
you. Except you never really believed that, did you? You
couldn't believe that or you never would've gotten out of
that hellhole. Soon I learned to resent them for being so
stupid, for not understanding the necessity, that it was going to happen anyway. It made it easier to do my job. If they
were recalcitrant I flashed a badge, took advantage of the
wide-eyed terror it produced to push my way into their
homes, ordered them out of the bathroom, the bedroom, the
covers thrown back, the still-warm bed smelling of sleep,
sex, babies suckling at their mamas' breasts, the dim little
bathroom with the bare bulb burning, the sink splashed
with water, a sheet of toilet paper on the toilet seat because
they were so scared they didn't have time to finish wiping
themselves. You terrorize them, make them understand in
an instant what they haven't grasped all their wretched
lives. Nothing is yours, nowhere is safe, any time, any
place, they, we, this fucking bureaucracy without a face, in
other words, your government, can come and take you
away, destroy your home, your life, leave no trace. / / / / / / /
/ /
I went around thumping walls, listening to the aged hot
water pipes banging and rumbling behind the plaster, fingering the cracks and fissures in the foundation, the frac-
tures spreading outward through the immortal stone,
while they followed behind me, afraid to speak, waiting for
an explanation. I never explained. I couldn't, not to them,
not to myself. I handed them a piece of paper, Sign this.

They didn't even realize it was an eviction notice until the wrecking crew showed up at their front door the next morning. Too bad for them. They should have figured it out a long time ago, found somewhere else to live, maybe one of the government settlements on the plain Frank was always raving about.

When I was still working demolition we used to pass down pieces of bathroom tile, marble, mosaics, mythical fish and beasts cavorting with maidens and nymphs, sometimes a chunk of plasterboard with some little kid's pink and blue crayon duckies, scribbles. After a while you start to sort it out, piece it together again in your brain, like shards of ancient amphorae, cooking pots. It's a game, you see, just to pass the time, like, what kind of people lived here and what kind of lives did they lead? Were they happy? Sad? Rich? Poor? At the end of their rope? Ready for suicide? Terrorism? Could they afford armed guards? Entire armies and navies at their disposal? Or were they wretches living like rats in dark hovels of despair? Without any culture? Without any art? Without any knowledge of who they were or where they came from? Without, in other words, a past? But you can always synthesize that, right? Put a few pictures on the wall, a couple of knickknacks on the shelf, this is great grandfather Jones, Aunt Matilda gave these to me the day before she died. Like I said, it was a game I used to play.

I got on the train, felt the darkness and depression slip below and behind me as I shot up onto a bright, tree-lined boulevard crowded with shops and pedestrians, all those good citizens leading a good, happy life, while the lonesome cowpoke, Sheriff Harry, rides off into the sunset after another day's good work. ///////////////////////////////// /// You have to understand, this is a normal response, Harry.

Resentment. Anger. Denial. Your brain cannot accept that you took part in the killing, especially when you were taught all your life that it was wrong. And suddenly you had this discrepancy, it was alright in certain circumstances. Of course you were afraid. Everybody was afraid. And then, on top of that, you got out of there, you made it home alive, and you felt guilty because you left the others behind, because you were living a normal life when you knew they were still out there dying (LAW & CIVILIZATION p. 193? 194? 195?)./// But that wasn't something I read in one of Frank's books, was it? It was that bullshit he dumped on me during one of those humiliating sessions. Yeah, sure, he was so high and mighty, all his great books, all his posturing and professions of concern for humanity. He was so smug, so certain he was responsible for my good fortune, this great fucking job. He'd invite himself over for dinner, the loving father, grandfather, hovering over the crib, cooing to the baby, his pale blue eyes moist, welling, a brief saltwater baptismal. Yeah, sure, the good father Frank, father to a revolution, all he ever wanted from me was the damn baby, to raise it up in the cradle of insurrection, nurture it and train it until it was old enough and crazed enough to pronounce itself king. Because even then he was manipulating me, working on my mind, guilt, sentiment, the baby. My dream is that one day you kids'll get out of this slum, move out on the plains where the air is clean, where you can see the sky, where you can breathe, raise a family, build a home. Yes, of course, home. Somewhere in the middle of his sermons he always managed to let slip that single innocuous word, home, like the lonesome cry of a locomotive hurtling across the dark countryside, the home he'd carved out of memory, dream, with ghost wife and children waiting for him in some sod shack, split rail fences, livestock and good green things growing in the earth. Because that was his method, wasn't it? The subtle indoctrination, the key words that clicked in your brain, made your thoughts, your heart and soul swell with visions of that home and that life of kith and kin, not just family and friends but an entire community, a civilization of like-minded men and women where everyone worked to the best of their ability and all enjoyed the profits of their toil.

Who knows, maybe I did believe that once, wanted to believe it. But even then I knew the truth was something altogether different. The communes he prophesied on the plains didn't mean egalitarian societies where everyone shared equally in the fruits of their endeavors. But cattle yards, concentration camps for vast populations of slave labor, not only his political enemies, but the victims of pogroms and purges, thousands, millions of innocent human beings, all those he held complicit in the death of his woman, wife, Cassa's mother. Besides, what were we going to do? Volunteer for one of those missionary posts on the plains? Live in a mud hut with a bunch of monkeys?

He was right about one thing. This neighborhood, apartment, all that had once seemed so bright and alive, now seemed dark, dim, overshadowed by the latest building boom. One evening the sun disappeared into a murky red gloom and never returned. If we opened the window at night the noise from the street below was too loud, the apartment filled with exhaust fumes, we went to bed with headaches, feeling sick, the baby was always crying. Christ! I'd yell, can't you make that damn thing shut up for once? I've got work to do! Cassa's painting had stopped altogether, ceased to be a part of her existence. Her life was completely tied up with the baby's. She'd sit on the couch with the baby at her breast in that protective, postpartum

alliance, her pupils dilated, her mind detached, drifting on
another plane with the soul of this blotchy, pooping, peeing
sack of flesh, trying to soothe its tears, smooth away the
outrage screwed up in its tiny red face, that pre-cognitive
sense of betrayal. /////////////////////////////////////
///
Later, after she'd taken the baby to bed, I'd make a fresh
pot of coffee, open a pack of cigarettes, sit down at the
kitchen table with my notes from class last night, a stack
of books from the library. Books, my one true secret, my
refuge and my resurrection when I was a kid hiding from
the old man's rage in a closet, when I was a man hiding in
a trench or a bunker on the plains in those interminable
lulls between the fighting, when I lay in bed at night afraid
to sleep, afraid of when the lights went down and the movie
started again. I read anything I could find, comic books,
torn paperbacks, skin magazines, weird holy scriptures
thrust at me by raving religious fanatics. But then I read
as an escape. Now I read to learn, understand, I absorbed
everything, drank, swallowed, gorged on words, images,
ideas. I'd never been so excited in my life, never felt so obsessed. It was weird to be so straight, so sober, to feel my
mind working so clearly. All these theories, ideas were beginning to come together in my head, poetry and art
founded on the structural realism of engineering, physics.
At least that's the way it seems to me now, the way I built
and pieced it together out of the graphs, the charts and
equations that covered my desk for months before I began
to make the least correlation between the work I used to do
with a pick and shovel and the soft blue, almost luminous
intersecting and divergent lines indicating archways and
abutments, suspension bridges, iron struts and trusses,
the skeleton of a city erecting itself out of the millions and
billions of tons of steel, lumber and stone hauled and car-

ried over how many months and then years by how many thousands and then millions of men and women according to the designs of dreamers, visionaries, the architects and builders, each generation shoring up the old, raising up the new, until centuries had passed and then eons of constructing and building. And how much of that before you began to conceive not only of the city and the creator of the city, but the creator of all building and creation? ///////////// /// I KNOW! you don't wanna hear this NOISE! right NOW! Brother Harry! There's no room for GOD! in your SCHEME! right NOW! Brother Harry!

I used to see this preacher on the street, he was probably in all the police files, government records, in fact, he probably worked for the goddamned government, he was out there scoping out every madman, every escaped convict, every down-and-out revolutionary who stopped to listen, doing a flimflam with a camcorder in his big black holy Book, a microphone hidden in his sacred icon, he was out there all the time, in the pouring rain, in the cold and snow, a lean, clean black man in a black suit and tie, railing against the world and the sins of the world, he looked mad, he looked completely insane, and then he looked right into your eyes and he said, We shall build the temple aGAIN! Brother Harry! We shall LAUNCH! our MIS!siles into the HEA!vens, Brother Harry, and they shall come DOWN! aGAIN! in an ALL!-conSUM!ing UN!ity of VOI!ces! Brother Harry! They shall SPEAK! to us as a CHOIR! of AN!gels, Brother Harry! Even those who seek to deSTROY! Even they seek GOD! Brother Harry! EveryTHANG! is a SEEK!-ing and deSIRE! to return to GOD! Brother Harry! We shall RAISE! up our VOI!ces, Brother Harry! We shall sing HAL!ayLU!ya in our FLAMES! Brother Harry! Are you LIS!tening to me, Brother Harry? I KNOW! you're listen-

ing, Brother Harry! I can see in your EYES! that you're listening, Brother Harry! Won't you get DOWN! with me,
Brother Harry? Won't you get down on your KNEES! and
PRAY! to the GOD! of salVA!tion, Brother Harry?! / / / / / / /
/ /
I'd drifted off again, gone off on another tangent. I felt so
tired, worn out, I'd pour another cup of coffee, light another
cigarette, try to pick up where I left off the night before, the
week before, whenever it was I felt that last burst of inspiration, experienced that last insight, epiphany into the
workings of the universe. But it just went on and on, an
endless string of beginnings, the whole mad mess evolving
out of control, I thought I'd never finish. I'd tear through
books, articles and essays, looking for a foothold, entry, I
wrote endless notes, tore up page after page. Suddenly it'd
stop dead, fall to pieces, I'd gone off on some digression, I
couldn't remember where I was going. I'd make another pot
of coffee, tear open another pack of cigarettes, sit at the
table and stare into space, my eyes burning, my thoughts
and my mind a wad of cotton gauze, nevertheless thankful
for these few moments of peace before the baby started crying again, woke Cassa. She'd come out to the kitchen with
the child in her arms, looking haggard, worn. Harry? Are
you still working? Aren't you coming to bed? I wanted to
shout, I haven't even begun to work yet! Leave me alone!
Go back to bed! By now I was completely neurotic, feverish,
my head aching, eyes blurred, convinced that I was going
to be a complete failure. Who the fuck was I trying to fool?
Everything I did was shit. I was never going to finish this
goddamn thesis. I put a tape into the machine, punched the
button, expecting to hear notes from last night's lecture.
But I'd made a mistake, put in the wrong tape, one of those
horribly demeaning things I made when I was still having
my sessions with Frank. As soon as I heard my voice I was

filled with self-hatred, disgust, I wanted to turn it off. At
the same time it fascinated me, I played it over and over
again, winding and rewinding it, listening to that frightened little voice I barely recognized as my own, lost in that
high-pitched garble and shriek, like a maze full of rats
screeching and running wild inside my head. Why the fuck
was I so scared all the time? Who taught me that? Was everyone else as scared as I was? That's when I first tried to
slow the voice down, when I resolved never again to capitu-
late to the babbling, to know always where I was and what
I was doing and what the voice in my head was really saying. But it isn't that easy, is it? You never get over that fear
entirely, it stays with you, haunts you, rises to the surface
again when you least expect it. /////////////////////////
///
When I was a kid I used to lie awake at night, listening to
the distant creak and howl of the freight trains rising up
miles and miles of bottomless black elevator shafts, scattering in their passing the newspapers and gum wrappers,
motes of dust, banana peels, lacy frilly baby dolls dropped
out of upper story windows by pudgy little hands, dead
dogs, cats, appliances tossed out by worn washerwoman
hands, laborer's hands, desperate, angry hands, the broken
bodies, broken in spirit, mind, hurtling themselves earthward in a last desperate attempt to fly, free themselves
from the horrible weight and oppression of their wretched
lives, all endlessly fluttering down like angels on tattered
wings, like moths descending into the light, all suddenly
scattered and blown away again by a freight or commuter
train roaring back down through the rotting black heart of
the hive. Sometimes I thought I could actually hear the
currents of electricity trickling and seeping down through
the endless centuries of brick and mortar, bearing long out-
dated messages, some urgent, some crying out in despair,

some mad, some drunken ravings of hope, exhilaration. Night after night there was an old woman's voice sobbing, repeating the same lamentation over and over again, no, no, no. One time a child's voice weepy and afraid. Who knows, maybe it was my own voice, a ten, eleven, twelve-year-old kid, even then with the terrible yearning in my body, in my mind, trying to figure things out, offering my pathetic little prayers to God, to whoever listened. I pictured myself falling on my knees, blubbering shamelessly in front of some wise old counselor or judge in a dark blue business suit, I'll do anything, take any job, work myself senseless, please, just give me a chance. ///////////// ///
A week after my thesis was published in NEW VISIONS I was invited to present a paper at a job seminar sponsored by Growth Group Industries. I remember everything about that day, how I woke early, my stomach churning, my hands trembling as I shaved. How I left Cassa with her face crushed in the pillow, her body twisted in tortured angles, waiting for her alarm to go off, the first howl of the baby. How I took the express up to the New World Station, grabbed a sky cab past the towers and atriums to the Olympus Hotel. How I stood there on the sidewalk with my shabby briefcase and overcoat staring up to the top of the forty stories of gleaming glass walls, terraces and columns, with marble nymphs and satyrs splashing in fountains and waterfalls, and runners and vines dropping green foliage and bursts of color onto the successive tiers and ledges hundreds of feet below. I felt like an impostor, a supplicant. I felt like falling to my knees and shouting to God. I felt like a conqueror hiding in the equine darkness of pitch and pine with the gleam of a sword in my eyes. ///////////// ///
After lunch I and a dozen other recent graduates boarded

the GGI tour bus, bounced and banged over the rubble and
rocks of the New World Boulevard, gasping at the sudden
gaping chunks of blue sky through the girders and beams,
the skeleton of a vast vertical metropolis swarming with
thousands of workers, installing the organs, the pipes and
wiring, plumbing, electricity, heating and cooling ducts, op-
tic fiber, phones, TV, security systems, computer hook-ups,
walling it in behind slabs of marble, great gleaming sheets
of green and gold and silver glass. During a stop at a construction site I wandered away from the rest of the group,
there was an unattended freight elevator, I stepped in, hit
the button, the motor whirred, I started up. I kept expecting the car to stop at the next level but it just kept going up
and up, the buildings, the tractors and workers on the
ground falling farther away and below. I felt my heart begin to beat and pound in my chest. I remember I had this
crazy thought, what if something's wrong, it never stops? I
could see myself flying off the top, launched into space like
a wild-eyed, screaming cartoon, and then—flop! splattered
on the ground like an inkblot.

A bell sounded. The elevator stopped. I staggered out of
the cage, onto the gleaming metal platform, clutched at the
railing. A cold wind whipped around me. The sun burned
like a bare thousand watt lightbulb in the pale blue sheet
of plastic stretched over the earth. I was at the very tip of
the missile, the spear. The acetylene heat and light blinded
me, filled my eyes with tears, made me look down. Below
me white puffs of cloud dragged their shadows over the
earth. The people on the ground looked tiny and far away.
An image flashed through my mind, a body falling through
space. What was that guy's name, Hank? No, Joe, poor Joe.
But it wasn't Joe you were thinking about now, was it,
Harry? It was you, and the paper you were supposed to deliver that evening. I'd worked on it for months, wrote and

rewrote until I was convinced I'd covered every angle. But when I thought of it now, suddenly it sounded like such a perfectly boring piece of shit. I could see myself standing in front of all those powerful people, I saw myself beginning to stutter and stammer and turn red in the face, I was going to fuck up, blow the only chance I'd ever get. What was I doing here? I didn't belong among these people. I felt a sickening urge. I let go of my grip on the railing, stood up straight. The pounding in my chest had subsided but suddenly it started again, the sound surrounded me, pounded inside me, I felt nauseous, dizzy, my legs were weak. I began to hyperventilate, I was gasping for air. Then I was screaming, AHHHH! AHHHH! AHHHH! //////////////// // Harry? Harry? Harry? I heard my name called, then polite applause, followed by a voice reading words on a page, something about building and construction, design, safety, codes. It was my voice. But something was wrong. I was starting to panic, my throat was tightening, my voice sounded strange.

Somewhere in the distance I heard a sound, a pounding, I felt the acetylene heat and light on my face, the cold wind whipped around me, I opened my mouth to speak, to breathe, to gulp the fresh air, and then it was roaring out of me and it was my voice and my words, and I could see them all turning to look at me, I could feel them listening to me, the words echoed in my ears like cannon fire, like grenades going off . . . The old way is DEAD! . . . many will lose their reSOLVE! . . . many will SUF!fer . . . fall beHIND! . . . nosTAL!gia! . . . DEATH! . . . deCAY! . . . we must not be aFRAID! to take this final STEP! . . . the FU!ture is NOW! . . . we are a RAD!ical EV!-o-LU!-tionary FORCE! . . . we shall CHANGE! the COURSE! of huMAN!ity! . . . LEAP! into the ARMS! of GOD! . . . it is our DES!tiny!

Of course I wasn't saying anything new, I was just re-
working the old, the obvious, giving force and cohesion to
the events that engulfed us now. It was the way I spoke, the
energy, the power and the light I felt inside me. I talked
until I was completely emptied, until I'd run out of light
and words and there was nothing left to say. Then I was
holding a drink in my hand, people were crowding around
me, they were patting me on the back, congratulating me,
asking questions, arranging interviews, appointments,
we'd like to hear more, Harry. Are you open tomorrow
morning? It wasn't until after midnight that I remembered
I was supposed to call Cassa. I asked the operator for long
distance, heard her making the connection, I was still
wired, full of light and energy and ready to yell into the
phone, Yayyyy! It went great! Then I heard Cassa's voice on
the other end, Hello? Harry? What time is it? She sounded
tired, irritable, suddenly I had to tone it down, make excuses, I'm sorry, I didn't mean to shout, what's going on?
Oh, but she didn't want to complain, it was just a virus going around, she was sick, the baby was sick, I could hear it
crying in her arms, making those horrible hacking sounds.
Yeah, I know, she wanted comfort, pity. But I resented her
for it. The fucking bitch, didn't she realize? This was my
night, I was a success, on my way up, couldn't she make an
effort to sound happy for me?

After I hung up I went down to the bar for a drink, then
another. I didn't feel like sleeping. I still felt wired, full of
energy, unwilling to relinquish the night and the success of
the night. Later I pulled on my overcoat and went out for a
stroll on the sky walk. Overhead the stars twinkled with
their distant suggestion of light and hope. I heard the
sound of heavy machinery. Across the valley I could see a
construction site lit up by spotlights. A tower crane swung
across vast chasms of shadow and night. Workers in hard

hats and goggles swarmed over the iron girders, silhouetted in the blue-white fog of arc welders. On the ground
tractors and earth movers growled over the earth. / / / / / / /
/ /
Brum! Brum! I hung off the chain link fence, watching the
kids in corduroy jumpers pushing toy tractors through the
sand piles, making rumbling tractor sounds deep in their
throats, and how could I not remember four-year-old Harry
splashing in a mud puddle with a fucking bottle or a block
of wood, his royal galleon, completely unaware of the filth
around him, infant God and king of his small universe.
Yeah, but now it was true, I was actually on my way up, on
the executive track. Sure, I was just one suit among a thousand other suits, but at least I was among my own kind, I
felt like I had a chance at last.

   Cassa coughed on the bench next to me, shifted the
child in her arms, buttoned its collar, letting me know by
every sign and signal that she wasn't terribly impressed.
You don't understand, I said. It'll mean a whole new life.
We'll get a place in the Heights, with clean air, and a view.
After he starts day care you'll have more time for your
painting. /
/ /
The truth is, I didn't give a shit about her painting. I was
just trying to appease her, appeal to her artistic instincts.
She'd developed a new routine when the baby was still
small, before it began to cry mama! and crawl around her
feet. She'd tie it up in a sling at her chest while she worked
at the canvas, like some kind of native woman or squaw
scratching at the barren earth, encouraging the dying
weeds to flourish and grow into food crops, the whole time
rendering upon her offspring that ancestral memory of
labor and the earth commingled with milk warmth and
mother's breasts, opening her top to feed the baby when it

woke bawling and flailing its tiny arms, laying it out on the couch to change its diaper, then tying it up in the sling and going back to work, the whole time singing it a little song in some private language only she and the baby understood. Yeah, I know, I should have been moved, maybe at one time I would have been moved, the Madonna, mother and child. To be honest, I found it disgusting, it seemed so primitive, crude. Besides, I'd always hated the smell of the oils, paint thinner, that toxic environment she created. I should have reported her to the authorities. She's poisoning my son! Now that I think of it, her work had changed too. It was less violent, more subdued. Ironic, that's the word I was looking for, the wildness gone, maybe mastered, controlled, transformed by her care and responsibility for the baby. Now she worked quickly, efficiently, applying confident, determined strokes. ///////////////////////// // At the edge of the plains a group of tall dark figures stood like statues, their shadows long, lean, like the spears they held at their sides, their eyes fixed on the distant walls and towers of a great gleaming citadel. Between them and the city stood a fleet of shopping carts. /////////////////// // And how many do you think will enjoy the privileges of this marvelous city? Hundreds? Thousands? Frank again, pontificating, puffing furiously on his stinking pipe. I'd made the mistake of inviting him for a victory celebration after my year-end promotion at GGI. I wanted him to see how well I was doing, I wanted him to acknowledge my success. I'd laid out a big spread, had some caterer deliver roasted game, exotic fruits, the piece de resistance some strange fish clad like an ancient warrior in its red and green mail, its dead eye a memory staring out of the past, out of the muddy brown water of a vast river snaking across the plains.

An endangered species actually, Frank said, raising a forkful of the fish's dark, smoky meat to his mouth, presiding over the dinner table like the progenitor and king of an entire race and nation embodied in the child he held in his lap, rocking it, cooing, talking to it, inculcating his nonsense upon its nascent brain in between bites of fish . . . a pre-historic creature that survived for millions of years among its natural predators . . . a bite . . . reputed to give long life and prosperity to those who eat its flesh . . . another bite . . . and then we came . . . bite . . . poisoning its waters . . . bite . . . thinning its numbers with nets and dynamite . . . a swallow of wine followed by another bite. It had never occurred to me before that there might be some contradiction between his radical philosophy and his appetite. He was as relentless in eating as he was speaking. He shoved it in my face as fast as he shoveled it in his mouth, reveling in his own decadence as he went off on another digression, his voice starting and stopping in staccato bursts, like the monotony of machine-gun fire in a bombed-out village, outlining for the hundredth time the endless diasporas, migrations, wars, clash of cultures, intermingling of races, religions, the contracts and covenants between church and state. But now that must change. You've got a voice, Harry, you've got passion. You can work your way up, take hold of the reins, give new meaning and direction to the word progress. I was only now beginning to realize what a lunatic he really was. He was completely convinced of my part in his conspiracy, so deluded he couldn't even smell the enemy's spoor right under his nose. Didn't it ever occur to him that I liked what I was doing? That my vision and the vision of GGI were one and the same?

By then I'd already put a down payment on a lot in the Heights, we were talking to architects, engineers, Cassa even got involved with designing her studio, plenty of light, with a nursery nearby for the child, a large living and dining area for the entertaining I'd have to do, all the time going on with our lives as if things were perfectly normal. Who knows how that works? Inertia, some underlying belief that things will get better? //////////////////////// // Cassa stood at the easel, poking at the bare canvas with an empty brush, stroking it, making a dry, hissing sound, sss . . . sss . . . sss, like an archeologist, brushing thousands of years of dust and debris from the bleached white bones of some ancient wanderer laid down for a night and then eternity in the sands of a riverbed in a barren wasteland. Remember when you used to tell me stories, Harry? How come we never talk anymore? It seems like we hardly even know each other. I can't even remember the last time we made love.

I sat on a chair, in a rumpled suit and tie, my hands dangling between my knees, surveying the crates and boxes containing the age-old wreckage of our apartment, her studio, listening to the sss . . . sss . . . sss . . . of her brush on the canvas, thinking about the work I still had to do tonight, proposals, presentations, contracts. And what was I supposed to say? When do I have the time? I work all day, come home and work again at night. Yeah, sure, in the old days, when I was a common laborer, then it was alright to come home, drink, smoke, get fucked up and make the bed bang against the wall—then, when things were more basic, when need conquered all. But that never meant anything to her. It was always her life, her fucking painting, then the baby. And all that time she was sucking at me, using me up, it all came from me, my words and my experience and all that I lived through. I was her fucking inspiration. And now that I was becoming a success she was afraid I'd leave

her behind. ///
//
I even tried to get her involved in company functions, seminars for employees' spouses, parties, fashion shows. Cassa
wasn't impressed. I don't like these people, Harry. Why?
What's wrong with them? Christ, Harry, can't you see?
They're stupid, they're boring, all they talk about is money,
things. They don't know anything about life. Oh yes, I could
already feel it evolving into another one of those hideous
arguments we were beginning to have all the time. The
fucking bitch. She was so goddamn stupid. She didn't have
any idea in the world where the real power came from. She
was always running around in those ridiculous costumes,
like some kind of fucking gypsy, vagabond. She knew nothing about fashion, about clothing or style. Oh, yes, of
course, she was an artist, she had a unique perspective on
the world. If I asked, When are you going to do something
real with your work? Why don't you ever try to sell it, make
some money? She'd look at me like I was crazy. That's not
the point, Harry. That's not why I paint. She had some
crazy idea, Frank again, I'm sure, she wanted to give her
work to the people. Yeah, sure, and what were those good
people going to do with it? Piss on it? Shit on it? Spray it
with graffiti? But if I said anything like that she flipped
out completely. Remember when you had a vision, Harry?
You were going to do things to help people? Build public
housing, community centers? What happened to that? I
wanted to scream at her, Shut up! What the fuck are you
talking about? That wasn't me, it was Frank, your father,
hammering at me all the time. Now it's you. She was always nagging at me, always on my back, always beating me
down with that whiny little voice that should have been so
cute, maybe even used to be cute, but long ago had become
a real whining drag, not just her voice, but her, Cassa. ////

///
The first time I had that thought I was sitting in the GGI
executive lounge, working on the house drink and a glitch
in the Glass Canyon account when someone hissed, Lenore
Nimrod! and I looked up from my notes and saw her coming toward me, insinuating herself among the crowded
tables in that costume, outfit, something red, outrageous,
like a skein of nerve fibers stretched over her naked body.
Then she was standing over me, leering down at me, asking in a very public way, Do you mind if I join you, Harry?
Suddenly my heart began to pound in my chest, not just
desire, but proximity to all that power, Lenore Nimrod,
CEO of GGI, power broker and headhunter combined, and
now she stood in front of me in front of the world or that
part of the world occupying the tables around us. Yeah, I
know, I should have been more cautious, exercised some re-
straint. But it felt so good, she puffed me up, preened my
feathers and hardened my beak, then left me dangling
there for everyone to see. Sure, sit down, I said, trying
to sound polished, tough. The truth is I was completely
ruffled. She knew everything about me, my resume, job
evaluations, promotions, the paper I'd given at the Growth
Group seminar nearly two years ago. Lenore lit a cigarette,
leaned closer for a sip of my drink, There's a situation
opening up, Harry. We think you're the right person. We'd
like to have you. Her voice was throaty, full, with an edge to
it, like my drink, an icy, menthol concoction with a trace of
something bitter, red. While you were drinking it you felt
wrapped in warmth and promise. You didn't realize how
much damage it was doing until the next day. I started to
say something but she uncurled a polished red nail in front
of her lips. You don't have to tell me now, Harry. You can
tell me in an hour or two, after I've had a chance to show
you some of the fringe benefits. I felt my heart begin to

pound again. Fucking Lenore. Just like that, in front of everybody, the show and the invitation to the show, Come on, Harry, give it to me, give it to me good. Not in those words of course, but in words that meant those words, pushing those bright green eyes in my face, pushing that soft red pout and hot, stinking breath. Too many cigarettes, too much booze, garlic, a real meat-eater, man-eater. I wanted to grab her right there, bend her over the table, fuck her, squeeze and fondle her tits, her ass, the way she swelled out of that dress, that membrane she'd painted on with blackberry juice and the blood of some dumb animal that had strayed too near. And now, when it was my turn, all I could do was salivate and raise my tail, because I knew, as certainly as I'd ever known anything before, that in ten or fifteen or twenty minutes, as long as it took to take the cab, the elevator, to go through some brief preliminaries, we were going to be in bed together, fucking, and it was going to be better than it had ever been in my life. ////////////
//
Yeah, sure, at first it was easy enough to tell Cassa some lie, another late night at the office, another big assignment. Which was true anyway. I was always busy, banging off the walls, caroming between board meetings, sales and strategy meetings, hitting luncheons, conventions, all the time selling myself and my vision in the name of God, glory and GGI. And still managing to squeeze in a couple hours between the sheets with Lenore. She'd stand in front of her penthouse window overlooking the city, peeling away the layers of silk and satin like onion skin. Her body was smooth, strong. We didn't make love, we fought, wrestled, pinned each other to the floor, the mattress, the wall, writhing and sliding over each other like serpents twisted up in a confused excess of killing and procreation, we sank our teeth into each other's flesh, threatened each other,

called each other names, you fucking cunt, you whore, you
filthy bitch, come on, fuck me, you ugly bastard, you prick.
We actually did it in her office, in the stairwell going down
to the stockroom, in the executive men's room with the
stall locked and her heels planted on each side of the toilet,
tearing at each other's hair, clothes, hot, panting, smothering each other's gasps, laughter. She had such a nice sexy
body and such a twisted little mind. In fact, she was really
quite a bitch, a sexy scheming bitch. In the middle of making love, or no, not making love, never call it love, war
maybe, or murder, or slaughter, she whispered, You know
we're doing a background check on you, don't you, Harry?
If you ever lie to me I'll fuck you up, I'll ruin your career, I'll
make it so you can't even find a job cleaning toilets. Of
course I laughed, in the middle of making love I laughed,
laughter, the alternate response to that stupid male mechanism hard at work below. Because it was a joke, right? Because she had no proof. All I had to do was lie and lie again
and compound that lie with still another lie until she
didn't know what to believe. The truth? The truth is whatever you want the truth to be.

Then I'd go home to our little house on the hill, the
dully gleaming glass and steel box we occupied on the
north tower of Aluminum Heights, everything still smelling of fresh paint, plaster, carpet and tile. Enter like a bur-
glar, thief, find the TV screen buzzing, Cassa huddled on
the couch with the kid asleep in her arms, a storybook still
open in her hands, her eyes on mine, watching me, waiting
for me to strike her, attack the boy, her progeny, whelp. / / /
/ /
Daddy! It's Daddy! Daddy's home! Yeah, sure, after a hard
week at the office Daddy finally comes home, drunk, crazy,
pounding on the front door so all the neighbors can hear.
Open up, ya fucking bitch, I'll kill you! He crashes through

the door, stinking of booze, he's dirty, torn, his eyes are
glazed, filled with hatred, he spots you hiding behind the
sofa. Fucking mongrel bastard I'll kill you! He knocks
aside your mother, grabs for the—telephone! Daddy's going
to knock your brains out with the telephone! No! mommy
shrieks. Get out of the way, bitch! Daddy punches mommy
in the face, blood spurts from mommy's nose, mommy sits
on the floor in a funny way moaning no, no, no! Daddy
grabs mommy's arm, twists. Shut up, bitch! You can hear
the snap and splinter. An hour later you're sitting in the
emergency room, worn out and afraid, a poor little poster
boy among a dozen other broken and bleeding bodies while
mommy explains in a dazed monotone, I don't know what
happened, doctor, there was a hole in the pavement, stupid
me, I wasn't watching where I was going. One day the old
man goes away for good and then it's just your mother, a
ruined old woman in dirty rags, trying to keep you all fed,
keep you all together in that tangle of brothers and sisters
piled up on some ratty, piss-soaked mattress infested with
bed bugs, lice, cockroaches running over your face at night.
But we know all about that, don't we, Harry boy? It's all
here on tape, with all the pauses, hesitations, searching for
words, for the breath to speak after another fit of gasping,
choking sobs. ///////////////////////////////////////
///
But Cassa wasn't buying that crap anymore, she refused to
listen to the old excuses. You haven't seen your own son in
a month, Harry! You act like a complete stranger! You come
home smelling of booze, perfume! What kind of life is this?
That was the signal I was waiting for, the key to launch a
counter attack. The kind of life you wanted! I shouted. The
kind of life your father wanted! I knew that'd get her, anything about her father, Frank, like he was some kind of totem, taboo. And then, when she tried to defend him, when

she shouted back, I changed my tack, played the serpent, snake, spoke to her in that smooth business voice, as if she was the one who was acting irrational. Don't you understand, Cassa? He's raising this stink. He's advocating dangerous things. He's causing trouble. He's going to ruin my career, just now when I'm starting to make it big. I'm a builder now, Cassa, not a destroyer. The people I work with know how to protect the world, especially from lunatics like your father. Then she really lost it, exploded, screamed all kinds of terrible things at me, her thin neck and arms taut with rage, her eyes blazing. Right on cue Frank walked in, his face frozen into a mask of shock, betrayal, that fury and indignation that lifted up his aging chest and shoulders like some angry, admonishing god. What's wrong with you, Harry? What are you doing? I believed in you, I thought you were one of us. Even if you don't care about Cassa, what about the boy? Your own son? Are you going to condemn him to the hell you're building now? Are you going to raise him up with these lies? / Yeah, sure, and what else was I going to do? Try to explain? I met this other woman, honey? It doesn't mean anything? Or better yet, tell her the truth—slam her on the head with that lead pipe—the truth, the truth, wrapped up and muffled in all those beautiful words I kept on reserve for times like that, You fucking pig, you whore, you ugly slut, and watch her face crumple into an ugly red mask? / How many men have killed to mask their transgressions, coldly, blindly, committing themselves to greater transgressions still (LAW AND CIVILIZATION p. 413)? / Yeah, sure, Frank again. Even when I wanted to be rid of him his words haunted me, intruded upon my private life.

All that bullshit he wrote, all those lies. Maybe if he'd told the truth, taught Cassa the truth, you have to be tough, you have to be strong, you have to be prepared to kill.

I lay on my back, a drink in my hand, a cigarette smoldering between my fingers, watching the smoke rise toward the ceiling. Cassa faced the wall, clutching her shoulders, her body trembling, her voice aching like a bad bruise, Why do you despise me so much, Harry? What did I ever do to you? And suddenly I did despise her, I hated her guts, I couldn't stand the sight of her. I'd never realized before how ugly she was. I felt a wave of revulsion rising in my stomach, a horrible gob of hatred and bile I couldn't hold down, I had to vomit it in her face. What's the matter, honey, I thought you liked monsters. / No, better to avoid that ugly mess altogether. Save it for the telephone, that wonderful instrument of time and space, distance and separation, so that she can't strike back at you with her fists, entreaties, tears. Hi, honey, it's me, Harry. Listen, let's try to get through this thing as quickly as we can, OK? I've found an apartment uptown. I'll send somebody down later for my things. Yeah, but you can't get out of it that easily can you? There are the prerequisite visits to the marriage counselor, the failed attempts at reconciliation, the resultant fights, connubial terrorism, the child as fulcrum in a dysfunctional equation, the battles, the bouts with the bottle. / I woke with a hangover, the bed empty next to me. Cassa? Then I remembered, felt the nausea rising again. Why did I drink so much, and what the fuck did I tell Lenore? All that stuff about Cassa and the war. And she wouldn't forget any of it, would she? She was a collector of details, she gathered footprints, drops of sweat, stray scents, broken twigs and trampled blades of grass and sewed them up inside a leather bag, stitched on it eyes, ears, nose and mouth and gave it a name, then commanded it to speak. Tell me the truth, Harry, tell me everything, and I opened up like a sieve, like a broken rain barrel. She was so hungry, she wanted it all, my entire life down to the tiniest fucking detail. If I said, I'm tired, I'm going home to bed, she shot out her web, put her stinger inside me, injected me with her little poisons, her truth serums and anti-coagulants, C'mon, Harry, and no bullshit this time. I want names, dates, places. You said you lost your discharge papers. But surely you remember your date of separation. //////////// /// I remember waking up in the back seat of a beat-up old school bus with drool pooling under my chin and a piss hard-on erecting its own little circus tent in my pants, much to the delight of my audience, the toothless, grinning peasant women in flower print dresses hugging sacks of garlic and squawling red-faced babies in their laps. Through the dirty yellow window I could see the city in the distance, the walls of glass gleaming in the fiery lurid sunset. I began to weep. Hot, heavy tears ran down my face. I felt worn out, exhausted, I never thought I'd make it back, I didn't know what I was returning to, if my old neighborhood was still there, if anyone would remember me, recognize me as one of their own, another unfortunate wretch who got dragged into that mess. Or would they despise me, spit on me, cry out monster, maybe even throw stones at me? // // Yeah, but Harry, Lenore scoffed, that was then, this is now. They'll call you a patriot, hero, they'll make you king if you want to go that far. Lenore's green eyes gleamed in the hot yellow slant of sunlight, the smoke from her cigarette stung my eyes.

Yeah, well I'd still rather not have it on record, I said.

But why, Harry? You aren't hiding anything are you? If there's something you aren't telling me you'd better do it now. I remember making some lame excuse, modesty, I didn't want to exploit a situation in which so many suffered. But she was so insistent, I ended up saying more than I wanted to, getting myself further entangled, every lie required another cover. //////////////////////////// // We were passing farm houses, gas stations, convenience stores, crossing a bridge, the black iron trestles flashed past in a chiaroscuro of dark shadows and dusty yellow light, and then the deeper canyons of shade as we entered the city. I watched the bus's reflection melt and flow in the molten neon glow beginning to come on in the bar windows, restaurants and cafes. Then I was getting down from the bus, my feet were touching the pavement, I felt like shouting, screaming, tearing off my uniform and running out in the street naked, Hey, everybody! I made it! I'm home! Suddenly I was in the middle of a traffic jam, crushed into a tiny square of asphalt, headlights and chrome. Horns honked, I heard a siren coming, people shouting, Heya fucking jerk, get outa the goddamn street!

I ditched my uniform in a gas station washroom, pulled on some sales tag civvies, a pair of baggy trousers, hawaiian shirt, a quick check in the mirror, ya look great, ya big lug. Yeah, sure, like some burr-headed idiot off the farm. But what the fuck, I was alive, I was a free man. Maybe later I'd get a bite to eat, look for a place to sleep. But right now, whooee! let's celebrate! Harry's back in town!

Two or three boilermakers later, not to mention a coupla hits off a joint some guy handed me in an alley, I walked the streets with my hands shoved down in my

pockets, inhaling the warm sweet and sour smells of exhaust fumes, raw sewage, garbage cans, frying pans, gin-
ger, onions and peppers in hot oil and vinegar. I'd have to
find a job soon. Right now I'd take anything, just something
to get started, save a little money. But tomorrow, right?
After I got a good night's sleep, caught my breath, had a
chance to look around. I stood on the bridge over the river,
staring down at the lights of the city glowing in the waters
below, and then up, through the iron girders, at the city
and the lights of the city rising above. ///////////////
//
A faint metal gleam touched chairs, lamps and tables. The
music was soft, low. Through the open drapes I could see
the city molten and glowing far below. Lenore stirred next
to me, her voice thick, her eyes oily, opiated. Beautiful, isn't
it, Harry. An's all mine, I'm the queen. I'd never seen her
like this before. She was fucked up, talking all kinds of
nonsense, she had this crazy idea she was descended from
some hoary old warrior-king who fought great battles, laid
the foundation of the city hundreds, thousands of years
ago, when a man could claim a continent as his own, en-
slave entire populations, command them to build empires,
temples, towers to God. And why not, Harry? They're animals, to be herded, to do our work, if necessary to be butchered, to feed us. In the dark her eyes gleamed, her mouth
twisted and writhed. Suddenly she began to sob. Shit, I
thought, now I've done it. I shouldn't have let her get so
fucked up, shouldn't have gotten so fucked up myself. I
tried to calm her down, but she pushed me away. You
fucking idiot, I'm not crying because of anything you said.
I'm crying because you're so goddamn stupid, because I
have to put up with assholes like you every fucking day.
You think you know everything because you've got a dick.
You think just because I can't unbutton my pants and pull

out a spear I don't have any other weapons. Well, I'm a helluva lot smarter than you are, Harry. I'm smarter than all of you. That's why I'm here and you're there. And even though it hurt, even though you resented her for it, you couldn't say anything, could you, Harry? Because then she laughed at you, mocked and ridiculed you. What do you think your wife's doing right now, Harry? Watching TV? Painting duckies and puppies with your little boy? What if she already has another man, Harry? What if it's our friend Williams? Shall we call him up and see? / Fucking Lenore, I hated her when she taunted me like that, hated her and wanted her that much more. The fucking whore, she was so goddamned sure of herself, so goddamned bored with everything else. She had no idea in the world what it was like to really work. Wouldn't she love it down on the line passing stone? I could see her naked, filthy, dripping sweat, her hair plastered to her face, the whites of her eyes every time the whip cracked across her back, every time she moaned, swore under her breath, because a scream or complaint would bring the whip down again and again until she was beaten to the earth. And then she'd be nothing, a piece of meat. I could see the men tearing at her mouth, her breasts, while she kicked and screamed until her body gleamed with blood and slobber and she couldn't fight back, she lay there and took it, her eyes dead black pools filling with the bloated faces of drowning animals. Yeah, but she loved it, didn't she? The fucking bitch, she was begging me, *please, Harry, please,* but not too long ago, *please,* maybe even last night, *please, Harry!* right here in this bed, *please!* between these layers of silk and satin, *please!* it was Williams, *please!* you fucking bitch, you were fucking Williams, *oh Harry! oh Harry! pleasepleaseplease.* Because that was the only genuine thing about her, that hunger, *please,* that need, *please!* it didn't matter who, *please!* as long as she got what she wanted, *Please!* Then she detached herself from you, pushed away your useless carcass, drifted off into sleep, into some dream world of her own, the whites of her eyes slipping like vacant moons behind the dark blue clouds of eye shadow in a languid act of dismissal. But I wasn't finished yet, I held her down, pinned her to the mattress. C'mon Harry, quit! she hissed, but I wouldn't let her up. Please, Harry, she whimpered, I can't anymore. The fucking bitch, she thought she was so tough, now she knew who was boss. Soon everybody else was going to see. As for that stupid fuck Williams? Set him up in auditing where his little fuck-ups might even come in handy? Better yet, put him down on the line with the working man, master become slave. I could see him, still dressed in that ridiculous tuxedo, dirty, sweating, a look of outrage on his face, passing stones down the line like a fucking valet with a tray of hors d'oeuvres, another brick, madame? ///////////// // Earlier that evening I'd run into Williams in the company lounge. He was really soused, sloppy, hanging off his stool. That Lenore'sh really something, isn't she, Harry? As long ash she's got a pair of shouldersh in a shuit and tie by her shide. And she can provide those shouldersh, can't she, Harry boy? One after the other, use 'em up, use 'em until they get too big for their britches, until they actually begin to believe they're in control. And then she removes them, replaces them in a seamless transition of power, another male face, another male voice repeating the company litany, each one as stupid as the one before, each one believing he's the one, promising her money, drugs, all the usual junk, and all of which I'm sure she accepted, deferring for one more day the inevitable slaughter. Because it wasn't Williams' drunken ramblings anymore, was it? It was me, my own suddenly too clear thoughts running wild in my head, piling up and smashing into each other like a train wreck. Why don't you do something about it? I demanded. For a moment Williams sounded perfectly sober again.

Like what, Harry? Make a fool of myself? Create a scene? Or should I run, look for a place to hide? Where would I go? Down? Oh no, I don't think so. Better to serve as the knight's squire than be an ordinary stable boy. Fucking Williams, even when he was drunk he sounded so polished. Of course his family had money, he came from good stock, like all these other fucking punks, the young gods, dressed in designer outfits, carrying expensive handbags, briefcases, flashing gold and diamonds as they guzzled their ambrosia, stuffed themselves with burnt offerings, the flesh of wild beasts. I heard a roar, the band was playing louder now. When the hell did they come on? Strobe lights flashed in my eyes, hot sunlight exploded in my brain, I smelled the hot stink in my face, tasted blood in my mouth. I staggered to my feet. I had to get out of there, get away from those people. Behind me Williams called out, Oh Harry, you are going to the big shindig tomorrow night? // // Overhead the stars twinkled in the sparkling champagne night, the perfectly clear, tinkling piano night. If only I hadn't arrived so early. Now I had to put up with all these fucking bores and I was already drinking too much. I stood in front of a concrete pillar for a good ten minutes, appraising its cracks and fissures like it was some kind of fucking statue, a fucking athlete carved out of stone, shouldering its burden for eternity.

Behind me the noise and the laughter swelled out to re-ceive me. Men circulated in tuxedos. Women glided across the cement floor in evening gowns. Candlelight gleamed off crystal and diamonds. If only Lenore'd get here. Was she really going to show up with that idiot Williams on her arm, even now when it was obvious to everyone that it was all a charade and he was already on his way out, a complete failure? And if so, that made her what? Black widow? Praying mantis? Shrew? I felt a delicious little gnawing at the back of my neck, the product of too much alcohol, adrenaline, the prospect of all that power. What if she came alone, entered suddenly, violently, her nostrils flaring, eyes flashing, disgusted with her whole life and everything in it up until the moment she looked into my eyes and recognized me as king, conferred upon me the ermine robes and jeweled scepter? Not by anything she said, of course, but her presence at my side, the intimacy with which she spoke to me, so that everyone could see, so they'd all know who I was and where I stood. //////////////////////////////// // At last I spotted her, on the arm of that new guy, Charles, the boy genius of marketing. When the fuck did he show up on the scene? He was acting so cool, so charming. With a drink in one hand and a cigarette in the other he glided along, staying with the group, prodding it and herding it, a word here, a word there, taking his cues from Lenore, the way she smiled, arched her brows, showed her teeth. If only I could get close, have a word with her. But wherever she went the group flowed around her, separating, forming colonies and cliques, then closing around her again. And that damned idiot, Williams, the way he kept staring at me, making those ridiculous faces, like a cow going up the chute to the abattoir. Suddenly the group changed direction, swelled around me, engulfing me and pushing me into the center. I felt their thoughts bending toward me, felt

their hot breath on my face. Suddenly it was very important that I say the right thing, I was just getting ready to
say the right thing when I heard a sound, a roar, like a coal
furnace thrown open for an instant and slammed shut
again, and Williams, poor deluded Williams said, What is
it, Harry? You look like you've seen a ghost. And Lenore,
suddenly cozy and concerned, put her hand on my arm. A
sound, Harry? What kind of sound? But when I tried to de-
scribe the sound it wasn't so clear anymore, I was getting it
mixed up with some jungleman on TV and that time my
father took me to the zoo and I heard that roar and looked
into those insane yellow eyes and the teeth driven by those
eyes. And then the motor whirred, and the teeth went clack
clack clack. But that was something else, one of those
stuffed animals my mother or grandmother or even one of
those anonymous uncles I remember hovering in the background stuck in my crib to make me stop crying because I
was still a wittle bitty baby, boo hoo, scared of the night.
But now, HaHaHa, I laughed. Everybody knows those animals don't exist anymore and probably never did. Then
Charles made some remark, and Lenore began to laugh,
that strange, almost hysterical bark she reserved for company banquets and other feasts. Suddenly I felt too vulner-
able, my throat too bare. I wanted to strike out at them,
hurt them as badly as I could and run away. No, better not
say anything. Better just to be quiet, fade into the crowd,
retain what shreds of dignity you can, maybe later make
alliances, strike back.

Afterwards, after everyone had refilled their glasses
and the conversation had turned to the weather and the
flag raising ceremonies next week, I stood on the edge of
the little group, listening with one ear turned outward to
the darkness that fell away and below and beyond the
infinite layers of culture and refinement, beyond the city

walls, the guard towers and barbed wire, across the plain, where the lights of the small towns and villages burned like watchfires in the night. What the fuck was I doing here? I wasn't fooling anyone. They all knew I didn't belong. I should've taken off that stupid monkey suit right there, swung from the chandelier with a banana in my hand and my pecker out. Yeah, sure, the ladies'd love that, maybe even some of the men. I signaled the valet, gulped another drink, felt the corners of my mouth drawing back into that twisted grin that used to greet me in the bathroom mirror when I was off on another binge. It was like the return of an old friend, the first edge of a good drunk, a drunk that could go on for weeks and months and maybe even years and still not be enough. ///////////////// /// Grubb Station! End of the line! It was sometime after midnight when the conductor woke me out of a daze. I lurched off the train, into the neon glow and smoky blue haze of bars and dives. It was late, everybody'd gone home. I felt sick, alone. Then I heard somebody call my name. Hey! Harry! I felt a rush of hope and warmth. A vaguely familiar face lurched toward me through the smoke, oh yeah, right, that guy I used to work with. Christ, what the hell's his name, Larry? Joe! That's it.

Harry, you old son-of-a-bitch! He was pounding me on the back, pumping my hand up and down like a fucking jackhammer. The whole time I was thinking, Jesus Christ, what a fucking ape this guy is, feel those fucking arms. Look at ya! he says, In a fucking tuxedo! Life's treating ya pretty goddamn good, huh Harry boy? Yeah, sure, I knew what he was thinking. Christ, is this guy some kind of fucking faggot? Was he always such a goddamn wimp? So whataya, Harry, in town for a coupla days? Looks pretty fucking bleak around here, don't it? Everybody laid off, outa work, all the action's up there, in the new city. What-about ya'self? And what else could I do but lie? You know how it is, I said. Just hanging in there like everybody else. Finally we shook hands, mumbled some understated male bullshit about getting together again. Good seeing ya, buddy, say hello to the wife and kids. / Yeah, sure, the wife and kids. A coupla months back I got a bill from the hospital. Cassa was listed as the patient. There was a lot of medical mumbo jumbo, chemotherapy, radiation treatments, cancer, the disease of civilization. When I called Cassa's old number Frank answered, his voice sounding tired, confused, ruined of hope. It was a mistake, he said. The bill was sent to you by mistake. Yeah, I know. I should have gone to see her, I always meant to go see her. But I was busy with important projects, company funds, meetings, blah, blah, blah. Besides, the fucking bitch, she set me up, sucked me into this mess. Her and Frank. Yeah, sure, they were all in it together. Not just Frank and Cassa, but Lenore, the company, it was all a conspiracy, they were channeling me, all my efforts and energy and anything else that could have been dangerous to them into a useful, a controllable mode, the status quo. Yes, of course, that's it. Ruin the brightest ones, the rising stars.

I pulled a bottle out of my pocket, raised it to my mouth, vaguely remembering having grabbed it from the wine cart on the way out of the party. Suddenly I heard a noise, a horrible hacking and coughing of phlegm. A dark form lurched at me out of an alley. AHHHH! I screamed. But just when I realized it was only a tattered old bag woman wrapped in layers of rags, I had another, even more terrifying thought. Mother! But that really was crazy, it was just some old hag, just the stench of cancer rotting inside her, just her words when she raised a filthy finger to my face and cackled with one eye cocked wide and the other a seeping wound, We're building ourselves away from God! A simple statement of faith and betrayal, a confirmation of everything I had ever denied to myself. I felt an impulse to call the cops. Haul her off to the city dump, officer! She's a disease! She's ruining society! Yeah, sure, more likely they'd haul me off. I started to raise the bottle again but the old woman made a grab for it. 'Ere, dearie, give us a drink of that, would'ya? I shoved her away, wandered up the street. All these weaklings who argue against the new order. You have to be tough, you have to be strong. Cassa's father didn't believe in our destiny either. He was old, afraid, he only had criticisms, complaints. But he offered no solutions, no vision, plan. Yeah, sure, my great plan. How is it possible that I could be so stupid, that I could retain the most infantile fantasies and dreams right up to the very end? Imagine, once I actually pictured myself as part of some evolutionary force, I saw myself struggling ever upward in search of God, truth, the source of light, like a supplicant holding my little book before me, my great plan for the city in the stars. /////////////////////// /// By now I was falling asleep on my feet. I staggered up the street in the direction of the old city zoo, looking for a bench, somewhere to sit, maybe lie down, take a little nap. It used to be nice around here, before they let all the riffraff move in. Now it's just a few clumps of vegetation, dying trees and shrubs stinking of garbage, human excrement. You gotta watch where you walk, there's hypodermic needles everywhere, used condoms, you can't see anything at night because the lights have all been shot out, nobody comes here anymore because of the madmen, the beasts, watching for somebody wounded, weak, foolish enough to

wander near the edge, the fringe of civilization. And then the beast comes, stifles your screams, tears open your throat, your belly, drinks the hot salty blood. But this is the best time to be here, the safest, in the first hours of dawn, when all the beasts are drowsing, drugged. /////////////
//
I sank down on a bench outside the wrought iron gates, my hands dangling between my knees, the bottle between my feet, listening to the yawning growl and roar of the street cleaning machines coming in at the end of the night, the waking roar and growl of garbage trucks starting out at the beginning of day. On my sixth birthday the old man took me to the zoo. I remember he didn't have enough money for the tickets. He looked nervous, afraid, like he was going to cry. Suddenly the guy at the gate jerked his head inside, Go on, it's free today. Who knows, maybe he felt sorry for us, maybe he knew we were going to pay for this visit for the rest of our lives. In my memory it's like a dream. The animals stand perfectly still in their cages, watching out of their tired old eyes, a heaviness in their bodies, as if they've outlived their usefulness, what they were in the minds of men in some distant past, not only magnificent creatures, savage and wild, to be hunted down and struggled with for food, dominion, but reminders of our bestial side, of evolution, the existence of God. Now nothing wanted them here anymore except the perversity of their keepers, hysterical old men and women who felt their own lives would be less without them.

I remember the lions' cage in particular, those wild wide eyes and that pink slop of tongue between the great teeth when it opened its mouth and roared. But the old man wasn't afraid then. He leaned over the railing, growling at the big animals, laughing at them, mocking them in that drunken boozy slur. C'mere, boy, he called, I wanta

show ya something. But I shook my head, no, I don't wanta. I was absolutely certain he was going to push me into the cage. Although now that I think of it there probably weren't any animals then either, it was just a bunch of tape recordings, inside they've got some old stuffed furniture covered in naugahyde, synthetic leopard and zebra skin. / / ///
It was almost light. Through the mist I could make out somebody lying on the bench across from me, he was just starting to wake. He sat up, stared at his shoes for a while, picked at the lint clinging to his dark blue sweater, scratched at his hair, his beard. Then he pushed himself to his feet, lurched toward me. Hey, mister! Mister! Hey mister! I felt my heart clench. Daddy! For one terrifying second I was absolutely certain it was my old man, his face ruined with alcohol, exposure to the elements. Go away, I growled, leave me alone! But he plopped down next to me, drenching me in the stink of shit, piss, booze. Hey, mister! Help out an old vet, mister? You know what it was like, mister. You was there. Yeah, sure, I know you was, mister, I can see it in your eyes. Hey, give me a pull on that, OK? I handed him the bottle. He took a deep swallow, handed it back. Whooo, man, that's the stuff, that's real good, you got taste, mister. Hey, look, you wanta buy sumpthin? Look! Look at these! I'll take ten for this one, OK mister? In one blackened hand he held a large curved tooth, in the other a brass cigarette lighter with a dent in it. From a spear I alwaysh tellzh'm, he grinned, toothless. But that lion's tooth, that un's real, mister, don't let anybody tell ya it ain't. //
///
Yeah, sure, those amulets, you can pick 'em up in any pawn shop in town. All the guys who were out there had one, carried 'em around for good luck. Brought 'em back with them,

sold 'em for a coupla bucks when they were short of cash.

Yeah? Well did ya ever see this guy? He ever come in here?

Look, Lieutenant, like I told ya, I seen hundreds, thousands of 'em. I wouldn't remember if it was yesterday.

Yeah, sure, fucking Lenore, following me all the way down here. She was so thorough, efficient, she'd track down the last shit you took in a public toilet if it'd get her anywhere. One time she showed me a dossier. It doesn't deny what you say, Harry. It just doesn't support it either. You claim you were the only one to survive in your platoon. But the records from that campaign were lost in a fire, it wiped out ten years of memory. There's no proof you even existed, Harry.// // I staggered to my feet, started down the street, the bum right behind me. Hey, mister, wait a second, where ya goin? I wanta tell ya something! I couldn't shake the guy, he was dogging my heels, trailing after me like a clown in his flappy shoes and torn sweater. What am I gonna do? I whined. Maybe I'll call Cassa, we can get back together, patch things up. The bum looked at me gleefully. Yeah, but Harry, she's sick in the hospital, remember? You were gonna visit her? You don't understand, I said. It was her father, Frank, he planned it that way, so he could get the child. For my genes of course, to renew the stock, to instill the hunger and the quest for power in the hearts of the tired intelligentsia, that's the only way they'll ever succeed in the revolution. I noticed some people staring at me, but the bum's eyes gleamed with recognition. Yeah, sure, that's it, Harry, now you're on the right track, it was her father, Frank, the old man. Cassa was just the bait. They made her do it. But all along she really loved you, Harry. She was good and beautiful. And now she's gonna die and go to heaven and be an angel. Yeah, sure, I growled, a fucking angel. The bum nodded vigorously, his mouth a cesspool of sores and rotting teeth. Yeah, well fuck 'em, Harry. Yeah, fuck 'em, I repeated. Let 'em have the goddamn brat. He'll grow up, he'll emerge, he'll find whatever life he can. If he's strong he'll fight his way to the top, get a lungful of blue sky and fresh air before he succumbs. That much he has me to thank for. It's in his blood, his genes, enhanced by everything I've endured in my own struggle to the top. I told you, didn't I? How I made it to the top? /////////// ///

II

hell squared

Maybe his name was Joseph or Peter or some other boy's name like that. Maybe the old man forgot to give him a name. They stood in the darkened doorway, not talking, the old man with his hands in his coat pockets, his eyes fixed on the yellow rectangle of light across the alley, the boy behind him, inspecting the white fuzz at the back of his neck, the heavy shoulders sunk with age, wondering if the old man was afraid, if he in turn should be afraid. He looked at the window again, began counting to himself, one, two, three. When he reached fifty the light'd go out and they'd step into the alley and then what? Go home? Sit around the fire and drink hot chocolate and tell bed-time stories? The old man didn't tell him that part, just, follow me, stand there, shut up. The old man who used to be such a great storyteller, dinosaurs, spaceships, anything to make him, a whimpering boy-child, a bawling dollop of flesh, forget the hunger and the cold and go back to sleep. Then the old man quit telling stories. He thought it was a bunch of nonsense, better to keep your mouth shut and your mind on business. Fifty.

The light was still on. He started to count again but the numbers got mixed up with his breathing, heartbeat, whatever it was that kept him alive while he pursued another train of thought. What happened to that old blue sweater? It was dark blue like the night with snowflakes falling down or were they stars? The old man told him the difference once but he couldn't remember anymore. Snowflakes were cold, wet, they smelled like damp laundry, burned your tongue. Stars were farther away, hot, they tasted like—he couldn't remember what they tasted like, just that they were so far away, so hot. He couldn't imagine a heat like that, a fire that burned across the centuries, across the cold black nothing of space. That part he understood. The cold black nothing of space was his room at night. The cold black nothing of space was the distance between the stars on his sweater. Although why he should think of it now, except that it was so cold and he sought refuge in that brief memory of warmth and the smells woven into that warmth, a big bright kitchen with a breeze blowing the curtains, and something else, the fragrance of flowers or maybe it was perfume, and the sunlight lying on the linoleum floor and a pair of rawboned female feet through the legs of the table, his mother of course, although now he was just imagining, he was daydreaming again, that was another thing the old man didn't talk about, his mother. Once he asked where the sweater came from but the old man refused to answer, raised his hand over his head, trembling with rage, his pale blue eyes like patches of winter beneath the shaggy snowdrifts of his brow, ready to strike him in the face. Then he relented, relit his pipe, retreated into the cold and silence again, into his books and papers, Don't bother me now, boy, I've got work to do. He didn't ask again, but he continued to wear the sweater. He wore it until it left his wrists and belly bare and the yarn had started to unravel. He wore it until he had outgrown it completely and there was nothing left to wear but rags, and even its origins had disappeared, something to do with a woman, some vague female entity on one of those stars in another part of the universe where people talked about life and love and the pursuit of happiness.

But the light, he'd forgotten about the light. He looked to see if the light was still on and in the exact moment of looking or immediately after that moment the light went out and suddenly he was struggling awake out of a sleep and a dream, the old man stepping into the alley and an explosion and a flash of light and the old man's only word a warning, Run! And then he ran or he saw himself running down a long black alley with the night exploding off the red brick walls, rusting fire escapes, banged-up garbage cans. He ran until he found his way back into the huddle of shacks and shanties, back to the pile of boards where he and the old man lived, where the old man used to live, and only then stopped, fell to his knees sick and vomiting up his disbelief, the old man is dead, is dead, he's dead. But those were just words, they still didn't have any meaning yet, they hadn't sunken in.

He lit a candle, held his hands over the glow, the tiny halo of warmth spreading out into the room, illuminating shelves, cardboard boxes, tin cans. There, it felt better already, he felt better. Activity, that's the thing, keep moving, don't think about it, don't think about anything, just do, be, act. Somehow he managed to make himself something to eat, burned up the last of the kindling in the scorched oil drum the old man had converted into a stove, put on a pot of water, adding to it what was left of the larder, a few scraps of vegetables, a drop of oil, something that looked like meat, on the side a crust of cheese, half a loaf of bread, along with a cup of tea brewed from the bark of some root the old man dug up out of the ruined ground, but don't say that, don't think about the old man anymore, just fix dinner like you would any other night, just set the table, sit down to eat.

And then he sat with the bread and cheese, the bowl of soup and the cup of tea steaming in front of him, and didn't eat, didn't drink, didn't do anything but sit and stare around the kitchen or that part of the shack that passed for the kitchen only because that's where they ate, because it was separate from the room in back where the old man slept, used to sleep, and the loft above where he slept, where he lay awake at night listening to the old man's labored breathing, wondering if the old man was sick, if he was going to die. But now he is dead, he's lying in the alley with his blood leaking out. But don't think that, don't say that, the old man not lying there in the other room or, who knows, maybe lying there somehow, his grinning corpse and those big muddy shoes and it's all a horrible trick. Don't think that. Just climb the ladder and get under the blanket without bothering to take off your clothes, without baring yourself too much to the night, the cold, without suffering even that moment of nakedness and chill undressing, and lie there and stare into the dark as if nothing has changed, and wait until tomorrow to find out if it's true, if anything is true. But it isn't that simple, is it? Sleep isn't always the refuge you want it to be. There's still dream and nightmare, things get moved around a little bit, the rocking chair here, the lamp next to the fireplace, the old man lying in bed safe and warm and asleep while you lie in the alley dead. But don't call it sleep, don't call it death. Call it gaps between I and I, between thought and not thinking. Although how can there be gaps? There is no yesterday, no today or tomorrow. The sun never rises, never sets, there is no sun, no days, no divisions of time, only the blackness and emptiness of space, of the vacuum, and the vacuum permits no entrance, not even the sound of your own breathing which is only an echo or a memory of something you once did or you think you once did. And still you speak to remind yourself that you can speak, that there is a you who speaks. Although why you keep saying you and not IIIIIIIIIIIIIIEE! Now am I, here am I, I and I, alone I, only I, I that exist, I that am, I who breathe the night, I who am the night, starless night, moonless night, night without shadows, night without doors or windows of distant light and hope, night without cries of anger, without whispers of love, light swallowing night, perfect night, now and forever night.

He woke with a gasp, lay on his back watching in a disassociated way as things began to appear out of the diffuse gray light, his breath hanging in the frosty air and the scrap of blue yarn caught on a splinter on the wall and the small black hole where the spider lived and his jacket and shoes inert on the floor although he didn't remember taking them off last night. But it was still too early, he didn't want to think about last night, didn't want to be reminded of last night, last year, whenever it was that everything stopped and then started again, that brief hiatus between what was then and what is now and forever. Even after he had climbed back down the ladder and stood in front of the stove with his hands out to the residual warmth of last night's fire, he refused to look in the direction of the old man's room, refused entry to that heresy and madness, because the old man is not in there, the old man is not lying on his bed, the old man is in an alley and soon the dogs will come or the wagon will come but you've got to stop thinking those things, you've got to stop dwelling on it, just get outside in the fresh air and the sunshine and take a nice little walk. But it isn't that easy, is it? It's never that easy. Where the hell are your gloves? And what about your rubbers? Those sensible black galoshes Mother made you wear to school, all the boys and girls laughed at you and called you baby, baby, baby, on the way home you splashed in a puddle, got your feet wet, Oh! Call the doctor! Chicken soup and a week in bed. Yeah, sure, something like that.

He pulled on his jacket, shoes, went out and walked and walked and walked with the chill at his throat and the numbness and burning in his feet, in those paper thin soles, passing shacks and shanties where dirty gray rags flapped on clotheslines and weary gray faces hung in the windows like deflated balloons, inhaling the pinched gray air, the sick rancid smells of raw sewage, burning garbage and charred meat, or not meat, not anything you'd call meat under any other circumstances. Quick, call the health inspector! The department of sanitation!

He stood outside a burger joint, his eyes and nose running, stamping his feet, watching some skin and bones junkie in a stained t-shirt working over the grill, his arms a failed skin graft of tracks, tattoos and grease burns, frying up something that used to be alive, something that ran around the gutters squeaking and twitching its whiskers, mm-mm, doesn't that smell good. But you can't just walk in and ask for a bite to eat. You can't just say I'm cold and hungry and expect them to plunk down a plate of mashed potatoes and gravy, because then someone else might get the idea, the chorus might get too loud, pretty soon the whole goddamn neighborhood wants a free lunch.

And still he did live, did breathe, did manage to eat, picking scraps out of garbage cans and off doorsteps, digging in dumpsters and trash cans and taking what he found back to the shack at night to gnaw, to crunch and grind like a contented cow waiting for the knacker's hammer to come down on his head while he practiced the most rudimentary form of thinking, now that it was his fire, his stove, his kitchen, shack, home, if he could keep it, protect it, claim it as his own. Because it was only now beginning to occur to him that he might lose even this, that at any moment someone, anyone, a grown man with a gun, or even just another punk like him, but a little bit smarter, a little tougher, faster, hungrier, could evict him, usurp his pile of boards. He lay down late each night, started awake early each morning, existed in the alternating conditions of cold and gray, cold and darkness, cold and fear, that's the word he was looking for, fear, fear the word he curled up and nestled with each night in his loft, fear the word that bent him over the table in the morning while he sipped his cup of hot water, fear when he should have said friend, when he should have cried out and advertised over the radio and in the newspapers for a friend.

Although what kind of friend would that be? In another life in another time some country boy knee-high in hay straw and brown from the sun who climbed trees and swam rivers? Who knew the names of all the plants and animals, insects, birds and stars in the summer night? What good would a friend like that do him here? Where did he dream up such a friend? Was that more of the old man's nonsense? Those long ago proscribed bed-time stories hovering in the back of his brain, along with an old blue sweater, a mother, the stars? Christ, kid, you're not gonna start bawling again? Listen, did I ever tell you about the time this kid, maybe he wasn't even a kid anymore, maybe eleven, maybe even twelve, thirteen, fourteen, with all the mechanisms for killing and copulation already intact, but still a kid anyway, see? And then one night he was out walking, he was alone, he'd lost track of time, he didn't realize how late it was, he was wandering around in a daze because he was so cold, so hungry. Suddenly a bunch of guys jumped him in an alley, they were laughing at him, playing with him, slicing up the night with their razor blades. And he knew he was in trouble, he knew it was bad, but he didn't know what to do, he'd never been in a fight before, never had to defend himself. He made a rapid set of calculations, went through all the possible delusions and lies, if I'm fast enough, if I kill that one and hurt that one before that one and maybe even that other one he could feel creeping up behind him, prying at his spine with a crowbar. But he still ended up with the same conclusion, they're going to kill me, I'm going to die.

But there was another possibility still, something he hadn't counted on at all, a shadow crouched on a window-sill, a body that leapt down into the alley, a pair of eyes that met his for a fraction of a second and made him an accomplice, then lunged past wielding a hot splash of silver that sliced through air and windpipe, blinded, hamstrung and disemboweled, then fled back into the shadows while he stood there like an idiot snapping black and white photographs to take back with him to the shack later that night, to develop and examine with a magnifying glass while he huddled over the table, searching the wreckage or the memory of the wreckage of arms and legs, skinny adolescent bodies and juvenile death masks for the eyes that met his, for the body that jumped down, for the hand that wielded the knife. But if that was the price he had to pay! If his life depended on that! And then all he could do was laugh or someone else was laughing but the sound came out of him, he was vomiting laughter and it wasn't even funny, he was just laughing because he was so scared, because he was still alive. Because it's only after the fear, after the hysteria, after the terror and laughing and not laughing when you begin to realize it can't be any worse than this, when you pray to God or whatever there is outside of yourself that it won't be any worse than this, that you ask yourself what this is, this blackness and night which is not like the darkness of a cave in the earth, without even the security of that, without even the terror of bats and spiders and monstrous howling beasts sucking you into horror and death, without even the more mundane worry of hypothermia or sudden flash floods when the rains above fill your subterranean cave with oceans and lakes and you smother and drown like a blind fish swimming in a universe without curves or light to traverse those curves, only you in your windowless night, in your starless bath, and a voice in a dream like an electric motor reviving itself from a long long sleep saying over and over again I am I am I am I am I am. And you go on saying I am until you are secure in that proposition and then you go on to the next which is something else still undefined that you must reconstruct out of memory and dream, out of nightmare and apocalypse, out of whatever must have been before for you to be here now.

But it wasn't his fault, he didn't kill the old man, didn't make those guys jump him in the alley, didn't invite that other guy to step in and play bodyguard, protector, alright, why not just say friend? Didn't the old man ever use that word? Wasn't it in his vocabulary? The old man who used to dandle him on his knee, anesthetizing him with fairy tales. Was the old man himself part of that fairy tale? Did that fairy tale have room for another kind of friend? In an unhappier life in an unhappier time some city kid who grew up in the street, tough and angry and ready to kill, who didn't care what a thing was called as long as it meant something to eat, something to drink, something to still the hunger, the cold, the night. That was the kind of friend he needed. The question was, why would such a friend need a friend like him?

It's just that every night after that night he felt that presence ranging near him, felt those eyes watching, following, extracting from him the slightest effusions of sorrow, guilt, whatever it was he was supposed to feel and didn't or wouldn't allow himself to feel. Stripped bare of the night, in the dim halo of streetlight, someone more or less his own age, fourteen or fifteen or sixteen, whatever the age of an almost man, of a man becoming, sinew and bone, fists and feet and aching genitalia, too much sorrow, too much loneliness, too much night. But that was him, those were his words, thoughts, ideas, that's what he felt. And that other guy? What about him? Who are you? he called to the night. What do you want? There was no response. What's the matter? Can't you talk? Still no reply. He tried a name, I'll call you Nakt. There was no objection, maybe because of the hardness of the sound, like a knock on the door late at night. He tried the name again, Hey, Nakt! Nakt drew forward a little from the shadows, his eyes hard, black, gleaming, his face skull-like, his shoulders hunched against the cold.

Still it felt good to have those shoulders next to his, they were lurch buddies, they lurched down the street like a couple of tough guys, all shadows and angles and geometry. But that isn't true, he wasn't a tough guy at all, he was just glad to have someone to talk to, the weather and how cold it was last night and the sun. Wait a minute, what about the sun? Was that Nakt's voice? Had he actually spoken? Yeah, the sun, he went on as if nothing unusual had happened. What does it look like, for instance? An egg yolk? An orange? A beach ball? How do you get to the beach from here, Nakt? Where's the beach? They were tramping through broken glass, stepping over bodies in doorways, nodding to the junkies lined up in the alley with needles in their arms and thin red lines flowing out into the night like neon, like the taillights of a car floating down the street in somebody's dream. The boys and girls were all bored, they hung out on the street corner, injecting alkaloids, inhaling hydrocarbons, burning holes in the night with glowing wands, playing with their shaving paraphernalia. The air smelled sweet and sour, fear, sweat and garbage. A radio was playing in a window. A disinterested thrum like the slow metabolic rhythm of some insect of death spread through the night. Someone coughed, someone moaned, the equation began again, the awkward geometry of bodies intersecting on a lethal plane. All around them people were getting shot, they were getting stabbed and beaten to death. It was just like being at the movies, like a bunch of lousy actors, so what if somebody gets hurt, so what if somebody dies? One less badly operating stomach, one less poorly functioning asshole. Besides, he had Nakt beside him, he had his bodyguard, protector, alright, call him friend.

He was pressed against the wall, watching Nakt dance, watching his eyes, his hands, the way they sought out weaknesses, tender spots—you aren't jealous, are you? You don't want that kind of love? You don't want to be fucked like that? Did he only think that, hear that inside his brain, or did Nakt actually say that, mouth that, whisper that in his ear as he leapt past, butchering and slicing, presenting his knife like an offering, see, here it is, the instrument of your destruction, and then the bouquet, the bright red blossom over the heart, the liver and lungs. While Nakt fought he went on with his own work, probing the leaking corpses, searching the ruins of ribcage and brain pan for decaying thoughts, experiences. What does it feel like to lie down on the wet pavement in some stinking alley vomiting blood and crumbling ceramic, still too young, too stupid, too ignorant and unformed to grasp that this is really it, the final and absolute abolition of yourself, of the thing that says I, even now, this very moment you cry out with

your last vapors and breath escaping into the cold night
. . . I . . . I . . . I. I what? Did you have something else to say?
Isn't it a little late?

But are you really remembering this? Is this the way it
really happened, or the way you're afraid it happened?
What if you're remembering the wrong life? The nightmare
of some little nobody who still wets the bed at night? Or
are you in fact creating it for the first time? And if so can
you play with it, distort it? Aren't you running certain
risks, that you will create monsters? Or worse, that you
will erase some vital moment and all the rest will crumble
and fade for the want of a smile, a frown, a cry of anger like
the gleam of a knife, like the edge of sunlight spilling over
the horizon of a vacant planet? And find in this life, create
in this life, put here a man. Is this the way to play God?
Will this be the first act remembered, the first word re-
corded in the blood of the poet? Better to be a painter, to
splash the world with blood.

Afterwards they stood around the fire, laughing and
drinking, singing their campfire songs. Little Franky got a
chain wrapped around his skull, tore off his face like a
halloween mask, little Johnny caught a dumdum bullet,
his heart exploded like a hot water bottle, little Rosie
Maria got gangbanged by twelve apostles of the night and
a truck driver who wandered by, now she runs an orphan-
age. They knew all the words, they all sang along. He stood
outside the firelight, watching the gaping mouths, the
dazed eyes. He didn't feel like singing, didn't feel like
laughing and drinking. He looked for Nakt, saw him standing in the shadows, still without a face, or with a face that
was just now beginning to come into focus. He felt an undefined terror, heard that single word Run! and he ran, he
had to get out of there, escape, find some kind of refuge. To
do what? I don't know what, think, try to think, under-

stand, escape from the violence of fists and guns in the street into the violence of words exploding in his skull. Murder. This is murder. You are a murderer. Where did those words come from? Whose voice uttered them? Was that the old man again, quoting from another of his fairy tales? Monsters and evil men? And if so, did that make those words any less real? Murder? This is murder?

He stood in a doorway, gasping for breath, his heart pounding. He heard footsteps, somebody running, then Nakt was beside him, his eyes full of moonlight, street-light, whatever light there was gleaming off the wet cobblestones, the damp asphalt, asking without saying, What happened? Why'd you take off like that? And what was he supposed to say, I don't know, I thought I heard a siren? What if he just skipped the bullshit, told the truth, I was scared. And then Nakt would say, incredulous, Scared? Of what? And what was he supposed to say then, Of you, of these people, this life. But he didn't say that, did he? He said, Let's go back to my place, I've got something to eat, drink. We can get in out of the cold. He'd never invited any-one back to the shack before. It was an honor, a sign of trust, friendship. But Nakt was already doing his little sideways shuffle down the street, his hands in his pockets, his face in his collar, Naww, I gotta go now, I got something to do, I'll see you tomorrow. Yeah, sure, as long as they were walking, as long as they were moving, then it was fine, talk if you want to, talk all day and night, but don't say any-thing about my place, my home, my stove, kitchen, bed, that's getting too close, too comfortable, too near, you can't allow yourself to know someone that well, can't allow them to know you. Besides, it's too hot in here, too stuffy, too small, and all this talk talk talk, it's not doing anything, it's not changing anything, it's just making me tense, you see? It's making me mad. All these goddamn questions, why you gotta know everything all the time?

He sat over the kitchen table, his head between his hands, his face a charcoal study of adolescence. He felt old, worn out, yeah, sure, without the white hair, without the lines and wrinkles and the big heavy shoulders sunk with age, without that moist, tired old light trickling from his eyes like a dying spring. But old all the same. He knew he should climb the ladder and go to bed, but even the thought of getting up from the chair seemed impossible, he couldn't do it, just go in and lie down on the old man's bed and go to sleep and worry about the consequences tomorrow, worry about the ghosts when they wake you in the middle of the night, worry about worrying when your life's over and there isn't anything to worry about.

He pushed past the blanket that hung over the doorway, entered that sanctum, that cell, and stopped, unsteady on his feet, inhaling the dark and the silence and something else, the lingering smells of aging and decay, of dust and machine oil and the slow oxidation of time, and something else still, the smell of personal refuge, of the unbaring of the body and the soul in the presence of no one but yourself and your God. But to speak of God when you yourself are nothing and no more than a voice in the night. To whom do you speak? What do you say? Excuse me? I didn't mean to interrupt? I'm not sure why I'm here myself?

His eyes slowly adjusted to the dark. There was a moment of almost terror when he became aware of a luminous growth spreading through the room. He heard a word sound in his skull, snow—not just snowflakes and flurries but piles and mounds of snow slumped and drifting over everything, the floor and the walls. And then the light grew brighter or his pupils wider, and the drifts resolved themselves into books and papers, dusty yellowed notes and

pages left open in the middle of work, investigations. On
the crate next to the bed the old man's tobacco pipe and tin,
a can of water long ago evaporated, an unlit candle, near
the wall a chair with some limp clothing, the old man
deflated, gone out of himself. He sat down on the bed, or not
even a bed but a couple of wooden pallets with flattened
cardboard laid over them for a mattress. On top of that a
blanket more tattered than his own. He'd never thought
about that before, never considered the old man's suffering
and needs. Did the old man feel the cold? Did he lie awake
at night shivering in his bones, riven with loneliness and
fear? There was something else, on the windowsill, some
kind of light, a faint green gleam, maybe a piece of metal or
glass. He wanted to get up, go to it, touch it, hold it in his
hand. But he couldn't move, he felt so tired, just lie back
and go to sleep. He thought of his shoes caked with mud,
and then he thought of nothing.

Then he was in the alley with Nakt again, he was saying, Come back to my place with me, Nakt, I'll make you
something to eat, my bed is warm. But what was he saying? Did he really say that? And Nakt, backing away in
horror, afraid he was going to make a grab for his cock, try
to kiss him. He could see Nakt's horrified face, his mouth
suddenly too big, too red, and filled with rotting teeth. That
part was right anyway. But why hadn't he noticed before?
Nakt was wearing lipstick, he'd painted his face with rouge
and mascara. But now he knew he'd fallen asleep, he was
in the middle of another fucked-up nightmare, dream,
there was something about the old man, the old man was
standing over him with a pillow in his hand, the old man
was saying, Stop asking so many questions, do you hear
me? And I don't want you peeing in my bed! Suddenly the
old man was holding him down, he was pushing the pillow
in his face, his lungs were beginning to burn, he was suffo-

cating, he couldn't breathe, his chest heaved and con-
vulsed, he tried to sit up in bed, but he couldn't sit up or
else he saw himself sitting up and sitting up and sitting up
in a kind of cartoon blur but no matter how hard he tried
he couldn't sit up. And then he knew, this time he'd really
done it, he really was dead, and it made him so sad, so terribly sad, he kept saying over and over again, he's dead,
he's dead, but it didn't change anything, the pressure continued to grow in his head. Isn't there a word for that? The
incipient pain of too much salt water gathering in your
skull for too many years? That sorrow and grief for your
own mortality, when you're still struggling to divide dream
from reality, when you feel the hot tears rolling down your
cheeks and you taste the hot brine and still you say, even
this is illusion, because a bodiless entity can not produce
tears, has no glands, no portion of salt and water to manu-
facture the dead rain, to make the universe gasp and heave
and wash it all clean.

And then, by sheer will of his sleeping brain, he was in
another place, a bright, open place filled with sunlight and
warm air, and something else, the sound of breaking glass
or no, not breaking glass, but liquid glass, molten glass
trickling over pebbles and stones, rivulets and streams of
glass splashing and burbling down through channels and
cataracts crowded with bright green moss and ferns, and
something else still, a chorus of trilling and toowheeting,
chirrupping and cheeping, and even if he'd never heard a
bird in his life, what else could it be but the sound of beak
and bill, the whirr and color of wings through the trees and
the leaves, and it felt so good, he was chuckling and cooing
like a baby, the tickling and silliness swarmed through his
body, burned in his head, it was beginning to hurt. There
must be a name for that too, that other ache and pain
starting in the side of your face, your jaw, the ache of un-

used muscles, the accumulation of unused laughter. And if you had laughed then your laughter would have filled the universe, like the laughter that fills the void and the universe inside the skull of a patient coming out of a coma after weeks and months and possibly even years of sleep. Because it was a joke, right? Or almost a joke, to wake up and find yourself not dead afterall, not dead and still not exactly alive, if life requires a body, a form to occupy, because the laws of nature as you were taught the laws of nature specify that it is impossible to place a man in solution, in a state of being that is neither here nor there but somewhere in between. Because you were still too stupid, too drugged with sleep and absence of thought to realize, to admit to yourself, because you thought it couldn't last, that it was something you could endure, that somehow there would be an end, a war or revolution or an earthquake, but something to intercede, to finish it for good, even if it was only God, even if only God intervened, but something that would release you from the hospital bed or gurney or whatever it was they had strapped you to, because you still didn't realize, you thought everything was the same and it was just going to go on like before, you were going to go on, eating and drinking, shitting and pissing your life away like some obedient little laboratory experiment under a microscope.

He woke with a gasp, a laugh, aware of a strangeness, a presence in the room. And then he realized, it was him, he was the strangeness and the presence, lying in the old man's bed, re-inflating the old man's dead and desiccated toad skin with his youth and life and breathing. He threw aside the covers, pushed through the blanket into the kitchen. There were still a few warm coals in the stove. He poked them into a flame, added a few sticks until he had enough fire to warm that smallest part of the room, to start the water boiling, to add to it the memory of a taste, mint or chamomile, sassafras or fennel, more words unbidden, words without origin or substance. Then he sat with the cup of tea, of hot water steaming on the table in front of him and his mind and his thoughts locked in reverse, there was something about last night, something in the old man's room. But he couldn't remember. It wasn't until he went out later that morning, it wasn't until he shoved his hands in his pockets for warmth, and he felt something smooth and hard, in the mute gray light a piece of stone, a green gleaming egg with deep black veins like canyons, like chasms, and then he remembered, oh yeah, right right right, the dream last night, with the water splashing among the moss and ferns, and the soft fragrances rising in the warm air, and birdsong, and it felt so good, he just wanted to let himself nestle and float in the warmth of those words, and if anybody asked, he was on vacation, he was taking a break from the dark and cold, he'd already forgotten all about the dark and cold, but something was trying to remind him, somewhere in the distance a little voice was calling him back, but it wasn't anything yet, just an itch, just a tickling in the base of his spine, a cold metal tongue licking and probing at his kidneys. Suddenly the voice was louder, it was shrieking, wake up! And then he woke or he was starting to wake, to turn, but it was already too late, he saw the knife and the hand that held the knife and then the eyes, not quite feline, eyes other than fox, other than serpent or snake, and still not quite human. Nakt! It was Nakt! And he was already laughing, he was starting to say you son-of-a-bitch, because it was only an-other joke, right? But something was wrong, it wasn't en-tirely a joke afterall, Nakt's eyes were sharp and gleaming, I saw you take something out of your pocket. And suddenly he was afraid again, he didn't understand this game they were playing. But he had no choice. He opened his fist. See? Just a rock, just a pebble, a pretty piece of junk I found. It's not worth anything. Nakt snatched it from his hand, held it up to the light, the green gleam filling the nighttime sky in his eyes, then handed it back again with a warning and an admonition, Not worth anything, you say. Not worth anything but your life if you aren't more careful, if you don't watch where you're going.

And he knew Nakt was right, he knew he had to be more careful, he had to watch all the time, he had to be alert and aggressive and ready to fight. What if someone was watching him, following? What if even Nakt and all this time it was just a trick, Nakt was leading him on, making him let down his guard, and one of these nights he was going to wake up choking and gurgling on the gush of hot blood pouring from his throat and Nakt's face hovering over him like some horrible monster mask caught for a fraction of a second in the camera flash. But that was crazy. It was just his own fear, paranoia. If Nakt wanted to kill him, dispossess him of shack, home, body and soul, he would have done it a long time ago.

You see? What kind of life is that? You can't even trust your own friends. You're tense all the time. It's like walking around in a pillbox, a concrete bunker, you keep waiting for the shell to hit, you keep waiting for the explosion, your guts are tied up in knots, you clench your fists and teeth until your head aches. After awhile you get tired of that, you just wanta sit down over a cup of coffee and a cigarette, maybe take in a movie, some escapist fare about a jungleman swinging through the trees.

He'd be striding down the street like some slackjawed pumpkinhead from the country who'd never even seen a tall building before, never taken a taxi, never been accosted by a cop, a pimp, a whore, when he stopped and stared, transfixed by a ragged spot of green pushing out of the dead ground next to a light pole. He'd bend down, pluck a leaf, crush it between his fingers, inhale the pungent green excess and explosion of chlorophyll into his brain. But a single clump of weeds in a vacant lot, a twisted, scraggly stump of a tree struggling to survive behind a blackened iron grate, did not translate into thousands of miles of forests, lakes, rivers and streams. No matter how hard he tried to relax and forget the dark and the cold and the fear surrounding him he could not forget.

He'd go home, put the latch on the door, warm himself by the stove a little before he went in and lay on the old man's bed. No, not the old man's bed, his bed now. Never again would he exile himself to the loft like a child. Never again would he be a child. He forced himself to breathe that air, sleep in that bed, inhabit that room, make it and all the things in it his own. At some point he'd started digging down through that brooding slump of snow, fingering through the dust and mildew of the old man's books, the life he'd lived on paper, in search of words printed on the page to match the torrent of words in his brain. It never occurred to him that he might not know how to read, his eyes met the page and there was a leap, a connection, and then he was sitting in the old man's lap again, his infant ears and eyes following as the old man's voice gruff and heavy with tobacco smoke pronounced the words on the page, teaching him without intending to teach him how to pronounce and decipher the insects and thorns, extracting from him, from the useless mechanism of tooth and tongue that he was, first vowels and consonants, then words, thoughts, ideas, until the old man stopped, ceased reading to him. But why? Had the old man realized the futility of his efforts? That the words in his books described things that did not exist in the boy's world, things that were al-

ready a memory in his, the old man's world? Sunlight,
stars, the birds singing in the trees, the cold, clear water
trickling down out of the mountains to the sea. What did
those words mean? Where was their analog in this life?

Even later at night, after he'd blown out the candle,
when he lay in bed with his mind racing and the blanket
clutched at his throat to keep out the cold and dark, when
just as suddenly he threw off the blanket again, lay naked
and writhing in the frosty air, tearing at his face, his eyes,
because of that thing growing and crawling inside him,
that almost panic, that need to know, understand what the
fuck is going on here and who the fuck am I? But that was
even more dangerous. It revealed a weakness that could be
used against him if he was caught, if he betrayed himself.
Betrayed himself as what? A thinker? Dreamer? What was
that? The old man mumbling in his soup? The old man
slogging through the frozen wastelands of his books and
papers in a daze of too many words and too many reasons
why and why not and never any answers and never enough
sleep? The old man who had left behind the world long before it evicted him? Not that the old man was weak, he
never showed any signs of fear, because there was something else, that strength, that almost fury that rose up inside of him, burned in his face and eyes, that lifted up the
hairy sagging chest and arms and filled the old man with
rage because of the stupidity of some idiot, some fool tor-
mentor who thought an old man and a boy would make an
easy target. But in the end it was true, the old man's vesti-
gial strength was useless, those words betrayed him, he
was completely unprepared for what came next, the explosion in the night and the last word Run! an empty bubble
of air held forever between the old man's lips, out of all the
thousands and millions of words that was the one the old
man chose to give him, don't stick around and ask ques-

tions, boy, Run! And that meant what? That in the end the old man recanted? Disavowed all those words? Realized he was wrong? His entire life wrong?

And then, in the middle of that debate, say She. Say She and create that distraction, as if that will solve any of your problems, as if that will add rudder and compass to your sail. How long does it take to make that leap from the concept of absolute aloneness and despair to the concept of maybe hope and maybe together? Seconds? Centuries?

He was walking down the street, he wasn't watching where he was going, he wasn't paying attention again, he was still at the matinee, the movies, the bleak little black and white newsreels running through his head, burned-out buildings and bodies lying on the ground and the old man's voice an echo or soundtrack crackling and popping like a cheap little transistor radio in the back of his head, Murder, this is murder.

He smelled salt water, fish, heard sails snapping and popping in the breeze. The sound resolved itself into flapping canvas, plastic tarps, he was in the market, wandering among the empty stalls, the ground was littered with fish scales, rotten fruit. The market was over for the day, the week, all closed up. Then he saw the girl, he hadn't seen her at first, and then he saw her all at once and in parts, her face and her legs and her breasts, or not even breasts yet but the first burgeoning and swelling of breasts. She wore a faded denim skirt, an old brown sweater, it was a cold, gray day, another cold gray day, I don't know why I bother about the weather anymore, it was always cold, always gray. And still she was barefoot, maybe she no longer felt the cold, her legs were thin, brown from the sun, but there was no sun, never any sun, why do I dwell on this? Maybe it's just that her legs were dirty, unwashed, the dirty, unwashed color of her face, her hair.

She watched him approach, followed his canine lurching from alley to lamppost and across the street to the market until he came and faced her and looked into her eyes.
Without saying anything she reached into her skirt pocket,
took out a piece of dried fruit, something that might have
been an apple or a pear ten or twenty years ago, and
handed it to him, watched him turn and walk away and
didn't call out, didn't try to lure him back, maybe didn't lie
awake that night writhing and turning in the surges of
heat and light, the image of her face flaring up and dying
like a match every time he pictured her in the market.
What about her in the market? That she was barefoot?
That it was cold? That her legs were thin, brown, like the
legs of someone who lives near the sea, who runs and
splashes in the surf and the salt spray, who hears the gulls
cry and the waves break and is not afraid, even at night
when the sea swells and looms over land with all its great
dark things and the foghorns moan and lament and warn
you to stay back? And her hair, if he buried his face in her
hair and breathed in would he smell golden cups of honey
overflowing with the warm hum and buzz of bees in a field
of clover in midsummer? Would it be like the smell of woodsmoke in that season and time of year when the fields
turned brown and ready for harvest and the moon rose and
pressed its swollen white belly down in the sky and filled
you with such loneliness and sorrow that you wanted to
cry? Or were those just more words, more of the old man's
fairy tales, the old man who led him right up to the brink of
nothing, then plunged in and left him behind, drowning
and floundering in nothing? The old man who never said
but whose long winters of silence nevertheless cried aloud,
oh God I'm so lonely? The old man who had somehow inher-
ited him, taken him on like a piece of furniture, an armoire
or an old clock, not as a thing to be loved and held in one's

arms and comforted, but as a thing to be watched after, worried over, a cause, in other words, for concern? Yes, but taken on from whom? But that's another dangerous question. It bespoke origins again, mother and father, male and female, the separation of I and I into polarities. But this is more nonsense, it has to stop, I was telling you, I was telling me, I was telling somebody about the girl.

And then, who knows, maybe the next day or the day after that he went out for a walk, stumbling over potholes and rocks with his eyes on the ground and his hands in his pockets, turning the stone, working it and searching it for a memory of something still to come, when the cries of the seagulls over water I mean the cries of the vendors in the market brought him back to the damp and the chill and he looked up and he saw her again, still in the faded blue skirt and brown sweater, still barefoot, but shivering a little now, feeling the cold a little more now, after waiting so long, he hasn't come in so long, is he already dead like the others? Or was that a fairy tale of his own making? That she should lie awake at night thinking of him, remembering him? That it was her sorrow and her longing and not the cold wind whipping through the market that stained her face with tears?

But even then he didn't say anything, he just took her hand and led her acquiescing and urging him out of the market and through the streets and back to the shack and through the blanket and into the old man's, into his, my bed, and her clothes were coming off and his clothes and their naked bodies and the clattering of bones and somebody was screaming, somebody was laughing and moaning, the sound exploded in the frozen air, echoed and pounded off the boards and walls inside his skull, inside that empty room called I. And now, to say She again, to say and create out of that nothing, out of that word, a child, a girl, a woman becoming, and then ask yourself what is she really? A photograph in your mind? A creation of your fantasy and need, to fulfill yourself, complete yourself, to fuck and use in all the thousands and millions of combinations and possibilities, you the steed, you the bull, you the swan, lion, serpent, beast, until there's nothing left but the bloody mirror you continue to fuck and empty yourself into to dispel that other pain when you lie down alone at night? And ask yourself, now, who is she? Goddess of the jungle, goddess of the forest, goddess of the night, goddess who bathes in waterfalls and deep pools, who walks among orchids and lilies, whose naked body is an offering of all the firm ripe fruits and all the hot gushing dreams of paradise you've ever had in your life, goddess who opens to you and calls to you and melts with you in the hot sun and the salt sea, goddess who wakes, goddess of moonlight, goddess of steel, you bloody bitch, you whore, will you lie down with me in my grave in my rotting corpse and hold me in your arms and say I love you, and hold me, and hold me, and hold me still?

I'm not saying it was wonderful, they were kids, they didn't know what they were doing, they just tore and clawed at each other until they got it right. And what did they talk about while all this was going on? Nothing? Neither said anything? Not a word? Is it actually possible they remained silent throughout the ritual, with only the animal scream and moan at the end, or were they silent even then? Did they stare into each other's eyes with hatred, defiance? Did they bury their faces in each other's shoulders and shudder with relief, oh my darling, my sweetheart, I waited for you so long, I wanted you so much? Where do you learn stuff like that? From books? Movies? Don't make me laugh. She didn't even know his name.

Luce, why did you finally decide on that? Was it something you read in one of the old man's books? And she, Mar, why attach that name to that face, that young, smooth, dirty face, tear-stained from the cold wind that blew across the open market?

Afterwards they slept, the blanket pulled over them, their bodies still joined in that moist warm cocoon, in the hollow and depression left by the weight of the old man's body, while the cold gray afternoon dissolved and passed into evening and then night and the coldest part of night when she woke, dressed silently and went out, back to her aunt's one last time to put together a few things, to say, I'm going now, I won't be back. And then what? The aunt cursing and screaming, You little bitch! You whore! I thought you were different. But you had to go out on the street, you had to give it to the first dog that came along. After I took you in, fed you, this is what I get? Finally collapsing on the floor in a weeping pile of rags, a frightened old woman begging in a tremulous voice, Please don't go.

And she ignored her pleas? She walked out on that poor old woman? But what else was she supposed to do? Stay home and play holy martyr and saint in that tyranny and hierarchy of too many bodies and too many mouths and never enough to eat? Somehow, impossibly, feed and wash all those sick screaming babies, cook and scrub and clean, and if she didn't nobody does? And then dear auntie calls her whore? Bitch? Besides, she didn't just walk out on her. She still went early every morning to help with the cooking, to clean and see that the kids were alright. She still went to the market every day to watch the stall, to count the beads and shells, the dross and dirty scraps of paper she took in exchange for memories of food, the hand-painted mangos and papayas, the rutabagas, carrots and onions carved out of wood, all those little delicacies she stuffed into her skirt pocket to take home at night, to share with him, her mate, now that it was her shack too, now that it was her home, pile of boards, cozy little cottage, with wedding pictures on the mantel and a piece of the cake in the freezer, lace and satin curtains and mom and dad over for dinner on Sunday afternoons, She burned the roast again, Harry.

Anyway, you get the idea what it was like. A marriage without words, without love or the symbols of love, a marriage like any other. He crunched and chewed and slurped the food she prepared. Later at night the frantic thrashing together in bed while it was still new, while their bodies still demanded it, unless there was something else, unless he was working. Wait a minute, what kind of work? You mean he got a job? No, not a job, not anything that brought in food, money. Well what then? But when she asked him that he shook his head, he couldn't say. What about pay? Benefits? Company picnics? I'm sorry, I have to go now, I'll see you later. He was already pulling on his jacket, already out the door, already off on another one of his famous peregrinations. And then she might not expect to see him until tomorrow or the next day or never again, and lie awake at night thinking about that without attaching to it the words suffering or pain, not his or hers or anybody else's, just lie in the dark and picture him sprawled on the wet cobblestones, on the frozen ground in some lot or alley with a string of neat black holes across his chest and the blood leaking out.

And then what? Go back to the aunt begging and pleading? Taking the kicks and abuse? You filthy slut, I told you. That, or accept the next in line. And who would that be? Yeah, sure, Nakt, she knew all about Nakt. He was good with a gun, a knife, he could use his hands and feet, but what would he do with a girl, woman? Fill her up with more cold, more darkness and night, then send her back out in the street with nothing but the fury of teeth and

nails and the protective clutch of the womb, of what might
fill the womb or already filled the womb? And you don't
need any government agencies or church ladies wringing
their hands, Oh the poor little babies, to tell you about
that, do you, girl? It's right there inside you, sprouting and
growing and eating up your insides, procreating and
spawning more hungry eyes, more swollen bellies, more
dirty, unwashed little faces popping out of the ground like
mushrooms. And then what's a mother to do? Dress them
in their finest rags and send them back out in the street to
play their miserable little games of survival, to peck at the
dead earth like sick scrawny chickens, to crawl into the
nice part of town and put on their wretched little dog cir-
cuses for the pieces of copper that fall out of the hands of
ghosts? But that was him again, those were his words, the
words he brought back with him from his most recent foray
into the night. She'd say, Where have you been? What have
you been up to? I was worried. But he just laughed at her
questions, her concern, he'd go off on some story to distract
her, something about the old man, how he used to wake in
the middle of the night, shivering with cold, listening to
the old man rustling about below, getting his gear together,
getting ready to go out. Then he'd wake again an hour or
two hours later with the gray light filtering in, knowing
the old man was already gone, who knows gone where? just
gone, out there, beyond the periphery, out there on the
plain, wherever it is they used to grow food, although
where can you go out there now, isn't it all desert ? wasteland? And then the next day or the day after that the old
man'd return, exhausted, looking older and more worn out
than ever, unshoulder his sack and empty onto the table
the roots and tubers, the nuts, seeds and berries he'd dug
up and collected out of abandoned fields and farms, out of
folklore and memory. The old man who first learned to sur-

vive in a world of parchments and scrolls, who made his living sifting through the dust and bones of other peoples' lives with a magnifying glass in search of words to explain origins, justify existence, the words he used to fill out endless pages of reports and requisitions, the words he wielded in front of leaders and administrators and finally a court and a tribunal before he fled, ruined, into the anonymity and quiet of the periphery with his books and papers and a boy, an infant barely out of the egg, to scrape together whatever living he could, to live long enough to give him, Luce, that boy, those words he had carried with him all those years like useless artifacts, truth, love, humanity. What are you supposed to do with words like that, Mar? How do you translate them into the snuffles and grunts that express hunger and fucking and pain?

Oh yes, pain, pain, pain, always plenty of pain, he could never get any further than that word, pain. His own pain, the world's pain, everybody's pain but her pain, lying there late at night, drawn into himself, not looking at, not moving toward, not touching, seeking out, searching for her. Why didn't he ever tell her truth? Tell her love? Tell her humanity? Why didn't he ever use the words sunshine and happiness and fill her up with examples? Or was that some crazy dream of her own, wound up on an old gramophone, on a spool of black and white celluloid, if only she could find the right button to push, the right switch to throw and fill the city and the streets with car horns and neon lights and fashion models on parade, fill up the bars and restaurants, offices, shops and department stores with soda jerks and shop clerks, businessmen in gray flannel suits, waitresses, bartenders and homecoming G.I.s, and in the middle of all that he'd shoulder his way through the crowd with a drink in his hand and his eyes bright and shining, and she'd be sitting at the bar, maybe bored, maybe smoking a cigarette, and he'd come right up to her, maybe he'd been watching her all night, and take her by the hand and lead her onto the floor, and the music would be soft and the lights low, and she would know, she was falling in love.

Didn't the old man ever write anything like that?

No. And even if he did, he, Luce, couldn't let it be like that. He had to drag in his demons and wraiths, he had to knock over his garbage cans, free his rats, let loose in the streets the lunatic, the raving and mad, and for escape give them bottles of shoe polish and paint thinner and tubes of glue out of which they might wring a few drops of poison, a few hours of hallucination and forgetfulness, too tired, too beat down and afraid to look up, to meet the eyes of the rich, the eyes of the law, because then there was the black leather, the boots and guns. Do they have faces, Mar? Do they have wives and children at home? Do they talk about love?

He lay on his back, talking to the ceiling, the night. She didn't answer, interrupt, he wasn't talking to her, he wasn't telling her anything new, it was happening right outside the window, the helicopters circling overhead, searchlights, loudspeakers, ladies and gentlemen, on center stage . . . a burst of automatic rifle fire rips open the night, little Danny down the street gets whacked backing out of a grocery store with a bag of worthless receipts in his hand, little Bobby who used to live above the laundry gets nailed to a brick wall while digging through the trash cans in some foul-smelling alley, little B-billy with the b-bad sta-sta-stutter gets cl-clubbed to d-death because the s-s-s-s-sight of a b-b-b-b-b-badge sc-sc-sc-sc-scared-scared him so ma-ma-ma-ma-ma-ma-ma-much he c-couldn't s-say his own n-name. He couldn't keep it to himself, he had to bring it all home to her, he had to tell her every little detail. She didn't know who he was punishing, her or himself. All she could do was try to ignore him, shut him off, until finally even he couldn't stand it anymore, he had to get up, get out, go somewhere, walk, look for Nakt.

He found him in an alley working on a bottle, a joint, searched his glazed eyes for anger, resentment, Hey boy, you don't have time for your buddies anymore, you're always hanging out with that little cunt. But Nakt never said anything like that, he just nodded, passed him the joint, Hey, boy, you're getting good, you found me. He wanted to say, of course I found you, Nakt, it was easy, you're all fucked up, you're nodding off like a slob. But he didn't say anything like that, he just said, Hey, what's up, what's going on? And then what? Maybe find the rest of the gang, hang out with the guys like the old days, get up a fire in a barrel and smoke and drink and do that until you're fuzzy in the head and rocking on your feet. But it isn't any fun anymore, is it? Maybe it was never any fun. Maybe all this time you thought it was fun you were hiding from the truth. Which is what? That you weren't so tough after all? That you felt helpless, you felt lonely and afraid?

It was like a dream, he heard this voice talking, saying all these crazy things, and he thought, man, this guy is crazy, he doesn't know where he is, these guys are going to kill him. Then he looked around the fire, he saw all those faces looking at him and he realized, it's me, I'm the one who's saying this stuff. He couldn't make himself stop, it was pouring out of the faucet in his head, out of the well and cistern of the old man's words, he thrust their own wretched lives in front of them, he spoke in words they could understand, he said shit, piss, fuck, he said God, damn, soul. The whole time he felt Nakt's eyes on his, narrowing and focusing, watching him, probing him, trying to figure him out, it was Nakt he was talking to, Nakt he had to convince. Someone coughed, laughed, started to interrupt, the firelight danced on Nakt's face, his eyes rolled in that direction. Who knows, maybe that's what made it work from the very beginning, maybe that was the combination, the words and the power behind the words, the promise and the threat. And because Nakt listened, the others listened, and he went on talking.

Pretty soon his audience began to grow, he went from fireside to street corner to stage and platform, there was never any program, no planned speech, you heard the murmurs, then the shouts, then he walked out on stage, a gaunt young man in baggy coat and trousers, a hand puppet with a bolt of lightning up his ass, sometimes he was solemn, stern, apocalyptic, sometimes he tore at his hair, threw his hands over his head, shouted, yelled, exhorted. He didn't know where it came from himself, there was some kind of progression, the words superimposed themselves on things around them, a cop's club coming down on a young man's skull, a red flag, a cry of freedom. The hall was filled, they were packed shoulder to shoulder, the air smelled of sweat, booze and tobacco, they came from the factories, the mines and mills, they came from the schools and universities, all those bleak, soot-blackened, worn-out, weary, exhausted and blankly staring faces, all those brilliant, hot, excited and enflamed faces. People are sick, he shouted, people are hungry, people are dying, what else do you need to know?

He made it seem so simple. In the beginning even Nakt believed, believed and didn't believe. Who knows, maybe he, Luce, really didn't see, the whole time Nakt and his soldiers, his conscripts were working the crowd, they moved up and down the aisles, bumping elbows, talking them up, getting them on their feet, getting them to shout. Luce! Luce! they cried out to him. Their faces shone in the torchlight, they were hungry, they wanted action.

Who knows how these things happen. Later somebody writes it all down, gives it scope and veracity, all the names, dates and places, how it began, how you gathered in boarded-up warehouses, in rundown shacks and speakeasies, how you pounded the streets night and day handing out leaflets and fliers, how you transformed gunshots and stab-wounds into slogans and banners, how you filled the streets and the squares with people shouting and cheering because for the first time in their lives they felt a kind of joy, a kind of hope, that something was really going to happen. And when it didn't, or it happened too slowly, you shot and killed again, planted bombs in candy boxes and baby carriages. And what did that have to do with the old man's injunction, thou shalt not murder? How did that fit into the old man's scheme of truth and love and humanity?

But when he doubted himself, when he had second thoughts, he heard another voice at his side, insinuating itself in his ear, yes, but is that what the old man really said? Is that what he meant? Isn't there another, more propitious way of interpreting his words? Not just bread, a warm fire and a roof over your head, but power and control and the wholesale slaughter of anyone who oppresses you, challenges you, gets in your way? But whose voice was that? Was it really Nakt saying those things? Who taught him that? Who gave him that voice and those words? Was he, Luce, responsible for that gift of speech? Is that what he'd been teaching all this time, the hatred? The killing? Or had Nakt simply misunderstood? Twisted it up in his own mind? What if it was something even worse? What if it was he, Luce, who didn't understand? What if that was what the old man had wanted all along? To let those words spread like a disease? To infect and persuade, to fill peoples' minds with thoughts of hatred and revenge, to light up the night with the flames of armageddon, to overthrow the old order, reduce it to ashes, and plant your own garden of fear and paranoia in its stead? Is that what you were struggling for? To find that button, to throw that switch, to put yourself on the inside and those who were in—out? And then what? Somebody else has to remove you, and someone else them and those who come after them, and so on and so forth? And call that revolution, call that evolution of the species? And still believe there's some reason to go on? Better just to shut up, close your mouth and nose, seal your eyes, ears and asshole and go back to sleep as quickly as possible without disrupting this monstrous harmony.

He'd wake in the middle of the night, panting, in a cold sweat. He used to have this nightmare. He'd find himself on his knees, in front of a tribunal of fat, fleshy old men in loose white robes and soft womanly breasts. They stared at him with disgust, utter contempt, and he was crying, not just crying but gasping and sobbing and blubbering apologies, I'm so sorry, I didn't mean to cause any trouble, I didn't know this was going to happen. Then he'd see Nakt in the wings, he wanted to ask, How'd you get in this dream? But Nakt was pleading with him, urging him with his eyes, Don't do it! Don't say it! Don't let anybody see! Because they all wanted him to be strong, they all wanted him to be so goddamn good and certain of his path, but he wasn't certain of anything. When he walked out on stage he'd feel that hot greasy thing sliding through his bowels, he felt like he was going to be sick, shit in his pants. Yeah, sure, everybody thought he had it all worked out, they thought he knew what he was doing. They didn't realize you could wake up in some cell in some basement with broken teeth and bones and clots of blood and God knows what else they can do to you, fuck you up for good with no hope of getting out of here or going back to that miserable little life you used to live, you and everybody else you've brought along with you in your little campaign for truth and love and humanity. Oh yeah, sure, we'll wage a war of flowers, overwhelm them with numbers, clog the treads of their tanks with our bodies, lie down in front of their guns until they run out of bullets. It's been tried before. The cemeteries are that much fuller.

If only he could tell someone, if he could just say I'm so scared, I don't know what's going on anymore, I'm afraid of dying. But not even Mar, not even those rare nights when she finally managed to pull him away from the drunken angry crowds, the madmen, cops and spies. Sure, in the beginning, when she thought they actually had a chance, she stood up there like an idiot, smiling and waving, encouraging the other women, the wives, mothers, daughters and sistuhs. Now she just wanted to scream, Why don't you go away and leave us alone! How was it possible? They used to be so much in love, they were just a couple of kids, they used to go from one bar to another with Nakt and the gang, it seemed like they knew everybody or everybody knew them. Something to drink, Luce? Something for the lady? C'mon, Luce, for old time's sake. And what was he going to say? Alright, OK, but just one, a tall cool something or other with ice clinking and a twist of lime, and raise it up and drink it down, and the warmth and fire spreading through his brain. And then he was primed, he was ready to go, bring on the next bar, the next table, somebody always wanted something from him, somebody was always asking a favor. Talk to Nakt, he said, talk to one of his men, they'll fix you up. By then he was already off and running with Mar behind him, trying to smile, trying to be nice, trying to keep up. But that's another dream, right? More confused fairy tales. It was never like that. Not even when she drew him onto her little island, when she led him, calling and whispering to him, deeper into the forest, into the redolence of lilies and orchids, when they dove down into that dark pool he swam up out of later at night with the moonlight or the starlight or just the light of some dismal street lamp shining on the wet pavement outside the window, when he lay there, staring into the dark, thinking, while she slept or pretended to sleep next to him.

Not even when the baby finally came, emptying her belly, transforming her screams of pain into cries for life. He watched her nursing it, holding it in her arms, this small envelope of flesh, this strange creature that came out of her body. Was that what enabled her to care for it, love it? Because it grew inside of her, sucked at her heart, her stomach, her lungs, taking from her breath and life and blood? Somehow her face seemed softer, younger, sometimes she even smiled. Was there a word for that? Goodness or kindness or even beauty? Could such a word exist, waiting for months and years and possibly even centuries for the rare moments when beauty was allowed? When some artist or sculptor chiseled it in stone or painted it on canvas as a reminder and keepsake for the next hundred or thousand years?

Yeah, sure, mother and child. What if she knew what kind of creature she held in her arms, suckled at her breast? Would she smother the child herself? Leave it on some barren plain or mountainside to die, to spare herself and everybody else the pain? Or would she hide it from the world, raise it in secret, deny and defend its every atrocity. What instinct was that? Who protected whom? The baby gave back life, validated life. Hers anyway. So why didn't he feel anything? Emptied, fulfilled, satisfied, complete? He stood over the child, staring at it, trying out the words in his brain, son, this is my son, even then knowing they were false, that he was only repeating past lies.

While she slept in the other room with the baby he stared into the fire, playing with the stone, turning it in his hand, feeling its smoothness and warmth, remembering the old man, that tic he had, that palsied, worrying, rubbing together of fingers and thumb, the old man trying to scratch an itch in the palm of his hand, in the back of his skull, an itch that corresponded to some truncated memory of his own lost childhood. Is that how it was done? A trap set first for the old man, and then by the old man for him, to give him just that much, the words and the key to the words, and then abandon him, turn him loose with that single word Run! Go! Now you figure it out? And if he couldn't figure it out, at least carry on, stumble and stagger along like a donkey in the night until he found or produced his own homunculus, instilled in its tiny brain that same sense of incompletion and longing, that urgency and need to carry on when he no longer could, to discover new words, to learn that madness, to foment more anger, hate, confusion?

One night he watched her holding the baby in her lap, at the same time working a ball of yarn and knitting needles in her hands. How did she manage that? Was that also some instinct, that allowed her to nurture that other, new life, while going on with her own? Or were they inextricably linked in a way he could never understand? Even the song she sang, some babbling baby talk only she and the baby could comprehend, her mind working on some other plane, governed by tide pools, the light of the full moon. The old man's fairy tales again, old wives' tales, the relentless chanting of tongues, knit and stitch, knit and stitch, needles and bones, needles and bones. Gradually it all began to make sense, the baby and the rhythm of her work and the ball of yarn in her hands, he began to recognize it, try it on in his mind, a tiny wool sweater, dark blue like the night with snowflakes falling down or were they stars. And then the unraveling of the night and something hot and wet rolling down his face. But he still didn't get it, he still couldn't quite understand, because the old man never used those words with him, she, your mother, love, when you were born. And what was he going to tell the boy, his son, when he was old enough to understand, to ask his own unanswerable questions? Make up the same old lies? When I was a boy I went out under the black winter night and looked up at the stars until my head spun and I couldn't stand on my feet? During the day my friends and I went out with our sleds and toboggans and trudged through deep white fields with tufts of dry brown grass poking up through the snow? But then he'd have to explain about sand dunes and the seashore and the flocks of seagulls crying overhead like the vendors in the market and a whole lot of other things that didn't make any sense anymore and probably never did. And the boy wouldn't believe him anyway, there'd be nothing in his world to corroborate his father's lies.

He was starting to cry again, the tears were rolling down his face. He could feel his pain pulling at her, drawing her eyes toward his, searching for the source of heat. But he looked away, he didn't want her to see, to think he was sick, weak, he was ashamed of his tears. But what if he was wrong? What if he had showed them to her, let her see? Would she have received them like diamonds, forgiven him everything, reached out to him and pulled him into her arms, crooning, What is it, my darling? Why are you crying? Speaking to him the way she did the child, telling her own lies, It's alright, baby, it's OK. What difference would that make?

He got up, pulled on his coat, went out into the night, hunched over, feeling frail, nervous, old. He had no idea where he was going or why. Papers and trash blew down the street. The last lights in the buildings had long gone out. He walked all night, walked and walked until the blackness began to crumble and disintegrate into a numb gray fog. His eyes were wet from the cold wind. He had his hands in his pockets for warmth, he was turning the stone, worrying it, worrying himself, worrying about what he was going to do next, when he stopped, came to a halt in the middle of an abandoned suspension bridge, a nightmare horror of twisted iron stretching across a steep valley. Far below a vein of raw black sewage trickled through a clutter of hovels and shacks, frost-covered weeds and burnt stumps. A pall of acrid smoke rose from a garbage pile, burned in his nostrils. He took the stone out of his pocket, exposed the faint green gleam to the dim light. If only he could generate or regenerate that happy idiot dream once again. But a shiny stone, a pretty pebble, couldn't substitute for a world, one deluded messiah couldn't resurrect a people, a planet.

He started to laugh. Suddenly he saw himself in a ridiculous monster suit with floppy rubber horns and the zipper showing in back, rampaging across the countryside, destroying everything in his path, trampling underfoot flowers and vines and strange cooing little creatures, fat, rosy-faced cherubim with freshly sprouted wings who beamed and chuckled and winked at him just as he brought his big black boots down on their curly little heads. Murder, this is murder. What? The old man again? Breaking his long silence? Talking through a mouthful of mud, the old man who belonged in another century, another era, who exhorted an impossible code of ethics, impossible in any time. Or was that just the way the old man wanted it to look? What if the old man was really a charlatan, a fake? What if all that time he was hiding out, running from the law, from past crimes and misdeeds? Did that make those words any less real? Murder? This is murder? He clutched the iron rail, felt the tug and pull of the chasm. There was a metallic ting, ding, the stone bounced off the metal plate under his feet, rolled over the side, and then he could only watch as it arced and fell and disappeared into the squalor below. But it was an accident, he didn't mean to drop it. Besides, it didn't mean anything, it was just a pretty pebble, a piece of junk, not worth anything, certainly not his life.

He'd started to walk again, slowly at first and then faster and faster as the little mechanism clicked on in his brain and the act of walking became the act of thinking and he was charging down the sidewalk with his arms and legs flailing and his thoughts mindlessly in overdrive, and any second now some cop was going to shout, Hey! Stop! Grab him by the shoulders and shove him against the wall. But it wasn't a cop, it was Nakt, ha ha, it was just Nakt playing a joke on him like the old days.

But something was wrong, it wasn't a joke afterall. Nakt was staring at him with horror, he was shouting at him, What's wrong with you? Where the hell've you been? We've got a meeting in half an hour, we've got marches and rallies to attend. Yeah, sure, maybe if Nakt'd thrown his arms around him, given him a big hug, Luce, buddy, let's get in out of the cold, get a hot cup of coffee, something to eat. But he had other things to think about, the organization, the movement, the hundreds and thousands of people risking their lives because of the madness raging in their prophet's mind. Maybe it was that pristine terror in Nakt's eyes that triggered his own fear, set him off again with Nakt beside and then behind him, trying to follow, keep up, keep him in sight. Form and shadow they lurched down sour stinking alleys, stumbled through crumbling labyrinths of brick and rubble, it didn't matter where they ran, it was always the same lousy fucked-up nightmare, dream, burned-out and abandoned buildings, twisted lampposts, the streets littered with glass, dead derelict machines. But now he was working on his speech tonight, practicing his lines, the words he'd use, ghetto, slum, riot, incendiary devices, casualties, loss of life. Murder. He heard Nakt hacking and coughing behind him, he smoked too many cigarettes, his lungs were shot, he told him to stop a thousand times but he wouldn't listen. He wanted to shout out, You'll never catch me, Nakt, I win! But suddenly he wasn't running anymore, he was falling, floating, collapsing to the ground. And then that other passage, Nakt somehow lifting his body, hoisting him over his shoulder, and then the jolting, staggering, drifting in and out of consciousness, followed by that abrupt thud and brief awakening when Nakt dumped him in front of the stove, the converted oil drum, like a sack of dirty laundry, and that word surfaced in his mind like a sigh of relief, home, that little stage, that board theater, lying on the floor with Nakt crouched over him like a gargoyle, an ape, waiting for the next scene, Mar's entrance with the baby.

And even if she did want to scream, to shout in Nakt's face, You bastard, you son-of-a-bitch, you did this! she didn't scream, shout, say anything, not when she put the water on the stove to boil, not when she knelt to wipe his forehead with the damp cloth, when she spooned the warm tea into his mouth, not even when he finally began to move, to show some signs of life and revival did she relent and let loose the hot gush of tears, Oh my darling, Luce, why do you do this to yourself? She only got him to his feet, got him to bed, then turned to face Nakt. But she didn't have to say anything, he was already going, he was almost out the door when he stopped, looked back over his shoulder,

stretched teeth and skin into some semblance of a smile.
But even if he was thinking, you fucking bitch, you whore,
he didn't say it, did he? Because even if she was a bitch and
a whore and anything else he could think to call her, things
were OK now, Luce was OK. For a little while longer the
fate of the organization was assured.

Yeah, sure, she watched over him, fed him, nursed him
back to health. But she couldn't watch all the time, she still
had the baby and her job in the market, she still had to
help out her aunt. Wait a minute, she was still working in
the market? Of course. Somebody had to bring in some
money, earn a living. She'd go to the market with the baby
tied up in a sling, the whole day on her feet, not even a five
minute break to sit down. She ate, bargained, bartered,
nodded off, even peed, standing behind her stall, the pale
yellow stream splashing between her bare feet, trickling
and running over the cobblestones, down the street. What
else was she supposed to do, day care? Join a union? Don't
make me laugh. That only happens in fairy tales. Then
she'd come home at night, find him up, find him bent over
those damn books again. He told her not to worry, he was
almost finished, he'd nearly reached the end, read everything the old man had ever written, he was convinced he
was going to find some kind of answer, solve his dilemma.
But things got worse, not better.

He didn't eat or sleep, he'd read the same page over and
over again, focusing on a particular word, a phrase, searching for some intricate meaning. One night he was absent-
mindedly toying with the old man's smoking paraphernalia.
He opened the tin box, crumbled the dried shreds of
tobacco between his fingers, inhaled the faint narcotic
aroma, a luxury from another time and place, from the old
man's past, from the plains, the country, where they grew
things to eat, to smoke, to drink, to still the hunger, the

cold, to give you visions of escape. He turned the pipe in his hand, inspected the chewed and chipped mouthpiece, the burnt black bowl. He could see the old man in his chair, the pipe in his hand, lost in thought, maybe contemplating the next act of the pen. But there wasn't another act, the old man was killed, he stepped into the alley and the explosion in the alley and died before he could write down that final word, Run! He'd read to the end of the old man's life, the last words on the last page crumbled into whiteness and snow, and then only the darkness and night outside. He felt abandoned, alone. He shuddered, hugged himself, on the verge of tears. His mouth twisted into a grimace, then he laughed. Was that the answer? Had he finally figured it out? Was it only necessary to die to end the madness and torment of words in his head? He laughed again, it seemed so simple. Then he realized he was still holding the old man's pipe in his hand, the bowl was cold, the ember long dead. He thought that was funny too, almost funny, he couldn't wait to tell Nakt, he'd think it was funny, if he could just remember the fucking punch line, how'd it go again? But he'd already forgotten, he couldn't remember. He stared into the fire, tearing at his face, his hair, counting again, one, two, three, four, searching for a stiller rhythm of heart and lung, some deeper silence within. How far did he have to count this time? To the end of night? But this isn't any night we're talking about, is it? Not a night measured in coffee cups. Not a pot of coffee night slumped over in the fluorescent mist of an all-night diner. Not even a river of coffee steaming hot and black through the miasmic night of whorehouses and honkytonks in some port city in some railroad district in some riverboat stop. But an endless, infinite, eternally insomniac night. You go from emptiness to emptiness, from void to void, with only those rare moments in between, laughter and tears punctuated by more nothing. Worn out and exhausted with nothing you collapse and pass out into nothing. Wake sick and aching with nothing. Stagger into the bathroom and dip your hands in nothing, splash your face with nothing, bathe and shudder awake again in nothing. But all this nothing nothing nothing! Why don't you get up off your ass and do something? What the fuck are you waiting for? Someone to light a candle? a match? the sun? Do you expect to hear the cock crow before you accept the fact that it really is time to go back to work? And what kind of work is that? The unraveling of madness? Only to replace it with another kind of madness still? Is madness salvation? Can you take refuge in madness? Live in madness? Call madness home? Hello, welcome to my madness, you who are madness, sit down, rest, I'll build a fire, would you like some tea? brandy? But this is madness.

Even when he did manage to fall asleep for an hour or two hours, when he slipped into that gray numb and nothing of sleep toward morning, when Mar came out because the baby was crying, because she had to get up, make something to eat, get ready to go to work, and found him slumped in his chair, when she stood over him, watching him sleep, awed at the transformation, the emergence of another face, a calm and peaceful face, a face almost like her baby's, and for those few moments maybe remembered who he was and what he meant to her, for a few moments maybe even loved him again. But then, when he started to revive, when that other transformation took place, when that soft smooth baby face he had rediscovered in sleep was suddenly disfigured, crushed by gravity and the weight of return to this world, and he started to rise from his chair, filled with hatred and rage at who or whatever had disturbed him. But it was only her, the woman, poking up the fire, putting together something to eat, trying not to

wake him. Although there were those times when he went
too far, when he couldn't quite make it back, when everything remained alien and strange for days, when he stared
at her without any idea who she was or what she meant to
him, when, suddenly, he broke down, sobbed uncontrolla-
bly because he knew she used to mean something to him.
By then she was sick of it herself, she just wanted it to be
over, he was already gone from her, he wasn't coming back,
she had to think about the baby.

Yeah, sure, for a while Nakt tried to keep things going
on his own, pasted and sewed together the torn flesh and
broken bones of the movement into a dead dummy he
shoved out on stage while a ragged band played some stupid marching song and the sisters' auxiliary choir sang
along. At night he sat alone in the empty hall, counting the
donations, the receipts, the promises of support when Luce
returned to the scene. Maybe that's when our agent
showed up, maybe he was one of you all along, maybe he
offered money, drugs, the usual routine. Listen pal, you
don't have to do anything, just meet up with him, give him
a friendly little hug, a kiss, just like you would any other
day, just so we know it's him, just so we get a positive ID.

There wasn't anyone to ask for advice, to tell him what
direction to take. He walked the streets all day and all
night, turning the thing in his head, gnawing at it and worrying over it with that shiny-eyed rat terror of too many
mazes, too many laboratory experiments, but no voice
came out of the sky bearing the right words and slogans to
get the movement going again. In the end he said yes, what
else could he say but yes? Who knows, maybe the greasy
little fuck thought he was going to save his own ass. Just
like he thought he was going to be the big man after Luce
was gone. Maybe he even thought he saw a way out, a trap
door within a trap. Sure, they'd have Luce, but on his,

Nakt's terms, as a martyr, saint. Maybe that was even Luce's plan all along. Besides, what if Luce survived? Wouldn't that prove him the prophet, messiah? Or was he only condemning him to more torture? A protracted death. And what if someone found out it was him who betrayed Luce? What then?

Ah, poor Nakt. He shouldn't have taken himself so seriously, another trait he picked up from his master, his benighted messiah, and for what? He wasn't the deciding factor, he was just a small fish, an errant radical in an already fucked-up equation. It was so much bigger than anyone had imagined. Perhaps if we—because we're in this together, you and I—if we'd all acted differently in the beginning, if we'd taken our reasoning one step further, if we'd seen that we share the same God afterall. Power, control, order in a disorderly universe. When things go badly one can not be weak, one can not wring one's hands in despair, one must rearrange the stars.

After that it was easy. Someone gave the order, sent the shadows slipping along the walls, they surrounded the little cottage, shack, pile of boards, the night smelled of nitrates and gun oil gleaming among levers and springs. Mar stood in front of him, the baby in her arms, her face ragged, worn with hatred, fear, fatigue. Are they just going to come in here and kill us? The baby? Aren't you going to do anything? And what was he supposed to do? Make a speech? Weave some miracle out of words? He touched her face, felt her recoil. He wanted to say something, make it right again, but what, run? That word was useless now, there was nowhere to run. Besides, Mar and the baby? Run? He opened the door, went out to meet them. But look! Who would have guessed? It was Nakt. Of all people, his old buddy Nakt. But he looked terrible, he wasn't eating right, he wasn't getting enough sleep, he looked tired and worn, his eyes eviscerated of all hope. He wanted to reach out to him, touch him, tell him, It's alright, Nakt, you did all you could. But it was too late, they were coming now, closing around him with their manacles and chains.

After that it was all standard procedure. We tossed him in the back of a garbage truck, hauled him off without any goodbyes, without even the sweet sorrowing kiss of betrayal. But the woman, that little slut, it took half a dozen men to tear the child from her arms, drag her out of there. Then they destroyed all, overturned the stove, torched the place, they didn't have time to mess around, they burned it to the ground, sent it all up in flames, the rat nests and cobwebs, the old boards, the old man's bed, the stacks of books and papers, the chorus of birds singing in the trees and the young lovers lying down among the rainbows and flowers and splashing streams, all lost forever in the orange flames rising in the cold black night.

Just having a barbecue, we told the neighbors. It's those damn space heaters, we told the press. Now go home, all of you, you've gotta go to work in the morning. And then the next day, in the cold gray light of day, we gave the public or not even the public but whoever might inquire (make sure you get their names, council) all the reassurances and all the bullshit lies. Of course he isn't being mistreated, of course he hasn't been shot. And then we got the little bastard in the back room and went to work. And let me tell you, boys, the technicians positively drooled, they rubbed their hands together with glee, they danced around our little Luce and cooed, Alright, mister messiah, now tell us the truth, all your plans, codes, names, dates, places, all your comrades, networks, blocks and cells.

To tell the truth, we were only going to scare him. But the little shit didn't blink an eye, he just gave us one of those insipid martyr smiles. Then the boys rolled up their sleeves, they got down to business, they gave him a little lesson in applied sciences, they applied his bare feet to red-hot frying pans, pounded his testicles into sour mash with a meat tenderizer, squirted wasps and scorpions up his nose with a turkey baster, nothing that hasn't been tried a million times before. Once again the old methods proved best, he couldn't hold out any longer, he was just like a baby, he opened all his doors, let loose the foul sludge and the hot yellow stream and the belated, the extraneous tears, babbling every bit of childish nonsense left in his brain. It didn't matter, they still weren't satisfied, nothing was true, the torture continued. But better not to talk about that here, better not to remember, to fill the night and the void with such fury and apocalypse, the lightning reticulations of a brain in chaos, in a thunderstorm of perverse creations, all the demons and monsters of all your childhood terrors, when you wake to find yourself swimming and struggling in a turgid black sea of slime and cold amphibian skin, of rubber blow-up fuck-me dolls and detachable tails and limbs, salamanders and eels and leering barracuda grins searching and probing and pushing their heads up your asshole, down your throat, to feel your body violated in every way imaginable, to watch—because they've fastened your eyelids open with fishhooks so you have to watch—as the scalpel draws thin red lines across your abdomen and thorax, separating layers of tissue, muscle and fat, membranes, arteries and veins, bundles of nerve fiber and white plastic cartilage, opening up the steaming black coffers of your chest and stomach until you pass into oblivion and night devoid of all responsibility while your sleeping brain revolts, denies all, spawning and scattering endless nightmares and creatures throughout the universe to destroy all, violators and innocent alike, in the final and forever pronouncement of doom, NEVER

AGAIN shall there be such a race and creation of monsters.

And after you have flayed the skin, blasted away the flesh, disintegrated the bone, drained the blood, collected eyes, ears, nose and mouth and pinned them to some dead doll's face, after you've eviscerated the tomb of the body and placed all the vital organs in various glass jars and containers, after you've obliterated the man, burned him into ash, destroyed all evidence of his ever having been, can you accuse the soul or not even the soul but the disembodied bit of fluff you call the soul of the crimes of the man? Can you call the soul criminal? Murderer? Abandoned soul, soul of God, of man?

But this is more nonsense, the deluded ramblings of a courtroom stenographer, some out of work scrivener hired to take down the confessions of one more in an endless string of criminals, dissidents, failed revolutionaries. Ha! Who did he think he was, the amanuensis of God?

But even that was part of the plan. We let the little four-eyed paperpushing creep sneak away into the night with his absurd little soap opera tucked under his arm to copy and disseminate among his miserable ranks, to give the populace a taste of what we had in store for them if they got out of hand, to set them on the right path, civil obedience, respect for the law and the will of God. Afterall, it was what our beloved martyr wanted. We were just helping him along.

He woke on his back on the cold cement, on a cold metal slab or block of ice. He was still too weak to think, to hope that it might actually be over. And then, just when that foolish idea began to percolate down into his numb skull somebody woke him again, splashed a bucket of ice water in his face, or maybe it was just the cold wind and rain. He heard a sound or not a sound but a voice droning on and on in a slow chanting monotone, a nice voice, a rich, deep, melodious voice that echoed inside the great stone walls, inside the vaulted ceiling of his skull. But he still couldn't quite understand what the voice was saying, or maybe it just took him a little while longer before he realized it was his own name, over and over again, his own name. But what did they want? They seemed to be asking him for something, they wanted his help. But how could he help anyone? He was so tired. He just wanted to lie there a little longer and sleep, it was so nice with the candles burning, thousands and thousands of candles, or maybe they were stars. And that wonderful fragrance, incense? Or flowers? And that voice droning on and on. It made him feel safe and warm, he felt a smile tightening on his face. But that didn't seem to be the right thing to do because the voice ceased. There was a moment of silence, and then the voice again, not so benevolent now, perhaps even a little piqued. So my friend, you think it's funny? You think we're playing a game? Well, just remember, we've still got your whelp and whore.

The warm whirring little motor of his dream stopped, he tried to squeeze his brain into some kind of cohesive thought. The voice spoke again, helped him along. Look here, my friend, open your eyes, what do you think of this? He opened his eyes or he thought he opened his eyes but it still didn't make any sense, there was a woman, and she didn't have any clothes on, she was writhing on the stones in a kind of slow motion parody of resistance, of flailing and kicking against an attacker or attackers who had long ago plundered her body and her mind of all thought and reason, and then—oh, it was a comedy, and here came a couple of big beefy men in starched white nurses' uniforms pushing a baby carriage. But that still wasn't it, was it? There was something else, some kind of monster, an alligator or crocodile with gaping jaws, like rotten logs studded with rows of rusty nails, and now the nurses were dangling the baby over the monster's head while its eyes grew mad with hunger and the woman screamed herself the rest of the way into insanity. And it didn't even matter if it was true or not, it didn't matter if it was just a little home movie and the woman and the baby were already back out on the street with a coupla extra bucks in their pocket and their whole lives still ahead of them, it made him so sad, so terribly sad, poor woman, poor baby. But now he was crying again, he was gurgling and sobbing while the nurses captured his tears in little glass phials. Such nice nurses. They were trying to be gay, to cheer him up. They'd slipped out of their uniforms and into pretty magnolia and rose-printed gowns. They'd put on their pancake and rouge and bright red lipstick. But they were just small-town girls and it really was too much, even for them. They'd both begun to cry, they were dabbing at their eyes with lace hankies and sobbing in falsetto voices, oh boo hoo hoo. But now they'd spoiled their make-up. They really were quite a mess. Their five o'clock shadow was showing through. Meanwhile, a little boy in a flannel nightgown or maybe he was an angel went up and down the aisles with salt and pepper shakers in his hands, sprinkling tears on the soundman and the cameraman and everyone in the audience, and then they were all weeping, they were sobbing and wailing, and it felt so good, it felt so warm and wonderful to let go like that and really cry your heart out while the symphony or maybe it was a choir broke out in a great big brassy flare-up of triumph and joy, he could feel the warmth and light closing around him like a red-hot sun, or maybe he was the sun, and then someone threw a black silk slip over his head or there was an eclipse, and he was collapsing back into darkness and night, but it didn't matter anymore, nothing mattered, he was floating in a dream or he was the dream and he couldn't wake up anymore, he couldn't move because of whatever it was they had strapped him down or nailed him to with a needle in his arm and that neat little hydraulic system pumping its infinitely slow poison into his veins, how long did they say? or maybe they didn't say, but he could guess, another thirty or forty or even fifty years, and then forever and eternity which was still only more darkness and night, but there was something else, something he wanted to remember, but it was already slipping away and he had to struggle, he had to concentrate real hard, he had to really try and say. What was it again? Oh, right, She. And for just a moment he saw her face, dirty and tear-stained from the cold wind that blew through the marketplace, and then it popped like a child's balloon and disappeared forever, but it didn't matter anymore, he was so tired, he just wanted to sleep now, he had to sleep, and maybe later, maybe later he'd remember, he'd try to remember again, but it'd be better, it'd be better if he remembered it differently, next time.

III

manhole

(ALSO CALLED babble on)

How long have you been digging now, Erde? Years anyway, crawling around underground like a buggering earthworm waiting for farmer John to stick his shovel in the dirt and take off your lid. And then what? All that sunlight and birdsong blinding you and assaulting your ears, news-hens and pic-turemen shoving their cameras and microphones in your face and there you are on the six o'clock news, popping out of the earth like a goddamn groundhog pronouncing six more weeks of winter you bastards! and your name in all the headlines. **Erde Recaptured. Erde Back In Prison. Erde To Stand Trial.**

Yeah, sure, think anyone even remembers you're still down here, Erde? Oh yes, of course they do, the scientists, the boys in lab coats. They never let go, do they? Plant their little electrodes in your brain the day you're born. Shove radioactive isotopes up your asshole and set you free like an otter in the stream, then they follow your progress through the earth with stethoscopes and other listening devices dropped down sewer pipes, abandoned wells, they analyze your shit, your breathing, heartbeat. That's how they know, of course, forensic sciences, spectrographs, tell you where you've been, where you're going, what you eat, read, think. They've got mom and pop and little missy putting their ears to the floorboards at night, listening for a damp cough, creaking elbows, the signs of consumption, arthritis, emphysema. Junior's in his Boy Scout uniform, standing guard next to storm sewers, steam grates, manhole covers.

What'cha doin', son?

Watching for enemy submarines, sir.

Junior's got a chestfull of merit badges, a yellow sash covered with ribbons and awards. That's right, boys and girls, let's put on our swastikas now, hob-nailed boots. Oh, but you mustn't say those naughty things, Erde. Somebody might be listening, who might be listening? You might be listening. But let's not get caught up in another futile debate, okay?

Every day they drag in a new suspect, some poor miner got lost following a vein of anthracite under the Appalachias, some bony old priest in black cloth and rosaries prowling the catacombs beneath the Church of Our Blessed Lady of Merciful Tendencies. Underneath his severe black cloth he's wearing silk panties and brassiere, nylons and garter belt, he's ready for a big night out. Suddenly a light shines in his face, machine guns, snarling hounds. Alright, Erde, you can take off the disguise! We know it's you! They've got the whole goddamn public up in arms. They've got the walls plastered with posters and bills. Mug shots all over the post office. Look out for Erde! Public enemy number one! Poor Mildred's up there clutching her dress around her knees every time she goes to the refrigerator, the kitchen sink, terrified of what lies beneath the linoleum, that horrible old Erde in black face, rolling his eyes and waggling his tongue, any second he's gonna make a grab for her ankle, Hey lady! Watch out! And then all that screeching and screaming and Call the police! Send in the ferrets, the sappers, the tunnel rats, have the whole goddamn pack on your ass. Who knows, maybe you're a fucking legend by now, Erde. Maybe they've got a new name for you, although God forbid, not Moleman or the Human Earthworm or some other abomination like that, next thing you know they'll have you playing the freak in some circus sideshow.

Oh yes, I know, you've certainly had your day in the spotlights, haven't you? Once everybody knew Erde. Poor little mannie, his name was in all the papers, they talked about him all over town, they made such a big goddamn deal out of it, interviewed his grade school teachers, dug up his baby booties, those poor little work boots already broken down and caked with mud a month after he learned to walk. They published all kinds of nonsense, excoriated him in court. He was always a strange kid. Never fit in.

Morose, said the girl who sat next to him in eleventh grade. Hmmm, and wasn't she a perfect little nihilist in her black bangs and alabaster face. Kind of cute actually. Hey, baby. Naw, too late. And that poetry teacher, what was her name, Mizz Fizz? Wow, what a knock-out. Like to see her lying naked in a bed of truffles. Liked you, too, didn't she? It's all here in her student files. Erde. One of my brightest pupils. Deep. Dark images.

In other words, your honor, a psychopath. The high school guidance counselor, Mister Wallstone, offering his years of professional opinion. It's all his family's fault, they fucked him up real good.

The boys in the pressroom flash a scratchy old black and white photograph on the screen. There's a dark young woman in a long white dress. She spends her days beating carpets, washing sheets and diapers by hand, stirring steaming cauldrons over a wood stove, ironing her husband's linens. Next to her stands a dark young man with furious eyes, tight lips, strong hands. He works hard, hates his job, comes home at night full of anger, frustration. The boy lived in fear of something imminent, the air trembled around him, at night he lay in bed, listening for the crack of the whip, his mother's screams, No! Don't! You'll kill him! You can't expect a boy to grow up normal in that kind of environment.

More horseshit. They didn't know a goddamn thing about his family, how many brothers or sisters or whether he got an extra spoonful of sugar in his breakfast porridge. Truth is, the boy was an orphan. Ah, too bad. His mother died young, he never knew her, he had only the faintest memory of that white dress, her face glowing like a cameo in the darkness surrounding his crib. As for his father, the old fool got into some kind of trouble. Murder. Embezzlement. Something awful like that. They sent him off to jail, the penitentiary, breaking rocks all day. No one ever heard from him again. Poor boy, he had no family, no home, no little rocking chair by the fire. He'd dug himself a little burrow in the ground at the edge of the woods near a farmhouse. Oh yeah, now I remember. There was some old woman, a real grandmother type. Now and then he'd give her a hand with the chores. Chop firewood, carry water from the well. Help her pull up her stockings in the morning, button her dress. Every once in a while he'd catch a glimpse of some horrible crevice or cave overgrown with moss and roots, just enough to ruin his outlook on life and the prospect of conjugal relations. Sometimes she'd give him something to eat, a bowl of soup, boiled potatoes, sometimes she baked him cookies, or a cake, then forgot to feed him for a week, a month. He'd go to school in the morning clung with leaves and grass, his pockets bulging with acorns, burdock roots, big fat grub worms. Hey Erdie, you

wanta trade lunch? I got peanut butter and jelly, whata
you got? No one ever suggested he go away to college.
There wasn't any talk of scholarships, fraternities, life in
the dorm.

After high school he ended up digging ditches, working
on construction crews, road gangs, whatever he could find.
He had a strong back, plenty of stamina, he could swing a
pick from sunup to sundown. Besides, he liked the work
and the rhythm of the work. It matched the rhythm of his
thinking. Remember, Erde? How sweet it was? Up there in
the sunshine? The entire day passing in a kind of celluloid
blur. The clouds and the trees and the birds taking wing.
Now and then you look up at the sun to see what time of
day it is, if it really is so hot. Sometimes a pretty girl goes
by. You can't even see her face, just her hair swinging and
her ass swaying, but it's enough to dream, to imagine for a
moment, to relish all the possibilities, if I had some money
in my pocket and a coupla days off, and a plane ticket down
to the Caribbean. Yeah, yeah, getcher self a sunlamp, why
don't ya? Girlie pin-ups on the wall, scatter some sand
around, plastic palms, requisition a case of beer. Ah well,
then the dream's over and it's back to work again, eh boys?
And man oh man! The hot sun on your back and the rock
and rubble at your feet. And you're swinging the pick
again, swinging the sledge, thinking about tonight, tomorrow, about nothing at all.

In other words he was stupid, lazy, practically an imbe-
cile.

No, that's not true either. He had ambition, desire, he
wanted to better himself. He just didn't know how things
worked yet. He was still young, innocent.

Objection, your honor.

Objection sustained. The court will determine the guilt
or innocence of the defendant.

Pretty soon he got a reputation as a hard worker. One day he went into the boss's office, asked for a raise. You know the scene. Boss's a life-long chump, hemorrhoids, high blood pressure, lousy sex life. He's balding, chomping on a soggy cigar. He looks up from his desk, What makes you think you deserve a raise, boy? Erde rolls up his sleeve, makes a muscle, I'm strong, I work hard, I know how to swing a pick. Boss laughs, points out the window. Down the road a piece comes a broken-down old mule pulling a wagon. Farmer John sits up behind with a switch in hand, Gee up, mule! Gee! Ya see, Erde? That old mule knows how to pull the wagon, but he don't know where the hell that wagon's going.

Erde went back outside with his face burning, his hat in his hand. Rest of the men are standing around, grinning their idiot grins. Say, Erde, who you think you is? You gonna be a dollar an hour mule the rest of your life, just like we is. Erde shrugged, raised his pick, went back to work again. Every chance he got he glanced at blueprints, engineers' reports, asked questions.

Wait a minute, what kind of questions? You mean like, what the hell are we doing here and what the hell's it all about and what came before God?

No, you simpleton, none of that. He was just trying to survive, get along in life. Pretty soon he began to figure things out. Hey, the bossman said, this guy's pretty smart, he works hard, learns fast, seems like a good company man. At the end of the day he called Erde in. I've been watching you, boy. He made him a foreman, gave him a dollar an hour raise, his own crew bristling with crowbars, augers and crates of dynamite, told him go here, go there, dig a ditch, a pit, a tunnel. The men worked hard for him. He was big, strong, he had that quiet authority, hard jaw, he looked older than he was.

One day they were building a bridge across the river that separated the town from the country. Erde saw right away they were making a mistake, sinking pylons in a sandbar that was certain to wash away in the next meteorological disaster. That evening he went into the boss's office with an empty lunch bag he'd scratched all over with a piece of charcoal. Look here, Boss, if we just move the bridge a hunnerd yards down stream we can anchor it in good solid granite and save poor old Mrs. Wingnut's hen house from eminent destruction. Erde was sure the boss'd be happy. Probably saved his ass, prevented him from making a huge blunder, maybe even a terrible loss of life. The bossman leaned back in his chair, puffed on his cigar a coupla times, looked out the window like he was searching for another mule to come down the road. Then he screwed up his eyes like a fat little pig at an empty trough, Listen here, Erde, yer a good worker and a good man but yer gonna get yerself in trouble if you keep thinking too much. Now get'cher ass outa here and don't come back! Erde went back outside feeling sick, humiliated, confused. The next couple of days he just tried to do his job, keep his thoughts to himself and his mouth shut. But even the men were beginning to grumble. What the hell we doing here, chief? First car goes across, this damn bridge is gonna be in the drink before I can drink me drink. That did it. Erde tossed his hat on the ground, stomped up and down. Now what the hell was he supposed to do? Rag on the men the way the boss ragged on him? Go back inside the boss's office and get tossed out again? Maybe even lose his job?

There was only one thing to do. He combed his hair, scraped the mud off his boots, bundled up all kinds of blueprints, geological surveys and back issues of the Sunday Times crossword puzzle and went to see the Commissioner of Public Works.

Sir, we're making a terrible mistake.

The commissioner was a big strong man going to lard. Obviously a working man once himself. He stood at the window with his coat off, his thumbs under his suspenders. Even with the AC going full blast his starched white shirt was damp with sweat, he looked like he'd been breaking rocks all morning. He peeled a pair of wire-rimmed glasses off his face, took out a handkerchief and mopped his brow. Yer a good man, Erde, but there are a couple of things you still don't understand. He pulled a roll of hundred dollar bills out of his pocket, tossed them on the desk. There's your engineers' reports, there's your blueprints and your planning commission. For one rarefied second Erde's brain drifted off to a warm little island in the sun, he heard ukulele music, the swishing of palms, girls in grass skirts. Only only only.

Only what, Erde? The commissioner had put his glasses back on. His face was big and shiny and mean. Erde felt like he was trapped inside a small glass booth and any minute they were going to turn on the gas. He took a deep breath, and then he laughed, hee haw! hee haw! hee haw! Something weird was happening. His ears were growing long and gray, his nose was turning into a furry snout.

Wait a second, you expect me to believe this? It's a trick, right? Animal costumes, magic mirrors, hidden doors?

No sir, it's all here in the medical reports. **Man Turns Into Mule Before Incredulous Public Servant's Eyes! Elvis Alive!**

As a last resort Erde went to see Mayor Muckly Marmalade, real understanding fellow, always glad to meet one of his constituents. Communication, that's the key. Tell me all, boy, social injustice, citizens' complaints, etc. etc. I stand on my record, I stand corrected, I stand for liberty and justice for the big guys and fuck the rest.

So, Erde, he said, peering from behind a paper mask of himself. Who gave you these ideas? Nobody? Really? You came up with them all by yourself? Hmm, good, good. You haven't gone to the newspapers have you? No? Even better. Alright, boys, get him outa here.

Of course Erde was out of a job. He shoulda been glad he still had his ass intact. But he couldn't care less. He was a good hard worker and an honest man. He wouldn't have any trouble finding another job, a good job, with good pay and plenty of self-esteem. Poor jerk. He still didn't understand how the system worked. The word was already out. He'd been blacklisted all over town. Guy's a troublemaker, send him on down the road, give him the bum's rush. Finally he did find another position, some sleazy outfit, they've got a real cush job, laying a pipe across town so Mayor Marmalade can get his beer straight from the brewery with the head still attached. Of course the foreman's a real fuck-up, rest of the crew stands around all day with their heads up their ass and their hands dangling below their knees. Every once in a while somebody sticks a shovel in a yellow jacket's nest for a little excitement. Erde figures what the hell, plants his shovel in the dirt and leans on the handle like everybody else, suddenly the foreman comes up from behind, whacks him on the shoulder, Get back to work ya lazy sonofabitch!

That got him. A malevolent little gleam crept into his eye. He raised the sledge over his head. He was going to bash in the little bastard's skull. The foreman was so scared pee was running down his leg. He was making a sound like an outboard motor—but-but-but. Then Erde had a moment of reason. If he killed the little fuck they'd hang him, sentence him to a life of busting rocks in a striped suit. At least now he had his Sundays free to lie around in the sun and pick his teeth with a wheatstraw, drink up his paycheck and chase women Saturday night.

Hey, I thought you said he was a good kid, practically a choirboy. Yeah, sure, he learned the gospel rolling in the hay. Hormones, you know. Ancestral genes. Just don't get 'em dirty's all. Spitting between his teeth he brought his sledge down on a huge boulder, smashed it into a thousand pieces. He kept on smashing those pieces into littler pieces until he'd made himself a nice neat pile of gravel, next to that a pile of sand, load 'er up, boys! Let's build some highways! All his anger and rage transformed into an afternoon's hard labor.

Yessirreee, the foreman grinned a mouthful of rotting teeth at the courtroom, I knows how ta make a man work. Ha ha ha, laughed the jury. Even the judge let out a guffaw, although the court stenographer transcribed it as a fart and the bailiff later recalled his honor having had a lunch of beans and a bottle of stout.

Erde wasn't amused. He glowered, glanced at the other men for support, but they kind of kicked their shoes in the dirt and laughed ha ha ha like a dog coughing up worms. Yeah, sure, Saturday night they got drunk with him, fussed and moaned, Who the hell that fo'man think he is? He say anything to me I'm gonna bust his butt. Monday morning they went back to work hungover and beat down and ready for the sting of the whip to push 'em through another week of drudgery. Just thinking about it made Erde angry again, he was swinging his pick faster and faster, his eyes bulged, his teeth were clenched, steam was starting to come out of his nostrils. Suddenly something popped inside him, a quiet little explosion, an idea that blossomed and swelled for half a second, men in uniform marching in the streets with picks and shovels and clomping feet, banners and slogans and angry speeches, and then it imploded, disappeared like an ash up the chimney of wasted dreams. He smiled, shouldered his pick, started down the road, Excuse me, boys, Mayor Marmalade'll have to tap that keg without me. Wait, the foreman called after him. Where ya going? Ya can't just walk out. You'll lose your job. Erde increased his stride. Please, Erde, wait, I'll get you a raise. And Friday afternoons off with full pay. Hey! You other men, get to work! Erde?

After that he went from job to job but the story was always the same. At first he was glad just to have a job and be working again. Then he'd start feeling that terrible depression coming over him, he'd start getting angry again, curse the boss, yell at the other men, C'mon ya lazy fucks, you'll never make it to hell if you can't swing a pick any harder than that. Pretty soon he'd quit or get fired again, go on down the road. You can always find something, picking peaches, digging ditches, pay's always the same, dollar an hour and all the shit you can eat. Wherever he went he managed to forge his way into the center of the crew. He was always the hardest working, the most driven.

Now they've got old Charlie Badger on the stand, lifelong ditchdigger, master of the long-handled round point, PhD—piled higher and deeper as they say. We'd tell him, slow down, Erde! You'll ruin yer back! You'd think he woulda learned by now, he wasn't a kid anymore. But he wouldn't listen. He just kept on swinging that goddamn pick. Then we got right to the point. Slow down, I tell ya! You're making the rest of us look bad, they'll expect us to work like this all the time. By then we were all huffing and puffing and soaked with sweat just watching him. But he wouldn't stop, he had this crazy look in his eye, like the sky before a tornado, and we knew we'd better shut our mouths and try to keep up or there was gonna be a storm to end the decade.

Objection, your honor.

Objection sustained. The court will strike the previous testimony from the records. Jury, forget you heard that.

Look, I'm not saying he was anything special. He just took his job seriously, it made him feel good about himself, it made him feel good about everybody around him. Pretty soon he'd start talking. Yeah, you know, the way people talk when they're working, just to pass the time, just to keep in touch with everybody else, maintain that thread, that neural connection, like where we at now, boys, and how far down the line we gonna be at two in the afternoon? When's the next break, fellows, and how's about a beer later at Rosie's saloon? He wasn't even thinking about what he was saying. He said whatever came to his mind. He laughed, he swore, he rhapsodized on the sunshine and the wildflowers growing on the side of the road. He whistled and imitated the birds singing in the trees. Ain't it wonderful, boys? To feel yer muscles working and the breeze cooling the sweat on yer brow? And to know the entire country's pulling together, everybody happy and proud of their work and really trying? And on top of that a nice long vacation each year with a month's pay? Don't that sound good? And the rhythm of his words laid down the rhythm for the other mens' work. The sound or the meaning of his words vibrated in their shovels and picks, trembled and throbbed in their worn and callused hands, traveled up their arms and shoulders through the bundles and fibers of sinew and nerves, finally penetrating their numb skulls and nestling there in the damp gray fog like fat happy cats. And the men worked harder than they'd ever worked before. And they believed in what they were doing. And at night they took the words home with them, spoke them again around the dinner table while ma dished out a big steaming pot of chicken and dumplings swimming in gravy, and a whole parcel of wide-eyed kids listened in awe as pa pushed out his chest and bragged, Yessiree, ma, ya shoulda seen me swinging that ol' pick today. We laid forty seven mile o' track and built that damn bridge pretty near the whole way across the river.

What? The bridge again? Haven't they finished it yet? No sir. I am sorry to say not. You know how it is, sir. Boondoggles, filibusters. One little snag and the whole damn machine comes to a halt.

There was even a rumor among the men that the whole project stopped the day Erde got laid off. Now he was back everything was flying along again. And the sun was a'shining up in the big blue sky and it looked so dadburn purty the way it musta looked the very first morning God hung it high above the earth, what's fer dessert, ma?

Very next day Erde'd come to work all grumpy and full of gloom. Who knows, maybe he even started out the day in a good mood, singing some silly little tune he'd heard on the radio or remembered from grade school, and then you could see that change occurring, that evil gleam starting in his eyes, and his voice turned sour like sweet meadow milk curdling in a glass. Oh yes, wouldn't that be nice, fellows, to believe all that? That we really are all in this together and those greedy bastards on top ain't robbing us blind and fucking up the whole goddamn country?

Look, I'm not saying he was a political genius. He developed his ideas slowly, methodically, like a mule pulling a load of iron ore across the desert. And then that little banjo string in his voice, in his brain, somewhere high up in his throat drew too taut and snapped, and the very next second all the sunshine and birdsong was eclipsed by an angry tirade that penetrated the mens' skulls and nested there like a dirty gray rat gnawing and chewing at their thoughts. At night they went home, slammed the door be-

hind them, hunkered down over the supper table, shoving
forkfuls of boiled potatoes in their mouths, chewing on
stale bread soaked in bacon grease, yeah, yeah, I know, I
know, cholesterol, calories, ah, too bad, that's all we've got
on sale today. Kids are sitting around the table with hollow
eyes, bony ribcages, afraid to say anything, afraid they'll
get a slap in the face, their ears boxed, wondering if they
might get something else to eat, hoping pa'll tell them
about swinging the sledge again, and building the bridge
across the river, and that funny man Erde. It's the only
moment of glory in their tiny little lives, those stories from
work pa tells. They don't even suspect yet that this is going
to be their lives and their childrens' lives after them. Black
lung, emphysema, cancer, heart attacks, oh stop it, please,
you're breaking my heart.

Well, maybe things'll get better tomorry, ma says, without any hope in her voice. Not likely, pa comes back. They
says we gotta have that damn bridge across the water next
month. 'Course the damn thing's gonna fall down anyway
'cause they're skimping on rivets and bolts and everybody
knows the design ain't right. And another section gang got
laid off today 'cause the company says there ain't enough
work to go around, even though they got the rest of us
working double time.

Next day the kids take the words to school with them
for show and tell. Ma and all the other mas exchange the
words over the back fence while they're hanging out the
wash to dry, while they're out on the front stoop darning
socks, peeling rotting potatoes. My man says that new
bridge is gonna fall down, he says it's just a scam for the
bankers and developers to get rich. Well my man says
there's talk of dynamite and government troops. Saturday
night at the tavern the men take the words out again, sip
at them and nurse them while they talk about the weather

and the game last night and everything else but, until they're finally drunk and angry enough for somebody to say and somebody else to shout, Maybe we should DO something! Get organized!

You see, he created an atmosphere of terror, he was a loudmouth, rabblerouser, stirring up the populace with his unfortunate talk.

No, that's not true either, he wasn't saying anything the people didn't think themselves. He had some kind of antennae, barometers and thermometers and all them other metric devices to read God's and mens' minds. Only thing was, he didn't understand how it worked himself. Shut it off! he'd cry to no one in particular. It was driving him crazy, all those damn voices in his head. He picked up all their thoughts, all their sentiments, all the darkness and night hidden in the crevices of their tired and worn faces. The entire populace was infected with violent, angry thoughts. The economy, health care, there was even talk of some horrible war or eclipse, cataclysms, the sky exploding in flames. They sought out fortune tellers, soothsayers, old Madame Hagess, looks like a congressman in drag, she's got her cards and tea leaves spread out on the table in front of her, she's rolling a goldfish bowl between her hands, I see trouble ahead. The town shut its gates, rolled up its awnings. Housewives called their children in off the streets. The dark came earlier at night, the cold crept in under the doors, around the windows. After dinner folks drew together around the TV in a dim blue circle of fear. At night their dreams were filled with caverns, caves, horrible labyrinths writhing with poisonous snakes. Really now? Ya don't say? Oh yes indeed, I read it in the paper, something to do with the libido.

The local constabulary was beginning to get worried. They informed the governor, the mayor, the county com-

missioner. What? Erde, d'ya say? I've heard that name before. Erde was starting to feel uncomfortable. Men with
guns leaned against light posts. Cigarettes glowed sinis-
terly in dark alleys. Everywhere he went he felt the eyes
watching him, following him, looking him up and down.
One night he heard a noise behind him, someone shoved
him against a wall, a billy club struck him behind the
knees, he sank to the ground, a blackjack smacked off his
skull, he sprawled on the damp cobblestones, a pair of
handcuffs gleamed, he vaguely remembered bouncing
around in the back of a paddy wagon, woke again with a
terrible headache and a bright light shining in his face.
Alright, Erde, speak up now and we'll go easy on ya. A
couple of beefy bully boys spent an hour or so knocking him
around, rearranging his face. Call it a crude form of plastic
surgery. Later on in life they'll hang out their shingle, cater
to the finest clientele, chisel the chins of kings, raise the
sagging careers of aging movie queens. Right now they're
giving a course in anatomy, these boys are really into their
work, they're demonstrating all the latest innovations in
the medical profession, love taps to the kidneys and spleen
with various hammers, mallets and ballpeens, palpating
the heart and lungs with lead pipes and iron rungs, caress-
ing the genitals and spine with forks and tines. C'mon
Erde, speak up, you had a lot to say on the street today.
Smack! They whacked him on the head again. Somewhere
bells were chiming. Up in the night sky the stars were
shining.

He woke in a ditch just past the city limits sign, covered with frost, his face a massive contusion, his eyes swollen shut, his entire body aching. Maybe if he'd held his
tongue, kept his mouth shut. But he limped back into town
the very same day. Got up on a bench in Central Park and
started blabbering away. Pretty soon he got beat up, run

out of town again, creating a public nuisance, jaywalking, they've got an ordinance for every occasion, a bludgeon or blackjack for every cranium. You get used to it after a while. Oh well, where'd we leave off. We were telling a story, right? Once upon a time. No! We're in the middle now. You have to tell it right. Oh alright.

After that Erde drifted from one part of town to another until they knew him in every neighborhood, in all the parishes, districts and wards. He'd panhandle a coupla bucks in small change, just enough for a bottle of chablis and a box of donuts, gotta get that sugar, you know, keep up yer energy, protect yerself against the harsh elements. He'd get drunk and stand on the street corner shouting Darkness! Shouting God! Shouting Fear! Anarchy! Magic!

Ah, Erde, was that really you holding out your cup of bile, of bitter rue to all who passed you by?

The truth is, he was performing a valuable social function. The good man gone bad. The poor example mothers set before the tender eyes of their dear little kinder.

Johnny! Jennifer! Did you take a piece of candy from that awful man? Spit it out this instant!

Mommy, what's that man doing with his pee pee out? And why is he lying in the gutter? Doesn't he have a couch? A TV?

Hmmph! mother sniffs. She's a good woman, really. Goes to church on Sunday. Puts up with hubby's little infidelities. As for Erde, ah well, poor man, he can't help it. Sooner or later he'll end up on some medical student's gurney. Cirrhosis of the liver. Bad lungs and a broken heart. There they are, carving him up like a Christmas turkey, tossing out wings and thighs, lizards, gizzards and giblets. Ah, where's our fair-haired boy now? Nothing left but some stuffing and gravy.

But wait a second. What if it didn't happen that way?

What if he cleaned himself up, got off the juice, got himself a job, joined the gentlemen's optimist club? Pretty soon he's giving seminars in universities, convention centers, he's called in as a consultant for big corporations. In his spare time he writes and publishes a highly successful tome called How To Succeed In Everything, accumulates stocks and bonds and huge estates. Incredible! A meteoric rise to riches. They called on him to run for president. He won every primary, he was elected by a landslide. He chose a cabinet, found himself surrounded by powerful politicians, members of the military, men in dark glasses. He gave orders, called a war council. They spread maps on the table, pored over logistics, intelligence reports. That night flight after flight of high altitude bombers took off from air bases all over the world, submarines slunk into foreign harbors, missile sites went on full alert. The following morning the world woke in the middle of a briar patch bristling with thorns. Earth is mine, Erde proclaimed in a message beamed all over the globe.

Ah well, and then the bridge finally did collapse, terrible loss of life, wives widowed, husbands bereaved, little Johnny and Jennifer orphaned in the streets. Too bad, eh Erde? Told them so, didn't ya? Yes indeed, those fateful words, uttered entirely in good faith. How they got twisted around, from Cassandra to mad bomber, not a prophecy of disaster, but a warning, a terrorist threat, violence against society. Sabotage! they cried. It was Erde! String him up, boys! Get a can of gasoline! The sheriff's men intervened at the last moment, dragged him off to jail again. The headlines told it all. **Erde To Stand Trial. Treason!** Imagine, they thought you were some kind of rebel, Erde, an agent provocateur in dirty underwear.

Of course the trial was a sham. The bereaved huddled in a corner like a flock of bats, sniffling and snuffling and blowing their noses in swatches of red flannel underwear, po' old farmer John won't be needing these no mo'. At the close of the prosecution's opening remarks the high school cheer-leading squad rose in tight sweaters and purple pom poms and led the jury in a rousing cheer. PROSECUTE! PROSECUTE! ERDE'S GUILTY! ELECTROCUTE! RAH!

Erde wasn't impressed. He rolled his eyes at the judge, made obscene gestures at the DA, waggled his tongue at the ladies in the courtroom. The ladies squealed, fanned themselves faster. Ah, what a rogue he was, eh? The tabloids bared everything, **Rendezvous! Adulterous Affairs! Liaisons!**

Yeah? I don't remember any of that. Last I heard our boy Erdie wasn't much of a ladies' man.

Yeah, sure, the prosecution even searched out his old high school flame, dragged her sorry ass into the courtroom, a pathetic, mousy little thing.

Miss Mayapple Millipede! the bailiff announced.

The DA circled, stalked. Now, look closely, Miss Millipede, at this . . . this animal sitting before you, this beast, known to have corrupted minors, miners, and mynahs.

Objection your honor, the prosecution is engaging the witness in bad vaudeville.

Objection overruled. Now tell us, Miss Millipede, in all the exquisite details, how this . . . um . . . monster had his way with you.

Oh . . . but, your highness . . . what I mean to say is . . . he didn't. I wouldn't have minded if he did. In fact, I always hoped he would. But he wasn't interested.

What? Not interested you say? You don't suppose he was gay?

Objection.

Objection overruled.

Oh no, your lardship, I don't think you could say he was

gay at all. In fact, he was often quite gloomy. As for sex, he balked. He liked it better when we only talked.

Talk? About what? Building bombs? Blowing up banks and churches and other revered institutions?

Oh no, your stuffiness, nothing like that. He talked about flowers and birds and God.

God? You mean he blasphemed?

Oh no, yer warship, he held God in highest esteem.

Hmm, not the answer they expected. Time to bring in the big guns. A team of psychos and shrinks, shamans and witch doctors danced into the courtroom in feathers and beads, bells, coconut shells and prescription pads.

As ... um ... you can ... hum ... see from the ... um ... charts here, it's really quite clear. Protracted adolescence, delusions of illusions and other misconstrusions. Mr. Wall-stone again, the high school guidance counselor, recently promoted, now he heads up the state hospital for the criminally and egregiously inane. He's got a tic in his eye, a twitch in his nose, he tugs at his ears, wiggles his toes, You ... um ... must ... hum ... understand, ladies and gentlemen, the ... um ... hormones, that is to say, a healthy young male, in the, uh, prime of his, um, life, that is to say, um, that deadly circus of flesh, I'm certain you know what I mean, ladies and gentlemen, aching hard-ons and wet pussies, not that I wish to appear a priss, of course, but life isn't all grunting and groaning in the bushes, is it? Of course not. Life is hard work and social responsibility. It's the family and job and unspeakable mediocrity. Personally, ladies and gentlemen, I don't give a fuck what this young man's accused of. I find him guilty!

Yayyyy! the public cried.

EXECUTE! ELECTROCUTE! the cheerleaders chanted.

Peanuts! Popcorn! the bailiff called from his concession stand.

In a brilliant move the defense called old Mamie from the church social to testify. Doesn't anybody here have one ounce of decency? It's not the boy's fault. His father was a drunkard, a bum. His mother ran off with some other man. The lad's an orphan, Miss Fortunato's very own bastard child. He lived in the streets, he grew up wild. If you run with wolves, you'll develop a taste for tender loins.

The courtroom gasped. What a naughty old lady. Yeah, well old Mamie was a sailor in her youthful days, she had a nautical way of putting things. The point is, she got her message across. The courtroom hung its head in collective shame. There were a few suppressed sniffles. The jury shifted uncomfortably in its wooden pews. For a while it looked like public sentiment was turning in Erde's favor.

He's been framed! cried the Carpenter's Guild.

Innocent! bleated the Daily Blat.

He only spoke the truth, whispered Pastor Poodlepump to the choirboy sitting in his lap.

That night Mayor Marmalade and the Commissioner of Public Works gathered together eight or nine of their most trustworthy sycophants. Now listen, boys, here's the plan. The next morning a troop of brawny men in brand new coveralls slipped among the tired masses surging toward the factories and mills, the mines and fields. Their tongues hissed like hot steel in a vat of ice water, whispered like scythes through a harvest of wheat. Lies! Distortion! Slander! Over the lunch hour men in brown suits and loosened neckties got up on soap boxes outside the factory gates shouting Outrage! Scandal! Next to the hayricks and metal discs men in open collars and rolled up sleeves demanded Action! Now! After work Rosie's saloon threw open its doors for an all-night bash. Drinks on the house, boys! Ladies night, girls! Mayor Marmalade's buying! Yayyyy! the citizenry cheered. The next day the jury deliberated over aspirin and bromo seltzer.

How do you find? the judge queried, adjusting the ice pack on his head.

Guilty, the foreman of the jury whispered, his face ashen, eyes red.

There was a collective gasp from the courtroom.

The judge banged his gavel, winced. The defendant will now rise for sentencing! Ouch! Do you wish to make a final statement on your behalf?

Erde nodded his assent. In an eyeblink he'd dropped his trousers, aimed his arse at the courtroom and let out a loud fart. BRAAAPPP!

I'll see you in hell! the judge shouted.

I'll keep your seat warm! Erde shouted back. The courtroom burst into laughter.

That evening on TV they showed a courtroom simulation with a rubber doll in flesh-colored tights, accompanied by an air horn. Showgirls in revealing costumes paraded with prizes provided by the station's sponsors. WIN! WIN! WIN! the announcer shouted into the microphone. The following morning the newspapers plastered XXXXXXXXXX across the front page. Meanwhile Erde was back in chains. Day after day he clutched the iron bars of his cell, watched the throngs gathering below. Look! someone shouted. It's the monster! Give us Erde! cried a man with a rope. Off on the side a small flock of women in black dresses with red roses pinned to their breasts yearned for him with their eyes, their faces porcelain masks behind black veils. A group of neo-post-constitutionalists started to chant, Free Erde! But they were quickly silenced by the majority.

On a warm spring day the whole town gathered in the cobblestoned square. Farmers leaned on their pitchforks. Vacuum cleaner salesmen demonstrated their products, Yessiree, ladies and gentlemen, this little baby runs on a combination of natural gas and wind power and let me tell you, folks, she really sucks. Nuns and priests in external lingerie promenaded arm in arm, pirouetting like music box figurines and kicking up their heels. Boy Scouts saluted. Girl Scouts sold cookies. The ladies auxiliary offered candy-coated road apples and fresh baked cow pies. At twelve noon the clock in the bell tower chimed eleven and a half times and a wooden oxcart creaked into view, bearing Erde naked and bound.

What? Really? Completely naked? Not even bikini briefs? A jock strap? Loincloth? Not a stitch? A thread? No? Nothing? Naked? Of course you always were a bit of an exhibitionist.

Wait, you've got it all wrong, it was the exact opposite. The idea was to humiliate him, shame him in front of the whole town, destroy his image. But things weren't going according to plan. The second Erde showed up the festive air dissolved like sunshine in the fog. Erde didn't look at all like the monster they'd proclaimed him. He'd gotten thinner, frailer, his days in jail had sobered him up, added something deep and soulful to his aspect. His eyes gleamed with an odd sort of light, like a lantern at the bottom of a very deep well. The townspeople were smitten by his nakedness, his beauty, their souls ravaged by the sadness in his eyes and the strange smile that passed over his face when he looked out over their heads. The word God passed through their minds. With tears streaming down their faces, they raised their eyes to the heavens. Ah, wretch, and to think, you actually felt sorry for them, didn't you? Sorry for yourself. Poor beasts all, driven mad by the notion of God, when you and the townfathers alike knew perfectly well that our Erdie was no god. Just some dark, forlorn man cast in their midst to remind them all how miserable were their puny lives.

Huddled in the shadows of St. Larry's Bingo Palace and Corporate Cathedral Mayor Marmalade and the Commissioner of Public Works conspired together, their faces buried deep within the dark brown folds of monks' habits, their eyes gleaming like venomous needles. Their tongues flickered in and out, whissspering fear, doubt. Maybe thisss wasn't such a good ideeea. We should have dealt with the little creeep in private where nobody could seeee. Now we've made him a martyrrrr. If we harm him the people will connnsssecrate usss with fiiire.

But their fears were unjustified, weren't they? They forgot human nature. Ha, remember when the ladies church chorale got up and sang that awful hymn? God, what a bunch of shrieking transvestites. By the second verse, the hymn had turned into a drinking song and the bloody whores were kicking up their skirts in a chorus line. Meanwhile, here comes a brass band marching down the street with tubas, strumpets and trombones glaring and blaring in the warm sun. Oom-papa, oof-mama. On the sidelines a bunch of bulging old burghers in beer bellies and lederhosen are swinging huge frothy steins back and forth in unison, ja ja ja ja. Und den efrybuddy in der whole goddum place getsh all mishty-eyed und shentimental. Pretty shoon we're all frothing at the mouth and shouting Gourd safe the Queen unt all dat rubbage. You can already see the derilection things was taking. A gang of juvenile delinquents circulated among the crowd, handing out baskets of rotten eggs, overripe tamaters. They're all dressed in their gang colors, khaki blouses, blue jeans and yellow bandanas, Still time to earn one more badge before the national jamboree, eh, lads? Some of the older boys had filled their pockets with stones. One or two of them even had blow guns. Ach, vat goot boys, eh mama? At that moment the band leader raised his baton and the crowd began to

count out loud, Ah-one! An ah-two! On three! a large rock
hit Erde in the forehead. Pebbles and stones rained down.
His body ran with egg yolk, tomato puree. He staggered,
sank to his knees, fell face down on the rough wooden
planks of the oxcart.

Hurray! Pastor Poodlepump cried. Another supplicant
of God! Death to the infidels! Convert the heathen! Another crusade!

Alas, poor Erde would've disagreed. Naked, bruised,
his head throbbing, his entire body a mass of aches and
pains, he was on the verge of passing out. Maybe if he'd just
stayed down, pretended he was unconscious, even dead,
they'd leave him alone. But he was in agony, if only he
could ease some of his pain. He picked at a splinter in the
palm of his hand, rubbed a bruise on the back of his head.

Hey! He ain't daid! An eagle-eyed youth shoved a
sharpened hot dog stick through the slats and poked him
in the ass. Ouch! he cried, jumping to his feet. Yayyyy! the
crowd roared. They were having a great time. They were
ready for more. An aged nun in oversized spectacles and a
snaggle-toothed grin reached through the slats and
yanked his pizzle. A young mother unbuttoned her blouse
and squirted a stream of warm milk in his face. Things
were really starting to get out of hand now. It was time for
the authorities to step in. A platoon of mustachioed men in
brass buttons and blue serge raised their truncheons aloft.
Alllrroit fokes, shurr and ye've had yer fun now. Stand
back the lot of ye. At that moment two dozen workmen
from the City Sanitation Department march into the
square, they're all wearing hard hats, coveralls, red bandanas and ballet slippers. They're carrying crowbars
at shoulder arms. They've got huge monkey wrenches
strapped across their backs. This is the cream of the crop,
ladies and gentlemen, the country's finest. For the next

hour and a half they contrive to pry open a manhole cover in the middle of the street, they're banging each other on the head with their crowbars, they're reading maps upside down, they've even got a guy on a backhoe trenching out the city gardens. Boinnng! Suddenly the manhole cover pops open and they all fall on their ass. Tweet! A shiny silver whistle blows. Side by side the high school football coach and the local army recruiter jog into the square, Hup-two! Hup-two! Hup-two! Grabbing Erde under the arms, they drag him down from the oxcart, hustle him around the square two or three times, Head up! Knees high! Keep 'em up! Keep 'em up! Keep 'em up! At the edge of the manhole they stop abruptly. Erde hangs over the void. The crowd fidgets. A buzzer sounds. A gang of referees run out onto the field. Nineteen! Ninety-nine! Hike! Hike! Hike!

Somewhere on the edge of consciousness Erde felt himself falling. Smack! His face encountered solid concrete. A little boy winced, covered his ears, That didn't sound like too much fun, mommy. The crowd grew quiet. The lights went out all over town.

Wait a minute. They threw him down a bloody hole? What kind of punishment is that? Yeah, sure, the black hole of Calcutta, I can see that. Or a black hole in space, that'd be alright, all that spinning around and disintegrating like a turd in a toilet bowl, like a bit of crud that got in with the egg whites. But a manhole? In the middle of the city? At the end of the twentieth century?

Erde woke with a terrible headache. His shoulder felt like it was dislocated. If only he could stretch out his legs. What'd he do, fall down a well? Brr, he was cold. Why didn't he have any clothes on? Look! somebody cried. He's still alive! Blinking up against the light he could barely make out a ragged silhouette of faces crowded around the small

blue circle of sky. Hey! one of them shouted. Ya want a banana? Ooka-ooka-ook?

For the next couple of weeks there was no respite. From
sunrise to sunset the little blue aperture over his head was
packed with bulbous noses, bulging eyes, gaping mouths.
The crowds were lined up for miles. All day long Erde
heard the shuffling feet, the cries of the vendors. Hot dogs!
Soda! Ice-cold beer! It was better than the circus. Kids
skipped school, secretaries took two hour coffee breaks,
businessmen missed important meetings, farmers came in
from the country with chickens and pigs under their arms,
went back home at night with sacks of sugar and coffee
and bolts of gingham. Saw the man in the hole today,
Martha, ayup. Bored young housewives leered at him, ran
blood-red nails over their breasts, between their thighs.
Post-menopausal matrons yearned for him with their eyes,
ached to cradle his poor head in their arms. Jealous young
husbands stared at his hairy chest, manly member. It was
enormous, I tell you. It hung down to his knees. He used to
hit home runs with it in sandlot baseball. He'd dress it up
in shirt and pants and tell his dates it was his little brother
Ernie.

Hey, just a minute ago you said he was practically an
angel. Now you're telling us he's some kinda ape covered
with mattress stuffing. What? I didn't tell you? It was all
the growth hormones in that meat they gave him. Each
night his keepers threw down a chunk of raw beef. Good
boy. In the morning before the crowds gathered they hosed
him down with cold water. Filthy beast! Can't keep hisself
clean, can he? By the time the first spectators showed up
Erde was in a rage, he hated them, glared up at them like a
wounded animal, tore them apart with his eyes, growled
and snapped. Grr! Woof! If only he didn't take things so
damned seriously. If he could just learn to relax and make

the best of a lousy situation. A sense of humor and a little playacting. Of course! In high school he lettered in varsity drama.

What? I didn't mention it before? Oh yes, quite the young thespian. Elected captain his junior year, all the girls after him, the boys envying him. Who knows, a little more encouragement from the faculty, proper guidance, a sponsor. He might have gone on to Broadway, Hollywood, stretch limos, his name in lights. **Tonight Only! Erde! In THE UNDERGROUND EXPRESS.** The scene opens on a frantic face, smudged with coal dust, who knows, maybe it's only charcoal, he got too near a barbecue pit, all you can see are his eyes gleaming in the dark, beads of sweat on his forehead, his teeth clenched. The camera pulls back. It's a miner. He's got an electric lamp on his head, he's swinging a pick in a dark tunnel. Somewhere behind him we hear a howl, it's some terrible monster, it's coming after him. No, wait, gas, it's gas, he smells gas and any second the whole damn place's gonna explode, if he can just break through this last wall, reach the ventilation shaft, he's working furiously, he's actually clawing at the rock with his bare hands, his fingernails are broken and bleeding. But it doesn't explode. It never explodes. And he never reaches the ventilation shaft. He just digs on and on for the rest of his life, frantic, driven, gnashing his teeth, with no hope of escape or finding his way out. The critics call it a fiasco but the audience goes wild. From coast to coast they're on their feet shouting Encore! Erde! Auteur!

Alas, t'was not to be. He never got the proper guidance. Nobody cared. Mr. Wallstone advised him to go into industrial arts, carpentry, welding, You've gotta build for your future, boy. Forget about that acting stuff.

Oh boo hoo. I'm so dreadfully sorry. I didn't know. Anyway, you get the picture. A hard luck story. Happens all the

time. Ah yes, and then—all of a sudden—a miracle! Old
Mister Peabody the school janitor cleaning up backstage
cranks open the sky and the gods look down, and poof, just
like that, the kid gets another chance.

The following morning he waited until a substantial
crowd had gathered around his hole. Then he began to
stretch and yawn and blink his eyes like he was just waking up. Suddenly, he snapped to attention, blew a trumpet
fanfare into his fist. Dooty-da-Doot-da-Doooo! Ladies and
Gentlemen! The most esteemed townfathers of the great
and prosperous city of Bumperville, in conjunction with
the International Brigade of Sanitation and Wholesome
Cuisine, proudly welcome you to The Greatest Show Under
The Earth! This was followed by a short burst of passable
calliope music. And then the show began. Drawing upon a
long latent gift for magic and mimicry and not a little bit of
mass hypnosis he was soon offering up a three ring circus
with barking seals, psychotic clowns on motorized tri-
cycles, acrobatic poodles in black leotards, dentally correct
lions and tigers. With a sweep of his hand he pulled a top
hat out of his ass, a rabbit out of the hat, and a fresh bunch
of carrots out of the mouth of the coney. The crowd roared.
They were eating out of his hand.

Hey! he shouted. Doesn't anybody up there have an old
blanket I can make into a cape? Tomorrow we'll do Shake-
speare.

Pretty soon he had bedding, draperies and linen, a complete wardrobe. No more shivering through those chilly
nights. No more exposing himself to prying eyes. Other
amenities soon followed. A box of imported cigars—Cuban
of course—bottles of good scotch, bourbon. Occasionally
someone lowered a magnum of champagne with a key attached. Couldn't take them up on the offer, of course, but it
was good for a little fantasizing later at night, after the

crowds went home, eh old sport? Mmm, that movie star in the tabloids, yeah, the blond with the big boobs. What was that bomb she was in? Oh yeah, and she'd just fallen into a pond and you could see her breasts through her blouse, and her nipples were hard and erect, and she was just starting to undress, but, oh yeah, that bad Indian was sneaking up with his lance all aquiver, oh rude brave, with thy flaming arrow unsheathed. Then he'd wake in the morning with a chorus of female giggles shattering like glass down the cement walls. More and more people were coming to town every day. Tourism was up, home sales were booming, business was great. The town was pulling itself out of decades of recession. This is our boy! the townfathers crowed. We've gotta get him in ink before he joins a union.

That night Mayor Muckly Marmalade in a cardboard cut-out Erde mask and The Commissioner in black tights and garters lowered themselves down Erde's hole on a length of good, strong hemp. Listen, Erde, we have a proposition to make. But our Erdie wasn't as dumb as they thought, was he? His eyes narrowed into slits, he drew his cards closer to his chest. Give me a little time to think about it, eh fellows? By the time the townfathers showed up again the next night Erde'd acquired agents, managers, accountants and attorneys. In a smoke-filled confab with plenty of booze and broads at hand, he hammered out a secret deal, signed contracts, endorsed products. He was given an unnumbered Swiss bank account, allowed conjugal visits by selected members of the Ladies Semi-Professional Volleyball League and Lingerie Guild.

For a while it was a good, if contained, life. Inevitably, though, the novelty wore off. He was fed up with the noise, tired of his fans' philistine adulation, sick of the scandal sheets prying into his private life. **Secret Bank Account! Girl Friends! Boy Friends! Alien Visitors From Mars!**

Erde Grows Tail! Barks Like A Dog! At night he sat beneath his chandelier of stars in a deep velour sofa with a laprug pulled over his knees, sipping cognac and smoking a heady Habana. But there was no pleasure in it. He was clearly in a rut. He felt like a lion in a pitfall with a bunch of pygmies poking spears at him. He wanted something new in his life, he wanted change, he wanted passion, he wanted to pound his chest and roar. But it didn't matter how he altered his routine, the crowds approved.

The next morning he strode to center ring, doffed his top hat, bowed deeply, flipped aside his tails and launched a highly perfumed fart up at his audience. Oh! the crowd gasped. What a bouquet! C'est magnifique! Il vapore della notte! Guano! Dropping his trousers around his ankles, he squatted down and shat a perfect chocolate petit four, half a dozen eclairs, and a box of cherry cordials. In another minute he'd filled several glass cases with red ribboned Christmas candies, chocolate Easter bunnies and Valentine hearts.

Bravo! the crowd cheered. I'll take a dozen! Hey, a box over here!

Tossing aside a chromed codpiece, he drew forth a priapic prop clothed in a banana peel and a red mop and began cuffing it about the ears. Malingerer! he cried! Cheat! Thief! Take that and that and that!

Et tu, you brute! the puppet protested in a Roman dialect.

The crowd roared. TV cameras dangled from helicopters. A team of doctors and psychiatrists offered considered opinions. He tried a new tack. He addressed his audience frankly. Look, ladies and gentlemen, this is absurd. You stand in line all day just to get a look at me, a poor unkempt creature, in the most abject of circumstances. And for what? Go home. Lock the door. You can perform these very tricks in the privacy of your own bathroom.

Hmmph! sniffed middle-aged Mrs. Mongoosian in pearls and foxfur.

Come dear! Young Mrs. Muffin tugged at her daughter's arm, It's time to go home.

He's ruining our business! Mister DeNero, the town banker, said, straightening his tie. That night the townfathers called in strategists, consultants. But it was too late. The lines had already started to thin out, the crowds all went away, the vendors closed up their carts and went off in search of traffic accidents and other natural disasters. Call it the death of vaudeville, eh boys? Erde's days in burlesque were clearly numbered. That night he discovered his booking agent had blown town on the noon express, his valise packed with the entire year's proceeds.

After that things began to get bleak. Erde had no more income, no supply of victuals and condiments. The city council cut off all funding, the treasurer refused to pay Erde's keeper to feed him. In a panic he tore open his reserve tins of caviar, sucked down cans of smoked oysters, guzzled bottles of sparkling wine. In a night and a day he depleted his entire pantry. Nothing remained in his humidor but the aroma of tobacco. On top of that it was getting late in the year. Red and yellow leaves began to blow down his hole. It got quite chilly at night. One evening he woke shivering, covered with frost. Looking up at the opening of his hole he could barely make out a cold, pale moon emerging from behind the clouds. Suddenly a foul-smelling sludge plopped down on his head, followed by a hot yellow stream. Hey! he yelled, his voice thundering out of the ground like a mine explosion. There was a startled cry above and a massive pair of buttocks lurched away from the hole and disappeared. For the first time in weeks Erde laughed. Not a healthy, hearty laugh, but a hysterical,

scary laugh, hee hee hee, ha ha ha, ho ho ho, the little shit
gets shat upon, the tiny turd gets trod again.

Erde's good humor was shortlived. Early the next
morning a lone worker from the sanitation department
showed up. Erde tried to engage him in conversation but
he was too busy munching on coffee and donuts. Finally,
after a short nap and another cigarette, the worker
stretched and yawned, then started rolling the heavy iron
lid toward the edge of the manhole.

Hey! Erde cried. What are you doing?

Putting the lid on, the worker said, laconical.

No! Erde pleaded. Don't!

But the worker only shook a plump, pink finger sausage down at him.

Shh! I'm not s'posed to talk to you. You gonna get me in
trouble. I lose my chob.

Yeah, yeah, I know, you think the guy's a heartless son-
of-a-bitch, right? Some lousy scab they picked off the
streets. But you know how it is, guy's got a wife and family,
he's just some scared little worm like you and me, he
doesn't wanta make too much noise, get in trouble with the
authorities, lose his situation. But try to explain that to
poor Erde.

Please! he begged again. But it was too late.

Clank! clang-clang-clang Clank! The lid caromed into
place.

Erde's little world sank into darkness. He leapt up
from his armchair, clutched blindly, madly at the unnatural night. But it was hopeless. The light was gone forever.
He fell back in his chair, his face wrenched with horror,
grief. They can't do this to me. I'm the star. I made their
miserable lives magic. I gave them comedy instead of mediocrity. Champagne instead of rye whiskey. Hey! Waiter!
Bring me a drink! A drink I say! Do I have to do everything

myself? On the top shelf sat his very last bottle of brandy. He'd been saving it for a special occasion, his little girl's communion, his son's graduation from college. Ah well, let the future fare for itself. Brushing away dust and cobwebs he uncorked the bottle, filled a crystal snifter to the brim and quaffed it in one fiery gulp. The bastards, they're punishing me for my impudence. Yes, of course, that's it. They'll come back when they think I've had enough. He downed another glass. Oh, please come back. I promise I'll be good if only you'll come back.

But what are you saying? Wretch! Did you actually grovel like that? Were you really such a snivelling worm? I can hear it still, echoing in my ears. That horrible whining, that shameless capitulation. Yeah, but it was different then, wasn't it, chump? You were still so naive. You didn't understand the game. You thought maybe you really had done something wrong. You thought maybe somehow you could atone for your sins. Imagine, poor little Erde sitting in the dark, sad, bewildered, alone. Why are they so mad at me? he moaned, pouring himself another shot. Was I really such a beast? Surely they're not going to leave me down here forever? Yeah, sure, a murderer maybe. He could see that. Or a war criminal, corporate executive, college chancellor. Hell, the list goes on and on. Why not all the bankers and lawyers, gym teachers and school crossing guards? What about the president? He's in charge. But a loud mouth? A common rabblerouser like himself? Not even that, just a lousy, two-bit failed comedian? An ugly drunk? You bastards! You'd better get me out of here right now! But his imprecations were for naught. No one came. The heavy iron lid remained fixed over the hole. You shee how it izh with public shervants? Never there when you need 'em. Oh, yesh, shure, come election day, then! Have a drink on me boys! And oh what a fine wee baby you have, Mrs.

Malone. Le's shee how long that lashts, eh? Hey, waiter! Another drink, do you hear me? Another drink, I say! But there was nothing left in the bottle. Erde's mood quickly turned sour.

In the absolute darkness his eyes gleamed like drops of poison. His mind was a bubbling porridge of hatred and revenge. He gloated over all of the gloriously awful, in fact, insane tortures he'd practice upon his captors if the tables were turned. Of course, we've had years to refine this little scenario, haven't we, Erde? Nothing quick, of course. It'll have to be a long slow process, the most excruciating pain, slice off a bit of tongue today, just a taste bud or two, enough to make every bite of sweet and sour pickle, every gleam of relish, dash of vinegar, pinch of salt the most agonizing dining experience. Then on to the rough stuff, eh boys? Floodlights exploding in your eyeballs twenty-four hours a day, fingers in the meat grinder, toes in the toaster oven, whack the ears, smack the nose, red-hot pokers up the asshole, writhing, decapitated eels down the throat.

Wait a second. Haven't we heard this all before? Ah yes, the sins of the fathers and all that rot. It's not really you screaming. It's somebody else, the old man they've got in the room upstairs, some martyr you read about in your high school history books. Oh, how ghastly, they didn't really do that stuff? The walls are covered with woodcuts of hooded executioners with naked hairy bellies heating up red-hot irons in a bed of coals, they're farting and belching, laughing and joking while they work over their clients.

Say, Fred, you wanta get a beer after work today? Hey, ya see that guy they got over in section D?

Roger's new case? I didn't think you could make a guy's head do that.

They're attaching swollen black leeches to pouty, pubescent lips, pouring molten lead down virgin throats, turning packs of starving gerbils loose on straining adolescent genitals, hacking off arms and legs with meat cleavers. Here on ze table today ve haf a plump porker of a man. Zeep! With a few deft strokes of our quality cutlery we disembowel him alive. In ze pre-heated ofen we roast up his intestines queek queek queek before he dies. Und voila! Before your very eyes—or should I say nose?—ve haf here ze piece de resistance, your very own soul food souffle. Care for a plate of chitlins, guv? A bite of scrapple? What? Not hungry you say? Nonsense!

Ah, but you see? This is all too plebeian, too absurd, too much like a silly little TV show. When what we really want is something truly horrific, something painful and protracted, something that nibbles at the remnants of your sanity like a huge, starved rat. A kind of autophagy, if you will, a hunger that eats and gnaws at your entrails, compelled by the lust for the endorphin rush your body produces to ease the pain you inflict upon yourself. Every drop tightens the screw another notch, every effort to forget, to turn away from your suffering exacts precisely that much more agony, the most you can hope for is a bearable, a continuum of pain, like the steady drip, drip, drip of the faucet at night. But let's not make it just any faucet, but a shiny metal faucet gleaming in the dark, and the water, those fat, metallic-tasting drops tap tap tapping on your shaved pate, that cold, chromium-tainted water saturating the heavy burlap cloth covering your face, your mouth and nose, so that you can just barely breathe, you feel like you're drowning, but you can't even kick or struggle because you're strapped into that hard wooden chair, your arms and legs so tightly bound they've gone numb, lost all feeling. Oh God! If you could only breathe! Open your mouth and shout for air! But it goes on and on for days and weeks. Months pass. And then years. Without even a solitary glimpse of another human being. Without ever being touched or touching again. Without even the jailer's slaps, punches and kicks. Oh, yes, please, hit me again. Just to be touched, to imagine each punch your lover's sweet caress. If only you weren't alone, if you at least had somebody to witness your suffering, to sympathize, to offer you a kind word, a warm caress. But no one even knows! Never again your mother's worn washerwoman fingers ruffling your hair. Never again the firm clutch of dad's big strong hand in a friendly wrestling match. Not even the chance encounter, the fuzzy, tingly rush and thrill of a complete stranger's bare arm brushing against yours on the city bus, it's called frottage, criminal code 666, You're under arrest, boy, come with me. The officer grabs you by the arm. Oh thank you, sir, thank you so much, you're too kind. But not even that. Never again any news of the day, the stock market, war, mass murderers, some well-known movie star caught in a sordid affair in some seedy hotel in the strip district. Oh dear God, what I'd give for a sound, a taste, a smell. There's poor old mom again, she's ringing the dinner bell, she's calling out the back door. Errr-diee! Time for dinner! ERDIE! You tramp inside, sullen, your head down. Aww ma, why do I have to eat now? The guys are waiting for me outside. But oh my goodness sakes, lookee there, child, there's a great big bowl of fried liver swimming in a sublime sour milk and vinegar sauce with a dollop of raspberry jam floating in chicken fat. And for dessert, salamander meringue pie a la mode, and a slice of key slime, and a cup of buzzard gizzard custard. And it smells so good. Suddenly you're overwhelmed with hunger. You yell out the window to your friends, See you tomorrow, guys, I gotta eat now, Mom made my favorite dish. But no, no eating, no drinking, no touching, no tasting. You're not even allowed to take a shit because after a while you'd learn to enjoy it, eat it, handle it, take pleasure in the foul, the impure, it would still be smell, taste, sensation, because you'll have to admit now that nothing starts out the day better than a nice big crap, empty out all the dregs and detritus of yesterday's bullshit and humiliations. Poop! Fart! Blap! Nothing, that is, but winning the lottery after forty-five deadening years on the assembly line, or lying down in the green meadow with some nymph or satyr and fucking your eyes out after twenty or thirty unrepentant years in a cloister or monastery.

But oh no, Erde. We mustn't talk about shitting and fucking. Especially not that. We'd rather have censorship, eternal suffocation and drowning. Let's go back to the torture chamber. Where did we leave off? With our hero suspended in absolute darkness, a single particle of breathing and light and consciousness suspended in the void. Alone. Oh yes, God, there is always God. Go ahead, my boy, call your God. Scream God God God over and over again until you realize how utterly absurd. Because you, wretched worm that thou art, you are not God, you are not even on intimate terms with God. You're nothing but a worthless little piece of shit crawling inside the belly of some giant worm. It's bombarding you with acids and digestive juices, its sucking proteins, fats and carbohydrates out of you, assorted vitamins, minerals and trace elements, it's ingesting you, squeezing you along the endless loops and coils of its alimentary canal, and at some point it's going to poop you out again, an undigested little turdlet, an ex-parasite writhing and squirming in the great yawning indifference of eternity.

Aw, yeah, but that's neither here nor there. We were telling you a story, a fairy tale actually, about a fairy prince who turned into a maggot. Another accident in chemistry class. Poor guy was just rinsing out the test tubes when—

bloop! Ah well, too bad.

    You see, he'd been down there so long it was driving him mad. He sat in the dark in his big stuffed sofa with his thoughts and his mind spinning out of control like a vile, twisted little engine, a swirling black vortex that sucked at the cement walls of his prison, whirled up and around and out through the manhole cover, growing and swelling into tornadic fury, drawing in everything in its path, tugging at the fringes of the city, the buildings swaying and bending like accordions, people screaming out of twelfth story windows, bodies flying through the air, the entire city beginning to stretch and tear loose from the earth, Mayor Marmalade and the Commissioner of Public Works just returning from the warehouse with a bundle of cash, merchants and businessmen clutching at loose change, politicians caught with their hands in the pockets of the constituency, secretaries and clerks stuffing cokes and candy bars and cold pizza in their mouths, in their machines, gumming up the whole goddamn works, sotted baby-machine housewives pushing double-decker perambulators up and down the streets of suburban nightmares, donkey-laboring workingmen slamming themselves on the head with picks and shovels, troops of brain-dead, TV automaton school kids marching to the mall, Pastor Poodlepump and the boys' choir lingering over the final strains of a traditional hymn,

do your balls hang high
do your balls hang low
can you tie them in a ribbon
can you tie them in a bow

    They're all spinning and whirling down his hole, sucked into the black omphalos, toilet bowl, bankrupt soul, they're swimming and doggy paddling among soggy clots of toilet paper, turds, slimy, diarrhetic masses, goldfish, alligators, baby booties, little brother Fred the fetus, baby Jesus in a whiskey bottle, kewpie dolls, plop! splash! there goes mousy Miss Millipede and Mister DeNero, flop! plash! Mister Wallstone and the court stenographer, one after the other, they're splashing and floundering among drooling condoms, grungy underwear, disposable diapers, wedding rings, earrings, kernels of corn, globs of peanut butter, tootsie rolls, cigarette butts, roaches, grams, pounds and packages of grass, cocaine, Jesus, it's the cops! People are shrieking, screaming.

But it wasn't what you thought, was it Erde, gloating in your little cell? Not the hysterical cries of a humanity terrified by your wrath, but rats! Hundreds and thousands of rats streaming around the manhole cover, pouring down the damp cement walls, a runnelling mass of fur squeaking and squealing and swarming over him, a nightmare horror of gnashing teeth and whiskers and beady eyes. He leapt from his chair, grabbed up handfuls of rats and began smashing them against the wall, he could feel their teeth sinking bone-deep into his fingers, his hands, they clung to his face, clawing and biting at his eyes, his mouth. He tried to scream but nothing came out, a big fat rat had plunged head-first down his throat. He clamped his teeth shut, tasted blood, guts. He felt dizzy, he was sinking into oblivion.

He woke again with a full belly, bits of fur stuck between his teeth. The floor was littered with pointy tails, whiskers and ears and shiny glass beads. After vomiting up the children of his insanity he collapsed into a deep funk. For weeks he sat in the rotting sofa, mouldering among his own stink and refuse. He was paralyzed, unable to move or do anything but stare into the dark, his mind torn, empty, like his stomach. Where's the nice nursey now? Won't mummykins come clean it up, make it all better? A warm bottle of milk, vaseline on his chafed bum, a soft, clean diaper?

He slept and woke and slept again. He had no idea how much time passed. His little circle of blue sky and sunshine was but a memory, the stars at night a dream, the clouds drifting across the moon but an ebbing fringe of surf in the dark waters of his mind. The street sounds, traffic jams, car horns honking, traffic cops whistling, people screaming, guns going off—it had all disappeared. No noise above, no sounds below. Only a languid sweet and sour bouquet seeping into his nostrils, wreathing itself around his brain, the long neglected remains of a desiccated Chateaubriand, a slice of mango cheesecake molding in the icebox. But even that failed to raise a rumble in his stomach. He no longer had any interest in food. His body had ceased to function. He neither ate nor voided himself. And yet he lived, without ingesting anything, without intravenous tubes connecting him to some anonymous machine or donor body strapped to a gurney in some state hospital or prison for the criminally insane located a mile down the road.

Wait a minute. Is that possible? Do I need to explain? You've studied your science. I'm sure you understand. It's a question of osmosis, molecular exchange. He derived nourishment from the foul, fetid air, sucked molecules of protein and carbohydrates from the black miasma that enveloped him. Call it the black dog, call it the blues. We've all been there before. And then one day you just get tired of feeling so down. You start to pick up the pieces again, you cajole and exhort yourself, This won't do, Erde. All this darkness, all this hatred and revenge. You've gotta pull yourself out of this funk. You've gotta turn it into something positive. Now it's the old coach again, giving us a pep talk, getting us back on our feet. Alright, boys, I won't lie to ya, things are looking bleak. I know, I know, you just wanta hit the showers and get a drink. Well, this ain't the time for tears, boys. You're gonna win this game, see? And you're gonna win big. But you have to really want to and believe, and tap your heels together and wave your magic wand in the air. And if you wave it long enough you'll get arrested for public exposure. Ha ha, that's it, me boy, humor, laughs. Try, Erde, try. But why? What's the use? The sun's set forever on our vacant little empire. Darkness reigns eternal. Yes, but just supposing it were true, that merely by willing it so or, no, it's not another contest of wills we need now, but faith, and believing it to be so, that's the only way you'll get out of this fix and find your way back up to the sun. But how do we begin? Simply part the molecules and pass through concrete walls like an earthworm through sandy loam? Through all kinds of intricate mathematical formulas and three dimensional graphics projected on the big screen? Or is the answer something more mundane still? Some simple and quite ordinary occurrence, like looking down and, hello? finding a map and a key on the ground?

Actually, that's pretty close to what happened. All this cogitation was giving Erde a migraine headache. He heard ringing in his ears, an incessant sort of grinding somewhere deep inside his skull, like a dentist's drill through the hazy distance of morphine.

But there really is a sound, I tell you. Listen, d'ya hear it, mate? Oh God, it's not the rats again? I can't stand it if it's the rats.

Now hold on a minute, chum, it's too regular for rats. There, you see? It's got a kind of rhythm to it, a sort of determination.

It was true. From an incessant whining, a somewhat

bothersome grinding, the noise swelled and grew, came steadily closer, like a thought taking shape in his brain, readying itself for that infinitesimal journey from the cerebral cortex to the tip of his tongue, just a tiny puff of air forced out of his lungs, and then that roller coaster ride up and down, over and around the simultaneous configuration of larynx, uvula, teeth, tongue and lips, F-f-f-foot! F-f-f-fart! I m-m-mean F-f-f-freedom! He heard a clanking and banging. With a terrible roar a huge metal corkscrew smashed through the wall, burying him in rock and rubble. A beam of light flickered in the cloud of dust drifting in his humble living room. He heard voices.

What's up, Hank?

Dunno, Joe, storm sewer, I think. Maybe it's a goddamn missile silo. Back 'er off a bit and change course—an' remember, anyone asks, you don't know nothing.

Yeah, I know, you think I'm making it up. Ya ever read the paper sometime? All those collisions in the East 31st street tunnel, right there where you're driving along and suddenly it makes that dog leg? Thank Hank and Joe for that little engineering feat.

At any rate, the drill withdrew. Dust drifted in the dim light. Water trickled somewhere. The air smelled dank, musty. Erde listened another minute, then poked his head outside. There was no one around. He stepped into the tunnel. His heart began to pound, he felt weak in the knees, he sank to the ground. Look. In their haste Hank and Joe had dropped everything, all their tools, umbrellas, kitchen sinks. He smelled a stink, not the smell of rotting garbage but something good to eat, a hoard of lunch bags and boxes, thermoses and bottles. His stomach rumbled with seismic activity. Hunger! He hadn't felt hunger in weeks. Suddenly, hunger blossomed in his belly like a rose in the desert. He tore through brown paper, aluminum foil, plastic wrap and rubber bands. In another second he was chowing down on barbecued ribs, his tongue lolled in a pig trough of tangy red sauce thick and swimming with bell peppers, red onions and jalapeños. He bit into a bratwurst and swiss smothered in spicy brown mustard with a clump of suaerkraut wrapped around a slab of kosher dill pickle. Mmmmmmm. He was enveloped in a spicy cloud of remembrance, lunchtime in the elementary school gym, food fights in high school cafeterias, sloppy joes, blt's, shit on a shingle. He took another bite, mm, yeah, the roach coach pulling up at construction sites, the lunch wagon outside factory gates. And for dessert, cream-filled chocolate cupcakes, mmmm, strawberry-filled jelly donuts with honey glaze. Wash it all down with a coupla quarts of pilsner frothy and biting with hops and malt. A thunderstorm brewed in his belly, his gut echoed with gaseous explosions, volcanic eruptions. He felt stuffed, drunk, he hadn't felt this good in years. He lit up a cigarette, inhaled the aroma of dark tobacco deep into his brain while he perused a little love note Hank's wife had wrapped around a pristine Polish sausage. Darlink, I vill be vatink—no, this is too silly— I'll be waiting in my black lace teddy. Oof, not that good. Rising to his feet he let out a loud belch, URUPP! Farted, BRAAAPPP! He patted his belly, scratched his head. It looked like he was on easy street. All he had to do was follow the tunnel back to the beginning and climb out.

But wait a minute. That's too easy. What if it was a trap, a little psychological jigsaw puzzle just to test his reaction? See if he was going to follow the rules from now on, or if he still insisted on playing the juvenile delinquent? What if there were men waiting for him at the other end with nets and guns and PhDs? He could hear them laughing as they dragged him out of the ground like some horrible little rat, kicking and biting impotently at their hands and feet. He could see himself on his knees, begging them between huge horrible sobs, Please, fellers, don't put ol' Erde back down in that 'orrible 'ole again.

Yeah, but it doesn't end that quickly, does it? They've got a little social agenda worked out. Radio, TV, talk shows, sound bites. Establish your image in the public eye, that's the thing. Let us know what dangers lurk in the soil beneath our feet. Ignorance! Bad Hygiene! The Forgotten Seeds of Communism! And then, Plop! back down the rabbit hole again, right? Another twenty or thirty years without TV privileges? Wrong. Because they're still not through with you yet. They allow you these infrequent escapes every year or so, put on these little neighborhood chase scenes, sirens going off all over town, squad cars swerving up and down residential streets, broadcasting warnings over their loudspeakers. Citizens! Stay inside! Lock your doors and windows! Erde has escaped, he's on the loose again! Do not try to take action! The authorities will handle this! Men with shotguns, hound dogs on your trail, crucified a second, third, fourth time, who knows how much longer this shit's going to go on. But really, Erde, this is absurd, they're not going to squander thousands, millions of the taxpayers' hard-earned dollars keeping track of a little squirt like you. You're entirely too paranoid. You've been crawling around down here too long. Good God, Erde, sunlight! Fresh air! Life! Can't we at least go up and take a look around? See what's happening above ground? Remember, Erde, what it was like to take a stroll through the park on a fresh spring morning with the daffodils and hyacinths blooming? Or the almost too sweet bouquet of lilacs when you began to feel summer in the air? Even the sulfury rotten-egg smell of mineral water burbling up out of that sooty old fountain, with pigeons shitting on your head while children scream and young lovers sigh, they're so in love with each other you can't pry them apart with a spatula. Young mothers fearful and overwhelmed and filled with awe at the living pooping bundle of nascent wonder and intelligence they hold at their breasts, somehow, impossibly, the product of their own bellies, loins. Old men parked on park benches, hacking and coughing and spitting up gobs of lung and phlegm, they're sitting on the very edge of eternity and still fumbling in their trousers for memories, one last bloom and arousal before they relinquish forever the fading scent and smell of life, existence, earth. Ah, but none of that for you, eh Erde? Alas, poor boy, you forsook it all, by all were forsaken.

Call it a curse, a noble cause, his course lay ahead of him. At his feet lay the tools of his trade, abandoned by the ever vigilant public servants, Hank and Joe. Lovingly, his mind flooding with memories of his years on the road gangs, he picked up the sledge, turned it in his hand, feeling its weight and heft. Ah, and the pick, with a nice shiny point at each end, obviously more an object of reverence than utility for the government men. And lastly, the shovel, a sturdy round point with a nice new handle. Despite his much weakened condition the tools felt natural in his hands, he felt the surge of steel in his veins, his eyes flashed, his jaw was firm. He strapped on the helmet, sent its light shining into the darkness, raised the pick over his head.

At first the going was rough. The blisters on his hands broke and bled, his joints creaked, his muscles ached. In the beginning, of course, he was just flailing about in the dark, hacking and chopping here and there, north, south, east, west, he was all over the map. It was like trying to read a goddamn bus schedule. He kept banging into elevator shafts, underground parking garages. He had to detour around sewer pipes, bargain basements, he could hear the enraged housewives tearing at buttonless blouses, one-legged trousers. Get your hands off my bedsheets, bitch! Johnny? Johnny! Take that plastic bag off your sister's head and stick these socks down yo' pants! Gradually, though, calluses grew over his soft skin. His muscles grew hard and lean. With his frail lantern light wobbling and flickering ahead of him, he pounded and picked, hammered and chiseled onward into the subterranean night, learning how to navigate the nether world, developing a kind of basement level street savvy, all the hot spots, happening places, where to flop, find a free meal. Five-thirty in the morning he popped up out of the grease trap at Doodle's Donuts. While Jim and Dave and Jesus Maria sat out on the loading dock, smoking a cup of good strong Colombian and sipping on a twist of senseless in that lazy, hazy, quiet in-between time when the baking was pretty much done and the first customers were yet to come, Erde was behind the counter pouring himself an extra large cappuccino, stuffing a cardboard box with half a dozen glazed donuts, three old-fashioned, uhhh, two raspberry-filled, and, um, a chocolate cake, yeah, and, uh, give me a bear claw, to go. For lunch he pushed aside a vent at the Metropolitan Art Museum and Public Cafeteria, slipped like a shadow over the gleaming white tiles, past the racks and stacks of cutlery and china, leaving but a faint grease stain on the stainless steel sinks, ovens and grills. His hand darted in and out like a ferret, sampling the tuna casserole, macaroni and cheese, this is an American dinner, boys, slap down some mashed potatoes and gravy, carrots and peas with a medium raw slab of beef. In the evening he rode the dumbwaiter up from the catacombs of the Hi-Tone Hotel, dining on pheasant under glass, smoked salmon with chilled vodka, champagne and caviar on the side, south Pacific octopus sauteed in sea cucumbers and ambergris and presented in a bed of rainforest insalata. The waiter lifts the lid on the chef's surprise and surprise! all that's left is a leaf of lettuce and a bone to pick. For snacks he hit the mom and pop grocery in the hood, sawdust strewn over the floorboards, little punk Danny Deus from down the street's hopped up on crack and adrenaline, his sneakers squeaking, trigger squeezing, he spins around with an oversized piece of metal in his hand, trigger itching, gunpowder on the verge of igniting into flame, slamming that heavy chunk of copper and lead into the head, the heart, the brain of whoever the hell you are, motherfucker! But Jesus sneezes! Here's Erde popping out of the potato bin like a body rising from the swamp, all you can see are the whites of his eyes and his teeth, he's dripping sweat and mud, he's got his pick raised over his head. Little Danny's so startled he trips over his own feet, stumbles, the gun goes off, shooting Danny in the hair. Madre! What'choo do, mon? My girlfriend gonna kill me. As the alarm goes off Danny runs out the door and Erde drops out of sight with a kosher dill, bagel and lox. Of course there's always the convenience store on the corner. Fluorescent lights. Air-conditioning. Shelves of candy bars, chips, cigarettes, refrigerator cases full of beer, thunderbeast wine, soda pop. Got all this one hundred percent, totally legal hopped-up hyperdrive-ya-nuts sugar and chemicals and alcohol treats. Got drug addicts, pimps, prostitutes, high school kids bouncing around like pogo sticks, punks, drunks, lunatic motherfuckers with machine guns, plate glass windows shattering, bullets flying, it's a goddamn shooting gallery. Erde grabs a bag of potato chips and a warm coke and drops his ass back down his hole just as an anti-tank shell hits, Ka-BLOO-ey!

Aww, that ain't nothing compared to what I seen.

Now we got old Mac talking into the cameras, he'll talk

to anybody who listens, he's a WW II war vet. Really? WW
Two? The big one? Christ, I don't know. Maybe it was Ko-
rea, Viet Nam, Afghanistan. Were we involved in that one?
It's been so g-g-goddamn long, who c-c-can k-k-keep up
with history these days? He's missing an arm, a leg, he's
got a patch over one eye. He pushes his lunch cart up and
down the street from seven a.m. to eleven at night, tramping through this goddamn, frozen fucking slush pie in winter, fucking melting tar and hot asphalt in summer.
Goddamn thermometer's over a hundred and one, poor
boy's got a fever, call the doc. Yeah, whataya want I should
call him? Nevermind, wise guy, just get me something to
drink. Yessir, what's yer pleasure? We got ice-cold coke,
lemonade. How about a shot and a beer. Drunk, fucked up,
Old Mac's talking to himself, doing this little gandy dance
on a bandy leg and a termite-eaten piece of timber he
carved himself out of the mizzenmast of some old schooner
he sailed on and sank in the middle of some piranha infested lagoon swarming with malaria while tracer bullets
flashed past his head like red-hot bolts of neon and his
body jerked and leapt like a marionette from every hit he
took. Once a month he gets a lousy check in the mail from
the VA, they don't give a fuck about the piece of lung he
coughs up every morning, that little colony of woodborers
eating at his brain. Call it a tropical disease, call it madness, call it a case of another good citizen who's been
fucked over once, twice, three strikes yer out! Ya know
what I mean, pal? It ain't the goddamn world series I'm
talking about. He's rocking and talking and one-hand
counting out change, slinging a red hot into a bun loaded
down with sauerkraut, onions and mustard in a cardboard
boat, how's that for a businessman's lunch? Lousy fucks
don't even tip ya, then they want a receipt for tax purposes
if ya can believe that. IRS keeps track of every dime, invis-

ible ink, radioactive iodine, they're threatening to take away my cart if I don't pay on time. He's so caught up in his spiel he doesn't see Erde's hand come up out of the steam grate. Whoosh! The doggone dog's gone, the customer's getting red hot. Hey, Mac! Where the hell's my weiner? he whines. By then Erde's half way down the block, two floors under, it's like double decker chess, ya gotta watch what's going on under the board.

There was even a brief spell when he'd show up at Hep's Downstairs in dark glasses and a beret, sit in on the combo with a cigarette hanging out of the corner of his mouth, he's got a shot of bourbon and ice on the side, banging pick and sledge, metal on metal for some of the hottest new sounds in cool jazz in the last forty years. He grew a little goatee, grooved on the chicks, the music, the scene. People on the street are saying, Hey, daddio, ya dig that cool new cat sitting in down at Hep's? Yeah, baby, I seen him uptown the other day. Pretty soon you start getting paranoid again. You can understand that, right? Cop car pulls up outside, lights flashing, maybe they're just hassling some bum, some poor guy got a bottle busted over his head. Erde gets all bent out of shape, thinks, Beat it, man, it's the heat! Scoots back down his hole. Wheww, now he's safe, he can take it easy again. Suddenly a coupla utility workers descend the manhole with flashlights and hardhats. They're just checking out a leak in the main. Of course Erde doesn't know that, he thinks, Nyahhh! They're after me! He takes off through the city sewer system. Every once in a while he pops up out of the toilet bowl in somebody's apartment, in the downstairs mens' room at the Overgrown Boy's Club, in the ladies' powder room at the Ladies' Billiards Club and Bordello, there's puddles of pee on the floor, shit everywhere, lipstick tubes, tampons, crumpled tissues.

Yeah, sure, you think it's funny now. You don't remember what it was like to be wanted, a fugitive, the newspapers blaring your face and your name all over the front
page, **Erde On The Lam**. Every time you start to relax,
forget, you think the heat's finally off, somebody fingers
you, a waitress in a coffee shop, guy at the gas station. Say,
ain't you that Erde fella they was lookin' for? Maybe
there's even a reward. Wow! Ten thousand smackeroos!
Dead or alive! Ssst, Mabel, run call the police while I keep
him occupied. But it's just your paranoia again, isn't it? It's
all in your head. It's the city, the noise, it's too intense
around here, everybody jammed together like rats, you
gotta drive all the way across town just to buy a washer for
the kitchen sink. Of course the traffic's bad. You tailgate,
ride the other guy's bumper. You've got a beat-up old bomb,
the front end's all banged up, the fenders are falling off, it's
smoking, burning oil, the rings are bad, blown head gasket,
cars all around you are rolling up their windows, giving
you dirty looks. What the fuck are you supposed to do, it's
the only ride you got. You're so angry you can taste the
blood in the back of yer throat, you feel like you're gonna
lose it, go completely crazy in another minute. That's when
the guy in front of you decides to park at the next light. You
admonish him gently, Hey motherfucker! Move yer ass! He
takes offense. Look out! He's got a gun! Not if you get him
first! Bang! Bang! Bang! Then you go home at night,
scream at the wife and kids, beat the goldfish. Man, it's a
jungle out there. If only you could find some peace and
quiet. People looking in your windows at night, listening to
the bedsprings creak when you're practicing your life-sav-
ing technique on an inflatable bedmate. They're sniffing at
your curried lamb, frying tortillas, they're inhaling your
pipe tobacco, cigarettes, herbs and spices. Officer? Concerned Citizen here. I wish to report a drug addict. Man,

you gotta get outa this city scene, Erde, find a place to hide, maybe a cabin in the woods, I hear the leaves are beautiful in New Hampshire this time of year.

Yeah, sure, in the beginning he used to tell himself, he hungered for and promised himself he'd get out of town, strike out for the country, for the dreams and memories of his infancy, of life on the farm. I told ya, right? How he used to help out ol' grandpa when he was a little tyke? Yeah, sure, milking the cows, slopping the hogs. Butchering sheep, goats, anything that moo-ooved. Plowing under fields of oats and wheat in exchange for government subsidies. It was a good clean life. An American life. Fresh eggs, milk and butter and home-baked cherry pies cooling on the windowsill. Church on Sunday morning. Rise early. Eat a big hearty breakfast before work, school, slurp down huge mixing bowls of Cheery Oats and Clogged Corn Flakes, you get your education reading the back of cereal boxes with pictures of golden-haired boys and girls spooning crispy golden flakes topped with an alpine dream of sliced strawberries and cream into their mouths. I get it, it's a commercial. Buy! Buy! Buy! Bye-bye! And now, back to the movie.

Here's the plan. Erde figured when he got beyond the city limits and out into the boonies he'd go back above ground, assume a new name, identity, maybe a disguise, put on a pair of horn-rimmed glasses, false nose, big black mustache, smoke a cigar, try to blend in with the local populace, maybe get a job somewhere, pump gas, load sacks of grain at the feed exchange. Yowsuh! The truth is, he was still hesitant to give up the city life, to exchange the urbane for the rural. He'd get all the way out into the suburbs, into some wretched little backwoods borough or township. For about an hour and a half he'd be telling himself, man, this is the life, fresh air, clean living. If only it wasn't so goddamn boring! Local sheriff sits astride his riding lawnmower, he's got a ticket book in one hand, a pint of bourbon in his holster. Behind a pair of mirrored sunglasses he's watching buxom little Clarabelle the county darlin' bouncing out to the highway in cut-offs and a halter top. She's gonna bum a ride to the mall with Elmer and Clyde, do a little window shopping, Can I help you, miss? No thanks, just checking the merchandise. Salesgirl looks the other way—zip! The watch goes under Clyde's jacket. Zap! Coupla rings down Elmer's pocket. Snap! A bracelet snuggles in Clarabelle's bra. Nobody sees nothing except the mannequins, the models staring out of the glossy magazines, the bum nodding off by the elevator. Hey, where'd he come from? Must've got off at the wrong floor. Hey, whazzis? Ain't no goddamn train station! He's filthy, bewildered. He doesn't know how the hell he got here himself, there's a crazed look in his eye, he's frantically punching the up button, the down button, the anywhere but here button. Here comes the security cop. He's got a giant skate key stuck in his back, he's swinging his baton, whistling a merry little tune, deutschland, deutschland, über alles . . . hey, hey, hey, what have we got here? A vagrant? This is just what he's been looking for, right? A little change in his routine, a chance to practice his people skills. Whap! Whap! Whap! He's whapping and thumping so hard and so fast, he's huffing and puffing and whaling his club, he's thinking, oh yeah, I'm so good, I'm so tough, he doesn't even realize it isn't Erde he's beating on, it's some blue-haired little old lady who stepped off the elevator just as Erde was ducking down the stairs.

As his tunnel progressed, however, and the industrial subterrain began to thin out, Erde found himself striding forth in the rich black earth. His eyes were clearer, his lungs expanding. He felt like he'd just spent a month at the spa. Years of stress, bad air and city life shrugged off with mud packs, sun baths, dips in icy waters, running naked in the snow, a little self-flagellation after with birch boughs, glug some ice-cold vodka. All the big city pressures of getting to work on time, of keeping some ridiculous schedule and making a buck fallen behind. No more smog, pollution, crime. No more rushing every morning to catch the bus or train. No need to worry about taking work home from the office, or leaving work on the desk undone. In fact, he was always at home, always at work, always on the job, his tunnel was his whole life. He didn't give a hoot about Nell and the kids wondering if daddy's coming home tonight. He was a good little company man, cog in the machine, confused Stakhanovite capitalist, setting the example, leading the way, ever building and growing and forging ahead into the future and eternity. They've got an old clip from his underground hit, **The Underground Express**, he's tunneling like a locomotive hurtling through the darkness and night, his headlamp illuminating wandering cows, invading armies, men from Mars, boarded-up towns and railroad crossings, the whistle's lonely cry a meditation on existence and a lament for all that is passing. And then you see the light coming around the bend and there's ol' Cap'n Erde at the throttle, he's furiously shoveling coal and blowing the horn, Tooot! tooot! tooo-wooo-oooo-ooot! And it sounds so lost and forlorn. In the damp black night ol' country cousin Erde's sitting on the porch of some ramshackle shack watching the train go by and thinking back to his younger days and what might have been, and God, it's gonna be good to go back inside later on and sit around the stove and talk with sister Sal and Aunt May, dear old ma and pa, or anybody at all, but somebody. Oh Erde, Erde, what are you doing down here? Have you truly lost your mind? Is there no elevator back above among your own kind? Can we return no more to those golden days of yore,

when our curly-haired Erde was but a boy who still believed in believing, when life was simpler, and looks less
deceiving. Oh Lord, how you gonna keep 'em, down on the
farm?

Sure, occasionally he fell into a cesspool or outhouse,
came up sputtering for air, covered with shit. But it was
good clean shit, real shit, none of that smart-ass ambigu-
ous shit some punk's trying to sell you on the street. No,
man, I mean it, this is baaaad shit! Now lookee here, boss,
this on the other hand is some gooood shit. Hey man, don't
gimme that shit! No hustles, no gimmicks, no fashions or
trends. Just the simple life. Food in abundance. Nothing
fancy, of course. In fact, dining had become a spontaneous
event. He'd find himself digging through the underside of
farmer John's vegetable garden, churning through a potato
patch, a field of lentils or turtle beans. All he had to do was
reach up and pluck a carrot from his ceiling, ehh, what's
up, doc? Beets and onions. Push his hand up through the
loam and he had strawberries, peppers and tomatoes.
Completely organic, you know. Always wanted to try a veg-
etarian diet. But when he thought about going up above
like he'd promised himself, he'd push the thought to the
back of his mind. He'd developed a new fear, another pho-
bia to supplant the old. It'd be too bright. The light'd hurt
his eyes. He'd been submersed in darkness for too long.

What, I didn't tell you? Yeah, sure, his lantern burned
out long ago. Whataya think, the battery's got a lifetime
guarantee? He dug blindly for weeks, months, he couldn't
even see to fill out an application for government aid, job
training, at least a seeing eye dog, a pair of sunglasses and
a white cane. Awful actually, a real tragedy. Poor boy, flailing around in the dark, directionless, without any guidance, no political agenda. Aww, save your tears. He was no
weakling, he had plenty of guts, he relied on his natural

resources. He'd developed an acute sense of smell, hearing. He forged on in the dark like a junior woodchuck. Follow me, boys! Moss grows on the north side of the tree! Mark your trail and keep going! Pissss. And then, in the very next breath, he'd panic, he'd cry out in a strangled voice, Help! I'm suffocating! I can't breathe! I've gotta get outa here! He'd chop and pick his way upward until he banged his head against the underside of a driveway, brained himself on a sewer pipe. Then he'd lie still and wait until all sound had died and ceased, Dad coming home from work at night in the old Nash Rambler, Mom washing dishes over the kitchen sink, the stereo on in Junior's room, flushing toilets, Sis in the bathroom for hours, trying on make-up, experimenting with tampons, this goes where? Fantasizing about that pink poodle skirt she saw in Lacy's. And then, when he was certain it was night and quiet and alright, he poked his finger up through the dirt and the cool night air poured over him like a mountain spring. Burbling and laughing to himself he put his eye to the hole and filled his brain with the impossible bombardment of stars in the night sky, his ears filling with the chirring and peeping of tree frogs and crickets, the tiny flitting of wings, of moths and fireflies twinkling and blinking in the misty night settling over the meadow where the shriek of a screech owl descending on a field mouse reminded all to live! now! and the breeze carried with it the scent and smell of new mown grass. It was an elixir, a cool tall beverage. It intoxicated him, numbed him, made him happy and sad. It was so unbearably delicious. He wanted more and he wanted less. It was like when he was a little boy and his big brother Bert or his sister Nan or even that mean old Danny down the street, but someone bigger or older than him held him down and tickled his belly, the soles of his feet, until he was laughing and crying no! please! stop! helpless and overwhelmed with so much ecstasy.

Toward morning, when the first birds began to sing and the first yellow lights appeared in the windows of the farm-house or tract home and the first gray light began to spread outward over the land, he'd hear the plumbing rat-tling and whooshing, toilets flushing, coffee pots perking, dishes banging, cars revving up, trucks roaring down the back roads, and he'd feel that old anxiety again, he'd aban-don his reverie, tear himself away from his hole and dig downward again, telling himself, just a little farther yet, and then maybe I'll go up for a look around. It doesn't even have to be for good. Just a week or two, a little visit. Oh, I know, you couldn't at first, Erde, it was still too soon, you had things to work out. But there's no reason we can't go up now, is there? We'll just pop up for a moment and see. Then he'd start to get angry with himself again. You sick fuck, it's just a game you're playing. You never had any in-tentions of going back above. You should have your head examined, see a shrink.

Ah, here's Mister Wallstone again. Recently appointed to the President's Board of Remedial Basket Weaving. Alright now, Erde, in your own words, whatever words they may be, tell the old witch decoctor why it is you don't want to go back up among yer own human-unkind.

But it was a hard case to crack, the patient was suffer-ing from psycho-paralysis, too much analysis. They tried everything, hypnosis, anti-depressants, mood alteration, here's old Mrs. McGillicutty the school nurse coming at him with a pin cushion and a measuring tape. Now just you hold still young man, a stitch here and a dart there and you'll look great. Even shock therapy. They've got him strapped down on a rubber mat, they're shoving glossy col-ored photographs of naked presidents in his face, they're whipping him with strands of overcooked fettucine, he's peeing all over himself, drooling and foaming at the mouth, no, please, stop! They've even got Joe the crane operator in there, he's got his rig fired up, blowing black smoke. Don't worry, pal, we'll get you outa that rut! Nothing doing. Erde won't budge. Look, the doc says, tilting a bottle of rubbing alcohol to his lips, I personally don't care if you stay down there forever, but yer making a fool out of yourself, it's breaking your poor old mother's heart. That's it, the old methods, guilt, derision, they'll make sure you never go up again.

The truth is, he was beginning to like it down there, he was starting to feel like he belonged. It was so cozy and close. And the air, so rare, so rich and full of earthy smells. And you couldn't beat the neighborhood, everybody so friendly. He was working away, swinging his pick and shoring up the roof of his tunnel with roots and fence posts when ol' Br'er Rabbit'd come hopping past, tipping his top hat and remarking in that kinda slow, country way, How ya doin' today, Mister Erde? Ol' Mister Mouse'd peek out of his house, Howdy, Erde, stop by for a game of checkers later? Ol' Mizz Possum'd come scurrying along with a sack of groceries under her arm, No time to talk, Erde, gotta hurry, mercy! winter's comin' on.

Wait a second. Winter? Is that, like, a seasonal thing down here? I mean, like, it doesn't snow, does it? I mean, I'm not so sure about this winter thing. Yeah, sure, the first snowfall's all right, in fact, it's kinda nice, get all bundled up in sweaters and coats, boots, jackets, gloves, hats and scarves—Ma, I gotta pee!—and go outside. And it feels so good, the frigid air pricking every pore in your bare face, and the big fat snowflakes drifting down and melting on your tongue, while your brain fills with the narcotic winter smells of damp wool, wood smoke and chimney soot until, overcome with so much ecstasy and awe, you let yourself simultaneously ascend and fall, you flop backwards in a snowdrift, flap your arms and legs in the crusty sugar meringue leaving the imprint of an angel, you fly down glistening sheets of ice on sleds and toboggans, crashing into trees and fence posts, screaming and yelling with the childish glee and presentiment that this can not last. Just when you're starting to feel cold Ma's at the door calling Errdiiee! Come in for some hot chocolate! Maybe you and sis gather up a great big bowl of fresh snow, mix in a little milk, some pure cane sugar and a drop of vanilla and presto! Home-made ice cream! Of course you can't do that anymore, can you? Snow's no good. Carcinogens. Toxins and dioxins. Yellow urine stains of dogs and reindeer. Spit it out! You'll poison yourself! You'll get cancer! Yeah, winter ain't what it used to be. The nights are darker, longer. It's always so cold, so dreary and drab, you feel depressed all the time, all you wanta do is get drunk and hide in bed.

Yeah, sure, later our boy learned to dig down to the coast for the winter. Oops, don't forget to feed the cats, water the plants, lock the doors and windows behind you. And then that long haul, the highway slipping past. Are we almost there yet, Daddy? For Christ's sake, we haven't even left the goddamn state. Ah, but the sea, the sea, the beautiful sea. You know when you're getting close, you can hear the distant roar and thud in the earth, the soil turns sandy and saline in your teeth, you're crunching through bones and shells, eons of accumulated coral, fossils of long extinct sea creatures, great great uncle Ook's ribcage, the sediment of ages, drawn on and intoxicated by the sea and the lure of the sea, not just the sun setting on the water in a vast autumnal blaze of colors, but muscular brown surf adonises and bronze-skinned beach madonnas splashing in the waves, shedding strings of pearls from sun-bleached hair flung back wet and unbraided. Mom and Dad and Sis

and Brother trudging up the beach like circus clowns off on
another humiliating family outing. Fat old Aunt Edna and
Uncle Ted like some kind of horrible carnival act in monstrous bulging bathing suits. Picnics and beach umbrellas.
Sea gulls screaming. Children shrieking, lean, brown-
skinned kids in wet-bottomed underwear chasing after the
receding surf, laughing and screaming and fleeing backwards in mock terror when another wave comes crashing
down. Maybe later go out for a drink and a bite to eat at
one of those quaint little seafood places, dine on lobster,
crab and oysters, fish frys, clam bakes, what a life, eh?
Nothing to do but breathe the salt air, eat and sleep and
catch up on your reading, who knows, maybe even meet a
nice girl, boy, whatever your persuasion. Oh God, Erde, it's
been so long since you last participated in humanity, that
dim and distant race you once belonged to. You can feel it
drawing you back again, calling to you, the way the sea
calls, whispering to you and speaking of birth, origins, God,
the great salty womb of eternity waiting to envelop you
and draw you in again. You're digging faster and faster.
You tunnel right down to the sea's edge. The salty, sandy
gray and brown water swirls around your feet, you can feel
this huge unspecified presence surrounding you and
pounding inside you. It gets so bad you can't sleep at night.
It haunts and terrifies your dreams, you lie there waiting
for the next big wave to come crashing down, to break
through your fragile wall. In your sleep you can hear the
last few inches of sand beginning to crumble and trickle
away like insects, and then the roar and rush as the entire
ocean pours into your tunnel, rushes along the narrow
twisting umbilical cord of your own making and overtakes
you, swallows you up sputtering and drowning in a great
wet oblivion.

Yeah, sure, but that first winter. Hooo, boy! Remember,

Erde? Gardens once lush and verdant with fruit and vegetables all dead and brown and tilled under, the muddy
rows crusted with the melting remains of the season's first
snow. Grapes and squash and tomatoes shriveled on the
vine. Corn stalks rustling in the wind. Icicles hung from
the roof of his tunnel. The earth was hard and permeated
with frost. His fingers tingled and burned. He'd poke a hole
up above, a dusting of snow'd fall down on his head. If he
was lucky he'd find a rotten head of cabbage, a few frost-
bitten carrots, onions, potatoes. Barely enough for a weak
vichyssoise. Then he'd get a whiff of woodsmoke, happy
hearths and homes lit-up and glowing with the warm yellow light of candles and lamps, it's one of those holiday
postcards, through the frosty windows you can see the tree
lit up with candles and ornaments, the family cat and dog
purring and snuffling at the feet of ma and pa and the little
ones gathered around the fire crackling merrily in the
hearth, all bundled up in their individual pockets of
warmth, roasting apples, the smell of pine, wreaths, bells
jingling, choirs singing, carols and hymns raised on high by
voices ripe with toasts and wassails. And there he was,
down in that filthy hole, hungry, wretched, alone, no warm
stove, no roasting turkey and giblets with all the trim-
mings. Shivering, distraught, he dug onward in search of
food, warmth. He was snuffling, blubbering, snot running
down his nose.

Christ, what a little whiner you were, a regular spigot.

Yeah, well that was a particularly dim period in our
life, wasn't it, lad? Just imagine. Lost in the dark, dazed,
confused, weak with hunger, with no candle, no flame, no
light at the end of your tunnel. He was on his last legs
when he heard a voice singing a merry little tune, Here
comes Peter Cottontail, hopping down the bunny trail.
Shhhh, he whispered to himself, it's Br'er Rabbit!

Why howdy-do, Mister Erde. Out for an evening stroll?
Erde's eyes gleamed.

Why Mister Erde, what is it? You look so strange. 'Ere!
What's this! Stop, sir! Desist!

Alas, too late. Without a word Erde had grabbed poor
Br'er Rabbit by the scruff of his neck and crammed him—
head and haunch, TV antennae, lucky charms and false
teeth—down his throat. It was only at the end of his repast
that he felt any remorse. What was he doing? He'd become
such a depraved thing. He plucked the fluffy little cottontail from his teeth. Boo hoo, poor wittle bunny. At least his
meager meal gave him the strength to go on again. He dug
for days, weeks. Finally one night—it was dark anyway—
he banged into a brick wall. The mortar was old, crumbling, the bricks loose. It wasn't anything at all to break
through with a blow from his pick. A faint ruby light
gleamed off endless racks of bottles. He'd tunnelled into
the wine cellar of some big estate. Erde was no oenophile.
He knew nothing of vintage or vintner, the difference between sweet, dry, dessert or table. Brushing aside the cobwebs, he pulled out his Boy Scout knife, uncorked the first
bottle he found and drank long and deep, the wine spilled
down over his chin, his chest. Ahh, paradise. This receives
the pick and shovel crest of good living. Mm, what's this?
Scotch! Well, although I know it's not in the proper se-
quence, let's have a sip. Hmm, excellent, a single malt with
a nice, smoky aroma, good fire, perfect after a winter
afternoon's tunneling. Now, how about a nice bottle of stout
to keep it company? Well, and lookee here, we've even got
comestibles. The shelves and corners were packed and
stacked with rounds of cheese, tins of smoked oysters and
sardines, barrels of dried fruits and nuts, jars filled with
pickled pears and chutneys, pretty soon he was fairly pickled himself. By the time he got through the ports, the

kirsches, the brandies and liqueurs, he was saying the most ridiculous things, schlurring hizh wordzh, breaking out in shong, ha ha ha, ho ho ho, Erde's a goof-o, dancing on his hoof-os, not a donkey anymore, eating like an epicure.

Just at that moment a door creaked on its rusty hinges. A candle flickered, gleamed off a bald head, a long, dour face, an immaculate gray livery.

'Ello! What 'ave we 'ere? A mouse is it? A bloody big mouse? Erde pressed back in the shadows, if he hadn't been so utterly filthy he would've been spotted. The butler stood not an inch in front of his nose, the candle held aloft, the dour face gleaming like a death mask.

Been sampling the guv'nor's cheeses again, 'as ya, mousie? Wot? And 'aving a nip at his lordship's vintage? 'Af to be a bit more careful next time, won't we Mister Mousie? Put the cork back after we've 'ad our little nipkins. All the while the wiley and quite unservile winophile was glugging down a bottle of port. Jamming the empty in a crevice he stuffed another bottle under his vest, glanced around, and went out the door. At the click of the lock Erde quickly exited the same way he came in. Closing up the bricks and mortar behind him, he staggered and stumbled down his tunnel, pausing for gulps from a champagne bottle and laughing so hard his stomach hurt. Hey, who turned out the lights! Haharho! Anybody got a match? Hooheeha! He was so smitten with his newfound humor he even contemplated a return to the stage, maybe he could revitalize his old vaudeville routine, re-work the punchlines, add a little song and dance, some stand-up comedy. Some joke, huh? He woke several hours later feeling cold, sick, with a blinding hangover. Grabbing his pick, he cursed and growled and groped forward in the dark, chopping and shoveling dirt again.

He went on like that for days, weeks, in a foul humor,

complaining all the time, bitching and moaning. Why don't they put lights in this goddamn hole? Man, I could use a cup of coffee and a donut. Where the hell's the manager? If he didn't find some kind of hostel or inn soon he was going to lie down on the side of the road and die. In a fit of frustration and anger he took a last desperate swing with his pick. The wall gave way in front of him, sent him tumbling into a pocket of warmth and light and sweet, spicy smells. He'd stumbled into another bloody fairy tale. But instead of some jolly old sot in red longjohns toasting his toes by the fire, Erde saw, seated in a deep leather armchair, a rather large bear dressed very smartly in a burgundy velvet smoking jacket with an heirloom quilt drawn over his lap, and on top of his big furry brown head a red fez with a gold tassel falling over one monocled eye.

Well? the bear growled in a deep, sleepy voice, exposing two rows of huge, jagged teeth. Aren't you going to introduce yourself, Mister . . . ?

. . . Erde, he replied, glancing around for hidden microphones, video cameras—Rhymes with merda.

Hmm, the bear drawled, examining his torn and mudcaked clothes. It certainly figures. Well, have a seat, Mister Erde. Care for a chocolate? Something to drink?

On the Chippendale table next to him sat a large decanter of blackberry brandy, a box of cherry cordials, and a rather dubious collection of smoking paraphernalia. Erde sank down in an armchair, plucked a chocolate from its wrapper and crushed it between his teeth. Numbing waves of rich dark chocolate and warm, rum-flavored black cherry enveloped his brain. He poured himself a glass of dark purple liqueur, raised it to his lips. The sweet, tart juice of blackberries washed in mountain springs and wrapped in a warm menthol blanket of alcohol swirled around his taste buds and tongue. Ahhh, he felt himself starting to relax, he sank farther down in the chair. The aches in his bones had already disappeared.

Mm-mmph! the bear yawned again, passing Erde a rather curious looking tobacco pipe—a particularly ferocious looking ursine fellow carved out of yellowed ivory with a silver cap on his head. It'll help pacify the bees if you know what I mean, Mister . . . what was that name again?

. . . Erde, he replied, putting the cracked and chewed stem between his teeth and drawing a thick stream of sweet, spicy smoke into his lungs. Hahaha, he coughed, passing the pipe back to the bear's great waiting paw. Ouch! A drop of blood oozed from the tip of his finger. He'd nicked himself on one of the bear's huge black claws. He had a moment of panic. Typhoid! Lockjaw! Rabies! But then he felt stupid, and the bear was really quite apologetic.

Oh dear. Please, excuse me, Mister Urdu, I forget some times.

Erde waved his hand in the air, grinned stupidly, It's nothing, nothing a'tall.

The pipe passed back and forth several times. The fire burned brightly in the hearth. A bayberry candle glowed on the mantel. Smoldering incense filled the cave with the fragrance of frangipani and jasmine, lotus blossoms and patchouli. Gesundheit! The smoke or the smell of the smoke made him sneeze or maybe it was the bear who sneezed, I can't remember anymore, it's so easy to get confused, all hung-up on memory and time. Wasn't there something I had to do today? Or was it yesterday? Ah yes, the dentist's appointment. And grocery shopping afterwards, and get the car repaired and see about a new showerhead for the TV or was it a toilet lid for the kitchen sink? Oh my God, and the job! That's right, pal, you forgot to go to work again. You still got another mile to dig, and half a mile behind you still gotta shore up. You'd better call right now and tell them you're sick, make up some excuse, your iguana has the measles. Aww, what're you talking about, chump? It's Saturday. You don't have to go to work today. Nothing to do but hang out and watch cartoons. Besides, what difference does it make if it's today, tomorrow or yesterday? It'll happen, right?

Huh? Erde snapped awake again. He'd been wandering in a cloud, drifting in a dream, when he suddenly remembered, the bear! He sat up in his chair, expecting to see the ursine lunging at him, fangs bared, claws curling. But the bear only stared at him through lidsy eyes, a knowing little smile drawing his lips back from his teeth. Hmmm, of course, I could have eaten you. While you were napping I mean. Isn't that what you were thinking, Mister . . . mmyawwwnn . . . Erté?

Hmmph! Erde snorted.

Come, come, the bear retorted. You humans, always on your high horse. We in the animal kingdom know very well how you view us. Beasts, monsters, murderers. Merely an excuse to chop us up into little pieces, bear grease and bear stew, bear skins and bear claws—mmmm, I like those. Tell me, Mister Erato, how many millions do you think we've generated in cookbooks alone? Not to mention the boost it gives your meager little egos to slaughter us in the wilds. Hmph! What wilds remain.

And what could he say? It was different in the old days? When men went around naked, with no guns or knives. We didn't have big teeth like you guys. We didn't have claws. We lived by our wits alone. We had to defend ourselves against you—beasts.

Oh really? the bear sniffed. I suppose you're referring now to the recently deceased, Br'er Rabbit? Besides, how exactly do we define beast? Is it simply a question of the fur coat and claws? Or is it one who commits beastly acts? What about all of mankind's tortures and wars? Destruction of the planet? Ah, insanity. Ha! I meant humanity. Or rather, inhumanity. But how inhumane if practiced by humans? Or is that what it means to be human, Mister Errare? To slaughter and destroy everything that doesn't suit your style? Do you know how many humans bears have killed and/or devoured over the long days and nights of eternity, Mister Errata? Exactly seven thousand, eight hundred and eighty three, not including businessmen and politicians. And do you know how many bears men have killed and/or devoured in that same period? No, I didn't think so. Would the figure seven hundred eighty million and thirty-three surprise you? Of course I've rounded off some of the figures, and taken into consideration the pandas' propensity for lying. But, all in all, that's a pretty accurate account. Oh yes, I know, the Good Book, dominion over the birds and the beasts and all that yeast. These are different times, Mister Erastian. You need a different book. Afterall, my boy, the Buddha, the Bible, the Bhagavad-gita, Moses, Mohammed, the Madonna's boy, Jesus. Whom are we supposed to believe, Mister . . . ummm, what did you say your name was again? Yerba? Sounds foreign to me. Don't you ever bathe, Mister Erebus? No, of course not. It's much too civilized a habit. By the way, did you say it was snowing outside? Ah well, never mind. Please, have some more brandy, smoke.

And that was certainly nice, making amends, smoking and drinking, cracking nuts, gnawing birch bark and sweet gum, chewing dried fruits, apples, pears and plums. Another chocolate, Erde? Don't mind if I do. More brandy? How can I refuse? It's the old story again, drugs and booze woven into the fairy tale fabric, esotericism, cabals, hidden meanings. The pipe went round and round as they went off on a rather drowsy, wandering discourse on the nature of existence. In fact, they were just on the verge of some major discovery, a sort of mathematical paradigm of the universe, with that old oak tree in the north corner of the woods as the fulcrum, and Brother Badger's fairly drunken meanderings underground as the course of light and matter through time and space, when the bear fell asleep.

Hey, Bear! Erde shouted. Wake up! We were just arriving at an answer.

Hmmmph? the bear grunted. What was the question?

After that there was nothing for Erde to do but get a little shut-eye himself. Only problem is, he couldn't sleep. Maybe it was all that Turkish coffee. He tried counting sheep but that seemed rather absurd in his present situation. Besides, the bear's snoring kept him awake. He lit the pipe again, took a couple of puffs. But what was he doing? He really should be going. What if someone came? Who, another bear? How would he explain? He took another puff. Aww, it's just your paranoia again. C'mon, Erde, relax, enjoy yourself. But what about the tunnel? You should get on with your work. He took another puff. You jerk, forget that working stiff stuff. Have another toke.

Poof! He woke in a great cloud of smoke. Had he fallen asleep? Hit a pocket of methane? He picked up his pick again, took a swing. Wasn't there something about a bear? What, a bear? I declare, Erde, you are in bad shape. You'd better find a decent motel, something to eat. He started digging again, but he'd lost all his drive, ambition. He couldn't get his thoughts straight. He was just sort of wandering around in a daze, stumbling over roots, bonking his noggin against boulders and rocks. The going was more difficult now. He was huffing and puffing and flailing about. He was digging and clawing with his bare hands.

Wait a second. He was digging with his bare hands? What happened to his tools?

His tools? Gone to the museum. Paleontology, archeology, they've got posters and displays detailing every advent of his progress, the simultaneous decline of his technology, his descent into planned obsolescence, grainy black and whites of his much treasured tools worn out on storm sewers, pylons and piles of granite. Here he is in a glossy nine by twelve promoting education in inner-city schools— Erde the public servant scraping the drool from the chin of some anonymous urchin with a teaspoon fashioned from his beloved round-point shovel. Here he is in a backyard family gathering, pitching horseshoes with the head of the pick pounded and bent into a scrappy little ringer! Here he is with the head of the sledge smashed into an ineffectual little ballpeen hammer, smashing atoms in his garage workshop.

No matter. His hands had developed into monstrous, horny things, his nails would've made Br'er Bear brown with envy. He dug and clawed and scraped forward like a mole, a gopher, a badger. It was actually easier now. He didn't need all that room to swing his pick, he kept his tunnel nice and tight—nothing vulgar now, OK, boys? Just enough space to crawl forward, shoving his hands into the earth like the perfect martial artist, dislodging rocks with a quick peck of the chicken beak, tearing loose roots with a tiger's claw, it's all a matter of applied science, prying at the right angle, with just the right amount of pressure, displacing so many yards of soil per hour. Erde was no geologist. He only vaguely remembered studying rocks in Mr. Maurice's sixth grade science class. Oh yeah, quite the teacher's pet. After school he dug around in driveways, rock gardens, stream beds, creeks and sewers, collecting quartzite and gypsum, feldspar and meteorites. He's thinking, boy, wait until the class sees this. Meanwhile little Becky Bumpercar's got a brass-bound chest of rubies, emeralds, all this junk her daddy brought back from an archeological dig in Egypt. That's what the old man says anyhow. Actually he's known the world over as a gun runner, drug smuggler. Only thing is, nobody can DO anything about it. He's got the authorities by the balls. In fact, he's got his hands down the pants of more pashas and beys, guerilla leaders, tribal chieftains and warlords than a frog has eggs. But Mr. Maurice doesn't wanta hear about that. He's not a politician. He's just a humble teacher, he's just doing his job the way he's been told. Don't forget to bring your rocks tomorrow, class. Limestone and granite, igneous and fatuous. It doesn't matter what you call them. Rocks are hard, dirt's soft, that's all you need to know. Find a good vein and follow it to the source. Soon Erde was churning through the earth like a dervish, drill, boring machine, he dug with the finesse of a sculptor, a diamond cutter, he'd become a zen master of digging, even chewing with his teeth.

His teeth you say? Now you've gone too far.

Not at all. When times were tough he gnawed on roots and tubers, grubs, worms and beetles and everything else eatable. He even developed a taste for dirt. Now and then he'd absent-mindedly pop a particularly tasty looking clod of clay in his mouth and go on his way working it between his teeth like a cud, like a plug of Richman chewing tobacco. Caliche, sandy loam, river bottom, top soil, soon he was operating almost entirely on a dirt diet. Yes indeed, ladies and gentlemen, you really oughta try it. It's got nutrients and trace elements, bulk and fiber. Besides, it was more expedient, no more interrupting his work for time-consuming coffee and lunch breaks. He had all kinds of charts and graphs demonstrating the precious minutes wasted looking for a decent diner or restaurant. The manhours lost at company cost. No more. When he was thirsty he lapped at trickling springs, raw sewage seeping from cesspools, septic tanks and outhouses, tasting the foul conjure of the bellies above. He'd developed an immunity to everything toxic and poisonous. In fact, he'd become a connoisseur of the rank and rancid, of putrefaction and decay. He ate his way through rotting animal carcasses, compost piles, boneyards, refuse pits behind glue factories, leaving behind a trail of castings that'd make an organic gardener green with envy. The perfect Buddha, right. It's all the same thing anyway, meat and potatoes, shit, piss and gallstones. It's all comprised of particles and molecules of breathing, life and consciousness.

In his spare time he was writing a book of holistic recipes, Eating Your Way to Apotheosis. Of course, there are some dietary restraints. Remember the first time you ploughed through a cemetery, Erde? Poor boy, he almost went mad trying to claw his way out again, tearing through crumbling, termite-eaten coffins, banging into mausoleums packed with mummified corpses and ancient bones stacked like festival loaves of sourdough, stale baguettes. Got used to it after a while. Still a coupla miles off he'd get a whiff of quick lime, formaldahyde, linseed oil, the sickly sweet redolence of wilting roses, orchids and calla lilies. Then he'd change his path, go off in search of greener pastures. He no longer thought about going up on top. At least, not as a goal or prerequisite. Now it was more of an existential pondering. In fact, it had become a kind of joke. He could see himself broaching the surface like a submarine after years under the sea, a little green around the gills, of course, his lungs grown with moss and mold, but none the worse for wear. Or, how about some strange insect, living and growing underground, his mind and his body surging along an accelerated evolutionary course, larva, pupa, chrysalis, imago, and ta da, one day Erde pops out of the backyard a beautiful moth or butterfly opening its stained glass wings to the sun? Yeah, sure, more like a dung beetle, or a seventeen year locust. Here comes old farmer John again, smacking you on the head with his rake, Miserable critter! Get back underground where you belong! And who's to say he's wrong? You're wrecking his garden, taking away his livelihood, insensitive clod, you've lost all sense of decency, your whole life centers around this mindless digging and eating. How long is it now, Erde? Months? Years? Ask a fish how long it's been swimming. All its life, since the day it was born, even when it hangs there, suspended in mid-air, so to speak, in that viscous twilight, treading water (let's be frank), trying to decide which way now, up, down, back or forth, driven by a motor that functions on the most primitive level, food, copulation, escape. And now ask, how long is it you've been digging, mate?

Clearly with the passing of time and a little keen observation, Erde had become something of a philosopher, a metaphysician, his entire life devoted to digging in that compost pile, that dung heap, that fertile nightsoil of his brain:

Sometimes I forget I am digging, I can't remember if I'm digging toward or away. I'm a fugitive, I'll admit that. At least I haven't killed anybody, not factually anyway.

And this:

Everything is a fabrication of mind, of thought, of blind, incorporeal existence. This dirt surrounding me, this dirt I dig, is not real. Can you dig?

For a while it looked like Erde was losing his grip on terra firma, he was still floundering around in the fish metaphor, splashing about like a madman, going out for long morning swims. He did the crawl, the breaststroke, he

even did the butterfly. For variation he'd roll over and
paddle along doing the backstroke with perfect ease. When
he got tired he simply quit moving, lay on his back and
stared at the ceiling, watching the tiny hair roots suck the
drops of moisture, the tiniest points of dew through their
skin, his brain swooning in a rich narcotic bath of earthy
vapors, while the ground shifted and moved around him,
heaving and breathing and sighing, eating and digesting
itself. All those little creatures inside it snacking and
cracking their mandibles and jaws, grunting and snuffling,
digging and clawing, fur bearing and reptilian, insects,
worms, parasites and microbes. And now he was one of
them. Just another one of the billions and trillions of good
little bugs doing their duty, eating up all the shit and garbage and turning it back into some kind of useful product,
it was his own little recycling program, airbrakes squealing, diesel wheeling, here's our public servant Erde haul-
ing and heaving boxes and bags and containers of cardboard, plastic and broken glass. Of course we'll have to get
him a proper uniform, at least a jock strap with the mu-
nicipal seal emblazoned across the pouch, can't have our
city servants performing their duties in their birthday
suits.

What, I didn't say he was naked before? Oh yeah, of
course. His threads had rotted away years ago. He was re-
duced to a state of blessed innocence, not a fig leaf at hand,
not a pair of breeches. And then all this crawling around in
the muck and the mire like a bloody worm, you can imagine! Every step he took, or rather, every inch he crawled,
put his body in contact with the earth in a most insalubri-
ous way, all that friction, all that rubbing, dragging his
truncheon through the mud, trapped in an endless oozing
orgy of semen and slime, memories of Milicent Mayapple
and the Ladies Semi-Professional Volleyball League and

Lingerie Guild swirling in his mind, every move forced him into another indecent act, Father Gropus, please, I can't stop touching myself.

Still he dug onward, mortifying himself with cold baths, fasts, acts of atonement and leather lashes. Singing hymns of deliverance he crawled through narrow crevasses, debouched upon enormous cathedral spaces hung with vast limestone draperies, the ceiling and floor studded with stalactites and mites cast and poured over thousands and millions of years in the forms of saints and angels with diaphanous wings and flowing beards. Of course they've got the whole place lit up like a whorehouse, lightshows, guided tours, there's the heavenly host on your right, folks. He was having a transcendental experience, the vulgar and profane metastasizing into a glorious reign. It must have been the giant fungus he ate his way through, psilocybe hallelucinata. He'd ascended from the earthly domain. Christ, he was inside a blinking UFO. It was in all the tabloids the next day. **Man Buried Alive For Forty Years. Rescued By Space Angels In Flying Sausage.** (Was the typo intended? Meant to increase readership among the red meat crowd?). On the cover you see a bunch of choirboys in flannel nightgowns and pigeon wings munching on hot dogs. Inside you get the whole terrible story . . . transported to another planet, slave labor, 'orrible experiments on his body, soap suds in his brain, a lifetime's surplus of energy extracted in seven minutes, then—zip!— back to earth again, a used-up husk of a man with another thirty years on the assembly line—if you're lucky, that is, if they don't hand you your goddamn watch and an IOU from social security, then kick you out in the street a week before the blessed birth of our savior. How the hell did that happen anyway? How did life pass us by so fast? Oh Erde, Erde, my son, my father, myself. Is this the path you sought when you set out? Is this the engine that drives your search? To hunt forever and never reach?

For some time now Erde had been tiptoeing around the back steps of a higher consciousness. Some inner light lit his way. In fact, he'd developed a kind of night vision, like one of those light gathering rifle scopes, like the feline contraction of pupil and iris, cinching the invisible halo hovering around an object into a skein on a computer screen outlining the form of a dog or a cat or a man with a gun. It didn't happen suddenly of course. It was just a gradual realization, like peeling successive layers of muslin from his eyes. Somehow his brain had learned to draw forth, to collect and gather the ten-billion-year-old particles of sunlight trapped underground among the particles of long and forgotten night. Everything appeared in a kind of phosphorescence, a penumbral light, perpetual moonlight, bonelight, the light that passes through wax, old flesh, alabaster, the light that fills ossuaries, mausoleums, the repository of worn-out machines, metal and calcareous skeletons oxidizing underground alongside ancient highways and animal paths.

One day he was tunneling along with his head bent and his nose to the ground when he came upon a set of tracks baked into the clay and sediment of a paleolithic stream bed. He followed it for a hundred yards or so when it was intercepted by another, much larger set of tracks that splashed behind in the limestone frieze of the long dead creek, until the two sets converged and became one. Boink! He bonked his head on a fossilized pile of ivory. He was trapped inside the ribs of some great saurian ship, its deck and planking long ago rotten away from its timbers and hull. He quickly thumbed through the pages of his sixth grade science book. Brontosaurus? Nope. Stegosaurus? Don't think so. Pterodactyl? Heavens no. Tyrannosaurus?

Much too large for the bad-tempered Carnovaurus. That leaves only the Imaginosaurus. The dragon or dinosaur or prehistoric beast of parade float dimensions he'd somehow twisted up in his post-infant brain with the horror of a Frankensteinian creature crackling on a black and white TV. The man-beast, sewn together out of body parts and occasional animal organs and jolted awake out of a shivering, tormented sleep of eternity by a bolt of lightning hurled across the synapse between man and machine by some manic, bespectacled genius, himself the creation of the fears of the masses, the multitudes, who could not survive, who could not otherwise find among themselves some common bond of brotherhood, if not for the monster, the hated enemy, raging across the landscape, destroying everything in its path.

Although why all this monster talk? You can't mean me? I'm not the monster. Ha, what a joke. One monster trapped inside another. That figures somewhere along the food chain, doesn't it? The apple in the boar's mouth? Turkey and stuffing? Ha ha ha?

But now he was getting hysterical . . . he was starting to panic . . . he had to get out of there . . . he was running around in ellipses . . . like a good little sub-atomic particle . . . hurtling around inside a cyclotron . . . headed toward a collision with another little piece of shit like himself . . . and he didn't even realize, he should have paid more attention in science class, he was blithely, blindly dragging his fingertips over the big beast's ribs, like Tom Hayseed plucking a picket fence, like a piano man making a musical plink, plink, plink. Hey, that's got a good beat. S'cuse me, ladies and gentlemen, while I sit down for a moment and tickle these eighty-eights, I don't mean to procrastinate, I'm just trying to escape my unfortunate fate, my subterrestrial destineeee. Following a quick and poorly received reprise of his days at Hep's he pried himself free from Mister Rex, leapt sixty million years ahead in the text.

With a final G minor he'd crashed through a rusty metal casing, tumbled headfirst into a large steel object. He was bathed in a viscous green light. A wave of clinical air washed over him, a bouquet of ether, sodium pentothal, nitrous oxide and menthol, cool and clean and reeking of hygiene. He lifted his head, his eyes grew wide, then wider as they rose high and then higher along the smooth white skin of a cylindrical body that towered up and up, ten stories of liquid hydrogen and oxygen, plumbing and wiring, finally arriving at the point of the matter, the tapering nose cone bearing its payload, a virtual explosion, the concept and the horror of a city disintegrating in three dimensional filmic glory. Quick, what is it? A missile? Correct. Fissile? You bet. He heard a hum inside, the missile vented steam. Had he disturbed its trigger mechanism? Was it going to go off? He turned to run, but something held him back, a strange magnetic pull. He stretched out his hands, placed them against the missile's metal skin, it felt so smooth, so cool, and the way it glowed, so luminous and white.

Yes, Erde, touch me, feel me, see how smooth my pelt.

Erde fell ackwards on his bass. Was it his imagination or had the missile actually spoken to him?

You can't imagine what it's like, Erde, the voice continued in a slightly falsetto, slightly sibilant whine. I've been waiting so long for one like you to come and set me free.

Erde cowered on his hands and knees. What do you mean, one such as me?

The voice turned coy. Oh, I don't know. Perhaps you wouldn't understand. It's just that I feel so . . . useless. Ohh, yesss, the deterrent factor. I know all about that. But it's such a slow game to play. It requires such cunning, such patience. How I'd love to just let go, to blast up into the ether on a plume of smoke and flame and breathe for one moment that rarefied air. Oh, those valorous souls who have sought God in rockets, shot themselves into space in tiny capsules, madmen all! How I would love to be one of them, for a few moments, anyway, before I began my descent, plummeted earthward again like God's own fist, smashing into some town or city, immolating myself and thousands and possibly even millions of others in a blossoming firestorm that roars over the earth, boiling rivers into dust, consuming forests and plains and turning vast continents into ash. How absolutely liberating! What catharsis! You can't begin to understand, Erde. For the poet, for the artist, every work, every attempt at recreating God's creation is a heartbreaking failure. Imagine, the absurdity, the presumption of mastering the omnipotent technique. But chaos and destruction! Sweet Lord, nothing tastes so much of success as does destruction. It doesn't have to be perfect to give you satisfaction. It only has to undo what has been done. To break the will and curb the spirit of whatever calls itself human. Please, Erde, when you go back above won't you petition your lords and masters for my cause? Surely you would like to return the kindness you have received at their hands?

In the powdery green light Erde felt the missile's hunger and its appetite. His lips curled into an evil grimace. His eyes gleamed with all the possibilities.

Come, Erde, the voice whispered in his ear. Let me hold you in my embrace. Let me share with you my warmth. He couldn't help himself. It seemed so modern, so good. He caressed the missile's skin, kissed and licked the metal fins. Plutonium atoms swarmed around his head. He felt drunk, drugged. Come, Erde, the voice said again. Come inside. If you press my button I'll take you for a ride.

Sweat streaked Erde's dirty face. He was on the verge of yielding when a light came on in his brain, a twenty watt bulb of reason. No! He shrank back in horror. I can't! I'll be damned forever.

Enough! the voice said, sonorous and deep, God and machine. Remember your destiny. It flows in your veins like the icy waters beneath the poles. Rise up, oh man, nation against nation. Hurl your bloody fists across the seas. One race destroy another until all are consumed. Only then shall you rise from the ashes of your own immolation. Fly Phoenix, upon newborn wings, no longer what you were, nor man, nor beast, but some element of God cleansed by fire, slipping among the stars in your new-found skin, satin-sheathed, messengers of truth and light, a race of perfect beings.

Liar! Erde cried. You offer us not life, but death. Not angels soaring unencumbered through the twilit universe, but minions of darkness, universally despised, our souls wraiths howling through eternity to haunt and torment those who yet live.

Oh Erde, please, enough of this horrible drivel. How can you defend this humankind who have despised you, forced you down here into this world of darkness? Do you think they think so much of you? From deep within the missile's metal skin he heard a rumbling, like the starting of its giant engines.

No! he cried. Please, not yet! But it wasn't the rocket motors firing up, it was laughter, the missile was mocking him. Humbled, horrified, he fell to his knees, crawled back along his worm trail, regurgitating every curie and crumb of contamination he'd ingested during his brief fling with the machine, leaving the walls of his tunnel glistening like the track of a slug on the back steps in the morning. Sick with fear and nausea, trembling with a strange, metallic chill that ached deep in his bones, he dug on, exhausted, until he couldn't dig any more. He sat and rocked on his heels in a dark little cavity in the earth. If only he had someone to hug him and hold him tight and tell him everything was going to be alright. But the missile was right, he was an outcast. Forget about life and humanity. Forget about going back up. He was down here for good. He'd made his covenant with God, the devil, whoever or whatever governed the underworld. He'd just stay down here forever, a monk, a hermit, an anchorite, and the hell with everybody else. But for all his bravado he finished his vow behind a veil of tears. The hot brine streaked his dirty face. How had he sunk from such happy innocence and hope for a better life to come to this wretched existence in darkness and gloom? It was true. He was a monster, a beast. He raised his eyes heavenward, every ounce of energy inside him devoted to a silent but fervent prayer for forgiveness, redemption. No angels' trumpets blared. No all-knowing voice spoke to him with reassuring words. In the bowels of the earth the darkness waited for him like a lover. He dug deeper still, where even with his overdeveloped night sight he couldn't detect a single particle of light. And yet it still felt too bright. The light came from inside him, not just light, but life itself that simultaneously consumed and illuminated him, this urge to live, to breathe, to go on when there was no reason to go on. Better yet if he just quit altogether, if he lay still, allowed himself to die, relieved the world of one less monster. He closed his eyes, drew himself up into a fetal ball, ceased all movement, turned his thoughts inward, preparing himself for the slow process to come, the gradual shutting down of all the power plants and generators inside, all the streetlights, the water works and sewer lines, the public parks, trains, subways and commuters. He threw another switch, click, and blacked out the entire city. Click, another switch turned off all the lights of the world. Click, the sun. Click, the Milky Way. Click, all the stars in the heavens. Click, night. Click, nothing. Click.

Down and down he sank, enveloped in an amniotic sac of dwindling intelligence, collapsing backward through the gestation and conception of a thousand times a thousand generations, the devolution of planets, solar systems, galaxies. But instead of arriving at that perfect dot of India ink that marked the conclusion of his journey and the death of a universe, something strange happened. He found himself squeezing out of the asshole of a giant octopus, a big squid that had spread its tentacles across the dark sea of the cosmos, capturing and consuming everything in its path, swallowing and swallowing until it swallowed itself inside out, spewing the contents of its stomach in a spray of black ink and silvery fish scales that ballooned in the vacuum, forming the stars in the sky of a new universe with a thing called I its nucleus, godhead, a pathetic little voice generated out of nothing, speaking to no one about nothing. . . . I . . . I . . . I . . . What is it you wanted to say? . . . I . . . I . . . I . . . We thought you'd gone away! . . . I . . . I . . . I . . . Is it true you're here to stay? . . . I . . . I . . . I . . . What miracles have you planned for today? I-yi-yiii! But that was somebody else's dream or nightmare, wasn't it? Some poor schmuck lost in a parallel universe, he's pounding on the windows and doors, he's shouting, help! somebody! let me out!

Hoo, boy, he must've fallen asleep. What a crazy dream. Man, he hadn't slept like that in months. He opened his eyes, or his eyes had been open all along but now things were coming into focus. He blinked, then blinked again against the unnatural light come down alien and unfamiliar through a narrow fault or crack in the earth, penetrating first the canopy of trees, and then the moss and ferns and large gray boulders tossed aside by the passing of glaciers thousands upon thousands of years ago. But this wasn't any rundown rockpile or randomly strewn rubble he was gazing upon, but cut stone, huge blocks of marble, limestone and granite. He stood at the gates of a vast city. Before him stretched a wide cobblestone boulevard lined with stuccoed and mortared buildings bordered and shaded by tall cypresses and plane trees. What was this place? A city once of dreams? Of empire? Entombed by war? Catastrophe? Time? Everywhere he looked he saw bones, disconnected skulls piled on top of femurs and fibulas. Entire skeletons sprawled face down, prostrate, in the final act of obeisance, their lives devoid of all life and still devoted to some lord or master. His curiosity soon overcame his awe. He stumbled forward, apelike, but upright, no longer a worm, some creeping thing, but a man, or at least manlike in form.

At the next corner a fountain burbled into a shallow marble pool tiled with scenes of sea and hunt, brightly painted mosaics of finned and feathered fish and sea monsters, ferocious boar and bear and other plural nominatives. He looked down at himself, at his naked body. He was filthy, a real mess, he hadn't bathed in years. Without another moment's hesitation he waded in, splashing like a baby, smacking the water with the flat of his hand and sending his rubber duckies flying into the lap of a toweled skeletal attendant. He came out of his bath as squeaky and clean as a salamander. He took the towel from the attendant's phalanges. Another skeletal valet held a comb and a bottle of cologne. Ah, he felt better than he had in years. Munching on a handful of petrified barleycorn he found in a wicker basket sitting outside a small granary he strolled along. When he was thirsty he broke the seal on a gleaming black amphora painted with scenes of ancient warriors and maidens plying lyres and lances, drank his fill of four-thousand-year-old wine, aged beyond age, a nectar and ambrosia that bore the nose and bouquet not only of vintage and vintner, but the must of time itself dissolving into dust. Drunk, he staggered down the street, shouting and singing, stopping long enough to piss against a stucco wall plastered with bills and graffiti. Gluteus Maximus for Senator! I love Aphrodite, Adonis. At the end of the street he entered a large square peopled by great piles of bones. Bones lay everywhere, occipita and mandibles mixed up with tibias and phalanges, inferior maxillas heaped with scapulas and crapulas. In the middle of the plaza a sundial had stopped at 6:15, its shadow pointing straight ahead to a set of broad marble stairs.

In a trance he began to climb, at every landing he encountered skeletons kneeling, in the act of supplication. At the top rose a great temple. He passed through the columns and pillars, approached the throne. Scattered around it were the bones of ministers and priests adorned in purple robes, chokers and chains hammered out of silver and gold. He sat down on the royal seat, placed a crown studded with emeralds and sapphires upon his naked pate, heaped gold and diamonds in his lap like a child burying itself in the sand. I am Erde! he shouted, his voice echoing over the great square, ringing off the walls and cobblestones. Rise now! Sing praise to the lord of the underworld, Erde!

Slowly, dreamily, the city began to come to life, the bones began to reassemble themselves into whole skeletons, they were laughing and chattering, they were getting up a chorus, they were beginning to sing, Oh the funny bone's connected to the . . . lazy bone, the lazy bone's connected to the . . . crazy bone. By now they were all dancing and swaying to the big band strains of the Nile Orchestra, palm trees everywhere, leopard skins, waiters in tops hats and red sashes were bringing drinks, skeletal anorexic girls in skimpy outfits sold gum, cigarettes. Now the band was playing a rhumba, followed by a bossa nova, the tango, the music was getting livelier, crazier, the skeletons were putting on their party hats, forming a conga line. Boom-boomba-BOOM! Boom-boomba-BOOM! Skeletons in loincloths beat on hollow logs, grinning at Erde, inviting him to join in. A bevy of bones in grass skirts and feather boas led him down a long passage reeking of quick lime, formaldehyde and linseed oil, ah yes, that old bouquet. But he was intoxicated, his nose led him on, drawn by the essence, the redolence of wilted roses and calla lilies, of a dark and dusky beauty blooming in the night—the queen of darkness called to him, she waited for him now in her residence, a long low villa where she languished upon a black velour ottoman, her body robed in a burgundy gown. She was more beautiful than he had imagined. In the dim light her skin seemed soft and smooth, almost luminous. A river of dark, shining hair flowed around her bare shoulders. His face felt hot, his cheeks were flushed, his chest heaved, he felt an impulse he hadn't felt in years, call it lust or love. Whatever it was, it stirred another voice inside his brain, arguing reason, caution, self-restraint. Go, Erde! Go now! Forget her, as you have forgotten all the rest of your hopes and dreams. But he couldn't, not yet. If only she weren't so beautiful. He had to look upon her awhile longer, and awhile longer still, to fill up all the years of emptiness inside with her beauty and perfection. Surely she'll forgive me this brief intrusion. Surely she knows what forgiveness is. She lay so still, and yet she glowed with radiance and life. He could see in her a love of wildness, of night-storms and lightning, of the wind in her hair and lying down in dark glades with satyrs and centaurs, laughing and wanton. Is that why she was condemned to this eternal prison at such a young age? Had she been persecuted? Censored by ignorance? The stupidity of the world around her? There was a look of melancholy about her eyes. The word beatific came to his mind. Those soft, long lashes kissing her cheeks, and her skin so smooth, and the flare of her nostrils, and her eyes, those closed portals, couched in their soft pouches, with everything they had ever looked upon locked inside—maybe even the image of another man. But he must forgive her that too, if she could forgive him his indiscretion, for being here in her private chamber. If only he could stop staring at her face, her eyes, above all her eyes, the lids diaphanous curtains barely concealing those shards of starlight, those bits of stained glass and butterfly wing fluttering in darkness, in a perpetual dream. Was it possible they trembled ever so slightly? That some life remained or reawakened beneath? He knew he must turn away, that if he looked upon her another minute he would cause those eyes to open and she would see him for what he was, a horrible worm, shriveled and naked, come to devour her, to render her into infinitesimal bits of breathing and life and consciousness, and finally, nothing. Erde, Godgiver, Nirvana bringer, Valkyrie and angel. No, he was none of that. He was a monster. He'd heard it all his life, the word echoed after him in his tunnels of darkness and solitude all these years. Monster, monster, monster.

Please, he moaned, don't think that of me. I've never known any kindness, nor love. Creeping closer, closer creeping, he took her body in his arms. Her flesh felt so cool, so full and heavy. He plunged his trembling hand into the dark eddies of her hair, raised her head from the pillow. Her eyes had fallen open slightly, revealing opaque pools of moonlight. From her parted lips escaped the faintest

breath of decomposition, sunken mines. He was intoxicated, drunk with ardor. He knew it was a violation of some
law of man or God, he should flee, tear himself loose from
her grasp, crawl back the way he'd come. But he couldn't
help himself. He raised her mouth to his, tasted the cool-
ness and fullness of her lips. Then he was kissing her bare
throat, pushing aside the velvet folds of her gown and kissing her cold firm breasts, his tongue licked and flickered
around the clumsy sutures climbing like a trellis from the
dark furze of her pubis to the arches of her clavicles.

Oh, my poor darling, your poor wound. Don't be
ashamed, it matters not to me. Let me heal you with my
kisses, my caresses. We, the corrupt, the monstrous, abomi-
nations even in our own eyes. Still, we must touch someone
so we touch each other. Run our rotting fingers over open
sores, leaking pustules. We put our mouths to lips and la-
bia rotting from Venusian mounts and faces.

As the flames of desire rose inside him he felt a concur-
rent warmth rising inside her. Had he infused her with his
own desire? Erde, she whispered. Oh my sweet Erde, I've
waited for you so long. Her voice surrounded him like a
menthol cloud, filled his brain with susurrations. But it
wasn't her voice, was it Erde? Wretch, it was your own,
twisting and mutating itself into an obscene falsetto
parody of female melody and song, her body become a
ventriloquist's dummy with your hand the genius working
her dead jaws. Oh! that awful sound, the snap, snap, snap
of those dead teeth. And her dead eyes staring, piscine and
wide. Suddenly her passion terrified him, the way she
clung to him, enclosing him in her corrupt embrace. He
wallowed in rotting gravecloth, in the protoplasmic jelly
oozing out of ribcage and hip socket. She wouldn't let him
go. She was pulling him down, joining him in her death.

No! he cried, letting her flaccid body fall from his arms.

Vomiting up his horror and revulsion he turned and ran from her tomb, fled down dark corridors, pursued by the clattering of skeletons falling from doors and hallways with swords and spears raised. Plunging into a pile of manure he dug down madly, clawing at the raw earth, afraid to turn, to look over his shoulder and see her flying after him with a legion of skeletons, her shrouds whipping, flesh dripping from her body. He had an insane urge to broach the surface, to burst out of the ground whether in some farmer's cornfield or a busy city street, it didn't matter, he'd embrace the first human creature he saw, cry out, Please, I'm not dead, let me live among the living!

Wait, Erde, stop! What are you doing? You can't go up there. Look at yourself, at what you've become. Do you think anybody will let you hug them? Do you think they'll be glad to see you dragging a dead body behind you? And what are you going to tell them? Uh, hi folks, I, uh, that is to say, I left my wife on the subway, I was just going back down to retrieve her? And then the cops again, the dogs and guns. They'll hunt you down like an animal. He didn't care, he'd turn himself in, go to jail if he had to—just let me clear the record once and for all, serve my time and go on with the few years remaining in my life, just to be back among the living, to watch the sun set and rise one last time. The thought of the sun filled him with a terrible melancholy. He felt like a seed that had germinated and sent out a sprout that refused to broach the surface, that went on creeping and crawling, growing thinner and more etiolated all the time, without ever knowing what it was like to rise up and turn green and flower in the bright hot light.

He started to dig again, slowly at first, then faster and faster, it was starting to feel warmer now, he was starting to sweat. He didn't have a fever did he? Yes, of course, spring fever! After years of winter, spring must have ar-

rived at last. Up above the birds were singing. The grass
was green again and overhead the sun was shining. He dug
even harder and faster. The earth around him was suffused
with sunlight and warmth. Somewhere in the distance he
heard ukuleles playing, the rustling of palm trees swaying,
girls in grass skirts beckoned to him with flowered lais falling over their breasts. But something was wrong, surely he
should have reached the surface by now, he was digging
madly, furiously, rocks and stones flew past, it was like
driving down the highway behind a gravel truck, like driving coast to coast and back again in the middle of a screaming psychedelic acid trip, the radio blasting, skull pounding, belly sick from coffee and donut overdose, greasy
spoons, Mom and Pop's Twenty-Four Hour DINER blinking on and off in big red neon, Mom and Pop've got twenty-
four daughters, Horae of course, they're named 12 a.m., 1
a.m., all the way around the clock, they're earning their
bucks on their backs in some bedbuggy old brass-framed
mattress, oh baby, I like it when you do that, it ain't me,
hon, it's that cockroach crawling up the crack of your ass.
The earth split asunder before his eyes, skyscrapers
tumbled into his dark abyss, bridges and overpasses
crashed down, dumping screaming carloads of flailing
arms and legs, tectonic plates groaned and shrieked like
colliding ocean liners, flaming rivers of lava flowed past,
hissing and steaming like dark-age dragons. By now the
heat was almost unbearable. A solar wind blasted over
him, turning his face bronze in the fiery light, slitting his
eyelids, sweat streamed from his body. Still he struggled
on. The sun! I've got to see the sun! At the same time a distant fire alarm was merrily, madly clanging in his brain. A
loudspeaker was warning, You idiot, it's not the sun you're
digging for, but the core, the center of the earth. You'll be
consumed in flames. You'll perish. You have to stop now,

you must go back up. But he dug deeper and deeper, the little gyroscope in his brain spinning madly, determinedly out of control, its inertial will driving him down and down.

Just at that moment the floor fell out from under him. Tweety birds tweeted in his head, stars shined, bells clanged. He'd hit basement, plunged through the roof of the boiler room. Clouds of soot and steam. Hell, of course. Not a daunting allegory of hell, but a simple cartoon hades with a bunch of clowns running around in red flannel longjohns. They've got on devil masks, plastic horns and tails and all the other prerequisite accoutrements of the underworld. They're leaning on pitchforks, sipping brandy alexanders and puffing on cigars, it's the usual goofing-off-around-the-watercooler routine with a lot of satanic bullshit and bluster. Then our little devil Erdie comes crashing through the ceiling.

It's the boss! a goblin cried. The others immediately jumped to their feet, began shoveling coal into the furnace.

Hey! another one said. It's only Erde!

Erde! the others laughed, dropping their tools. They were cracking open six-packs, pouring whiskey and gin and lighting cigars off the tips of their horns. They were waving their pitchforks in the air and dancing in the flames, their eyes gleaming like oiled frying pans, their teeth shining like butcher knives.

Yikes! Erde turned and scrambled back up his tunnel with the pack of demons right behind him, he could feel them clawing at his ankles, raking his spine. A voice rumbled after him like a charge of dynamite in a coal mine. But the goblin's words were garbled. Did he say, You can't escape up there? Or, It's not safe up there? Instead of asking himself such stupid questions he should have been paying attention to his driving. The wall in front of him gave way with a roar, his body was enveloped in a great cloud of steam, he was tumbling in the cold rushing water of an underground stream that carried him up and up, mile after mile, sputtering and coughing and gasping for air, his lungs were on the verge of bursting, when, whoosh! He exploded from the water like a rocket, he was gulping great lungfuls of fresh air, gasping and drowning in pure ether. And the light, the light was so bright he couldn't see. But where was he? At the bottom of some well or cistern? Blinking away his tears and treading water he caught onto a clutch of roots, pulled himself up onto a narrow ledge. Collapsing on a bed of moss, he immediately sank into a deep and exhausted sleep.

He woke on his back, looking up at a small blue circle of sky with white puff clouds drifting over. Suddenly he heard again the laughter and derision, saw the leering faces crowded around the hole, remembered the shower of rotten eggs and tomatoes, gobs of spit, douche bags and used diapers. His immediate impulse was to do a swimmer's turn and dive back down. But something about that small blue aperture made him hesitate, a simultaneous sense of revulsion and sanctuary, like a leper returning to the sanitarium years after he'd been miraculously cleansed of his disease. There was a kind of security in it, a familiarity. Somewhere up above he heard birds singing. Around him there were green reeds and moss, growing, living things. Frogs chirred and croaked, fish swam by. The water was fresh and clear. Life could be good here, there were plenty of good things to eat. And that view of the sky. He could lie here and stare at it forever. He felt like a lotus eater who had stared into his belly button so long it had turned inside out and swallowed him, sucked him through a horror house ride of imagined monsters and mangled bodies and opened again like the petals of a flower upon a safe, friendly world of sunshine and blue sky. A moment later his reverie was fractured by another sound, human, someone singing, coming near. He ducked under the ledge just as a wooden bucket splashed down next to his head. Then he heard the voice again, female, he was sure of that now. And young, full of field and meadow and rocky green hills, with strong arms and legs, and laughter in her eyes and her strong white teeth. Probably some milkmaid or shepherdess. No doubt a half-wit, some inbred, bastard child, her father said yeah! and her mother said baaaa! and she dropped on her ass with a preference for grass, and a coat with a curly white nap. Oh, how awful. Lock her up in an institution. Chains. Padded cells. Keep her drugged, sedated. Once a year you stick candles in a gooey lump of birthday cake with a rye fescue icing, it's all yours, babe, eat away. Thirty, forty, fifty birthdays go by. By now she's this huge, gross creature. They would've turned her out to pasture if she wasn't such a money maker. Every spring they give her a good shearing, weave sweaters, blankets and tweeds out of her wool, for the tourist trade, you know. But are you still insisting on this guise, Erde? If you weren't such a cynical wretch you would have realized right away that she was a nice girl. Her voice sounded so melodious and full, even though the song she sang wasn't happy at all, in fact it was actually a very sad tale of far away lovers and pining souls. She was just pulling on a horned helmet and shield and launching into an aria when Erde sneezed.

Oh! the girl gasped. But she didn't seem afraid. She leaned over the well, her breasts squeezing out of her bodice as she called, Who is it? What are you doing down there? Erde peered out from under the ledge. He was terrified, he hadn't spoken to another living human being in years, and certainly not one so pretty.

Ah-choof! He sneezed again.

Who are you? The girl demanded. Answer me or I'll call the police.

Ummmm, he cleared his throat.

Why, it's a frog, the girl laughed. Humm, but a strange-sounding frog. Are you really a frog?

Well-ummm, not actually, he muttered, finding his voice at last. That is . . . umm . . . there was, humm . . . an accident . . . an errant chemistry experiment . . . in the Biology department . . . in the lab . . . just as I was about to perform a vivisection.

Hmmm, the girl pondered. And now I'm supposed to come down there and kiss you, right? And you'll turn into a PhD with management prospects at Burger Box?

Harroom! Erde bellowed. Nobody said anything about kissing! Besides, there's no reverse clause in my contract. A frog I am and a frog I shall remain for the rest of my life. I just have to make the best of it.

Oh my, how brave you are, Mister Frog, she repented. If only I could accept my fate with such stoicism. You see, my Tom is off in the war, and I haven't heard from him in so long, I'm afraid he's dead.

Harrummmmph, Erde grumphed, still trying to digest the Mister Frog appellation. Is that all that's bothering you?

I know it's not much, she apologized. Now she was starting to cry. Her tears dropped on his head, plink, plank, plonk. Soon it was a regular torrent, the water around him was turning salty, it was beginning to rise.

Oh, please, stop! he coughed. I'm sure your Tom's alive.

The rain let up for a moment. The girl's face brightened. Oh Mister Frog, do you really think so?

Of course he didn't think so. In fact, he was quite certain the young fool was dead, blown to pieces on some smoky battlefield in another one of those endless wars he heard rumbling overhead. But if he told her that she'd flip out completely, and this brainless wailing of hers was already driving him nuts.

Listen, lady, if you stop that horrible racket I'll help you find this hero of yours. But please, enough of this Mister Frog business.

Of course, Mister Frog, sir. But do you really mean it? You'll help me find my Tom? Her face clouded with doubt. But Mister, er, Sir Frog, I don't mean to question your abilities, but . . . how?

Howwwmmmm? he repeated. Howwmmm? Well, he could . . . that is, to put it briefly you see . . . by word of mouth, you understand . . . he might contact his frog friends all across the land . . . by way of water, that is. You know, lakes and rivers, channels, canals, sewers, swimming around in all that horrible shit, condoms, tampons, Colonel Corncob's Patented Hair Restorer and Cure for VD. That is to say, with a little luck and a lot of hard work, we'll find out what happened to your young man.

Christ, Erde, can't you ever shut up! What on earth were you telling her? Your frog friends? And who the hell might they be? Some renegade gang of amphibians? Newts, toads and salamanders? Is that the kind of company you want her to think you keep? What if this Tom fellow never shows up? She'll be broken-hearted and it'll be your fault. Probably get in trouble with the law too. Breach of promise or some rot like that. If you were a real man you'd do the honorable thing, run like hell, leave the little bitch to her fate.

Too late. She was laughing and jumping up and down with such bouncing, bubbling joy, one loose button or stay and this story was about to turn X-rated. Oh thank you, thank you, Doctor Frog. How can I ever repay you? Would you like me to bring you some flies?

Flies? Too phleabeian.

Or grasshoppers?

Unsettles the digestion.

What about grubs, mealworms, maggots?

I'd rather brown bag it.

Of course he'd dined on all the above at one time or another. But the truth is, he was hoping for a little more haute in his cuisine. At last the lass began to catch on. Since it was still early in the morning she decided a little breakfast was in order. After an interminable delay she lowered a basket laden with toast and marmalade, bacon, eggs and home fries, with a steaming cup of coffee and a tall glass of orange juice on the side. He'd barely had a bite before she started to pester him.

I know it's still early, Learned Frog, but have you heard anything from my Tom?

Nom yet, he grunted, picking a piece of bacon from his teeth with his fingernail.

For lunch he had fried chicken, potato salad and a fresh-baked cherry pie with a stein of lager to wash it down.

Any word this afternoon, Kind Frog?

Nom yet, he said, chomping on a thigh. But I expect— yum—to hear something soon.

For dinner she brought a pot roast, mashed potatoes and gravy and a bottle of stout.

Hey! he called up the well. Bring me a napkin! And another piece of pie. And some coffee, and make it fresh this time. And don't you have any brandy?

You sure are a strange frog, Mister Frog, the girl muttered, lowering the bucket with his requests. Haven't you heard anything of my Tom yet? If he's alive why doesn't he come home?

Ummm . . . Erde said, stalling for time. Maybe something's happened to him, he can't contact you, he's afraid.

But why should he be afraid to see me? I'd do anything to have him back, no matter what's he's done.

But what if something's been done to him? What if he's lost an eye or a limb?

Oh, but that doesn't matter, Mister Frog, I'd still love him.

Wellummm, he muttered, I'll get back to you tomorrow.

Soon she was coming to the well all the time. She'd already used up a year's rations, now she was pilfering old Auntie Asparagus' fruit cellar at night. At least she didn't seem quite so melancholy anymore. She'd even stopped asking about Tom so often. Erde started to think she'd grown fond of her Mister Frog, or Froggie, as she sometimes called him. Whenever he opened a bottle of wine he always sent her up the first glass by way of the windlass. Sometimes he'd send along a water lily or hyacinth. One day as they were finishing a magnum of champagne she leaned over the well and said, You could just hop in the bucket and I'd pull you up, Frog. Wouldn't you like to feel the sun on your skin? It must feel so smooth and cool, your skin. I could dry you off with a nice soft towel, and rub you with oils and creams.

Erde's chest heaved. He felt warm and trembly inside. At last, the moment he had dreamed of. But her intimate tone frightened him, that single sultry syllable, Frog. In a flash he saw himself as she would. Hairless, naked, an amphibious sort of thing. In other words, a monster. But if she could love a frog, or at least the voice of a frog, maybe she could love the creature who supplied that voice. Besides, it'd been so long since he'd held a real live woman in his arms, put his mouth to hers, felt the warmth coursing through her body, her breasts, her thighs. But what was he thinking? Why go on deluding himself like this? If she saw him she'd scream, she'd lose her mind. Then it'd be the authorities again with guns and dogs. Besides, she didn't love him. She was only lonely.

Poor Erde. His dilemma was decided without him. He heard the sound of heavy boots crunching up the gravel drive, and then the girl's voice, laughing, hysterical, crying.

Tom! Oh Tom! I thought you'd never come. I thought you'd been killed!

And the young man's voice, I thought you'd given up hope. I thought you'd forgotten me by now and found another man. He sounded tired, worn out, like he'd been walking a very long time. He tried to explain. The battle had been raging for months. Somehow he got separated from his platoon. He thought they were all dead. He tried to find his way back behind enemy lines but everything was destroyed. There were no landmarks, no trees or houses. Everything was gray, mud, smoking craters. The air was filled with the stench of rotting meat. He had no idea who was winning. He couldn't even remember who he was fighting anymore. At night he lay under the canopy of stars, the first clear night in months. And there was a kind of calm, a tranquillity he hadn't felt in such a long time. And then—he could've sworn—he heard a voice. He thought he was dreaming. It was such a strange voice, a sad, deep voice. It said, What are you doing here, Tom? Why don't you go home, see if you still remember what love is. And he just got up and walked away from the war and came home. He didn't care if she despised him, if she'd taken another man. He had to see her once more.

Then there was a lot of mushy stuff, osculations and postulations underscored and duly enforced by contractual agreements of eternal love. At the bottom of the well Erde spat something bitter from his mouth, a dragonfly or mosquito. Hmmph, just like that, goodbye Frog and hello Tom.

He was just about to swim down when he heard the girl's voice again.

Come with me, Tom. There's someone I want you to meet. It's my dear old Mister Frog.

Mister Frog? Tom sounded skeptical.

I know it sounds crazy, Tom, but it's true. He lives down the well. It was he who made me believe you were still alive, he who brought you home. Hey! Mister Frog! she shouted down the well. Come out and meet my Tom who's come home at last.

Ohh noo, Erde groaned. I hate formalities. But he couldn't help himself. He had to have one last glimpse of that beautiful face.

Oh! the girl gasped.

What is it? said Tom.

I don't know. I thought I saw a monster. I guess it was just my own reflection in the water. I wonder what could have happened to Mister Frog?

By then he was well on his way again, swimming back down along the underground stream, searching for a likely port or harbor to lay anchor, to tie himself back to land, to find a dim little bar or tavern to drown his sorrows in, to bend whatever ear he might encounter with his tired old fairy tale of love, the milkmaid and Mister Frog. Yeah, yeah, yeah, I heard it all before, save it for somebody else, sap. Hmmph, Mister Frog indeed. And wasn't that a nice little goodbye she gave you. Monster. And if her good Tom only knew how close I came. Who'd be calling whom monster then? Ah well, thank God that episode's over. It's too goddamn hard being nice all the time.

But it was no use. For all his posturing and putting on a gruff demeanor the brief encounter with the young lass had left him feeling hollow and sad. For a month he sat on an underground island in the stream with his chin in his hands and his elbows on his knees, pondering his next move. How fortunate those unfortunate soldiers abandoned by time and shifting alliances, not knowing the war had ended twenty-five, thirty years ago, they went on hiding on their tropical isles, hoarding their few corroding bullets to shoot at an advancing enemy who never came. But at least they had the sea at their door and the jungle on fire with parrots and bromeliads, and the chattering of monkeys in the trees to remind them of the society back home. Maybe even an occasional glimpse of another human being, some native boy or girl paddling by in an outrigger canoe. The truth is, this island idyll was getting to be a drag. He was sick of eating blind fish. His skin had taken on a decided fungal tinge. And the amenities! No guided tours. No coconuts. No bare-breasted native girls. Not even a decent radio station. All AM, the same poopular pop tunes—I mean, the same popular poop tunes over and over again, DJs yakking incessantly, mindless recitations of the news.

Oh yes, the news, the news, even down here we get the news. Don't ask me how. It trickles and seeps down through the earth like some horrible disease, teeming with all those poisons and carcinogens that wash down in the rivers and streams. It was so quiet at first when I turned off the TV. But then I started to hear them again, the voices in my head, newsmen, anchorwomen, news, news, news. I shut off the radio. Ahh, silence again. But it didn't last long. Sirens, explosions, traffic in the streets, screams, bombs going off, guns. You see, you can't ignore them. All those horrible things going on up there. They happen whether you like it or not. They encroach upon your fragile little existence. You can't hide. They'll come to you, plug you in again, they'll use the most subtle, insidious means. Knock, knock. Hello, Mister Erde? John Q. Republic here.

Mind if I take a few moments of your precious time to ask some questions vital to the national welfare? Of course you don't, Mr. Erde. Now then, answer each question as quickly as you can, without thinking about it, you see? Ready? Let's go. What kind of breakfast cereal do you eat?

Um . . .

Who'd you vote for in the last election?

Uh . . .

What's your favorite TV program?

I . . .

Whataya mean you don't watch TV? Everybody watches TV. You don't? You're sure? We'll fix that. Head-screws, braces and racks, you wake up eyeball to eyeball with a brand new sixty inch, super panoramic instamatic, lights and cameras, soap opera addict, colored TV screen, electrodes in your brain, IV tubes feeding a highly volatile mix of LSD, sodium pentathol, glucose and adrenaline directly into your veins, they've got you plugged in twenty-four hours a day, seven days a week for the next six months, they're giving you a megaboost of pilots, summer reruns, soap operas, sports specials, sitcoms, morning, afternoon and evening news breaks. Now, Erde, tell us, what kind of breakfast cereal do you eat? What's your favorite program on TV? Who ya gonna vote for in November? See what I mean? They've got you back in the groove again, unemployment, the economy, the war, don't ask me which war, there's always a war. You should be up there fighting like a man, do your part for the country.

Well, I suppose I could made flapjacks. Or eggs and sausage, biscuits and gravy.

What the fuck are you talking about?

Breakfast, of course. Or dinner, or lunch, brunch, hors d'oeuvres. Open a soup kitchen, an inn for weary travelers, divide up a can of tuna fish and a loaf of white bread and feed the multitudes of mindless, the soulless and re-soled, all the damaged, lost, injured sojourners of the planet.

Aww, quit it, you're breaking my heart.

Finally one morning—it must have been a Friday—he came upon a set of tracks that circled round and round the island. He followed them for hours until he began to suspect that it was not he who was following them but they who followed him, he started to run but as his stride grew longer so did that of his pursuer. It's after me! he screamed to no one in particular. Panting, exhausted, he fell down in the sand, lay there waiting for the monster to overtake him. But nothing happened. The air was perfectly still. The only sound he heard was that of his own breathing. Suddenly it was upon him. Erde, it's you—I mean, it's me. All this time you've been chasing your own tail like a canine or chimera. You really have been down here way too long. You've lost your mind. You need a vacation from your vacation. You really should go up now, back among your own kind.

Always a man of action Erde splashed back into the roiling waters, swam on again with the purpose and determination of a bloodhound, putting his trust in his nose, following storm sewers, drain pipes, underground steam ducts and utility tunnels, sniffing out the bouquet and aroma of civilization, wherever people congregate, make noise, the lights and sounds of the city, the laughter and music of twenty-four hour juke joints, bars and taverns and nightclubs, pawn shops, peep shows, pimps and prostitutes, pin balls, pool halls, street preachers converting the lunatic, the crazy, the drunk and lazy, the uninformed, deformed and hazy, Yas yas yas, brothers and sisters, join the parade! And for employment, give them tin cups, pens and pencils and government manuals on how to masturbate with a prosthesis, alright, Ace, you're on your own now,

we'll be back in a year or two to see how you're coming.
Street musicians with drums and guitars and saxophones,
banging and twanging and HONKing, it was all pouring
down his hole, that syncopated beat, that bop, that be-bop,
Bam! He was back in the city again, and oh dear God, he
was so excited, he was thumbing through the entertain-
ment pages, theater listings, nightclubs, comedy acts,
maybe he could get his old gig going at Hep's Downstairs.
As soon as I get in I'll get a room at the Hi-Tone, shower
and shave and call Leo, maybe meet at the Ritz for a bite to
eat.

Yeah, but Erde . . .

Erde, merda, that little schmuck doesn't exist anymore.

He was on a roll. Ready for the big time. Poor fool. Of
course it was all a dream, a fabrication of his addled brain.
He was completely deluded. It was all those good smells
wafting in the air, roasted chestnuts, baked yams, candy
canes in their little cellophane wrappers, hot soft pretzels.
It's winter again, snow's drifting down, winter wonderland
and all that Christmas fairyland stuff. He stood outside
the window of a downtown restaurant. It's all lit up inside
with a warm yellow light, crowded tables, waiters carrying
silver platters and trays, while a string quartet played and
flames leapt and danced in the fireplace, in the chande-
liers, off the mahogany and oak railings and banisters, everything hung with holly and mistletoe, red berries and silver tinsel, lights and ornaments and a little choo choo
chugging around a dark green tree—even through the
glass he could smell the turpentine pungence of dark forests where little elves tapped their toy hammers on tiny
shoes. At a table near the window a huge, manlike creature
bulged out of a suit and tie, obviously a refugee from another fairy tale, the barnyard in rebellion, the failed coup,
his accomplices turned into chicken and dumplings, leg of

mutton, beef stew, a master of disguise he's managed to pass himself off as a local citizen, with his skull boiled and scraped clean of all hair, and his pointy ears and narrow eyes hidden behind dark glasses, and that fat fleshy mouth sagging among folds of yellow wax, relentless in his eating, dipping thumb and forefinger into steaming silver boats and tureens, plucking out the delicacies, sucking gleaming eyeballs and genitalia into his gaping mouth like stewed prunes, smacking and slopping his lips over every morsel and bite. Oh, and look, here's Donald the doorman in gold tassels and brass buttons, Good evening, sir, howdy do, ma'am? And who are you? Erde, you say? Do you have a reservation, Mister Merda? Credit cards? Political connec- tions? So sorry then, but you can't come in. Meanwhile, he's holding the door for a procession of ghosts—what else can they be but ghosts, they certainly come from another world than you, n'est-ce pas, Erde? The faces of ghosts floating above tuxedos and gowns woven out of memory or dream, the bodies of ghosts exhumed from the silver screen. He smelled something sweet, a scent out of place, a fragrance out of time, lilacs, roses, the faintest mist and intimation of spring squeezed from a cut glass atomizer by a long and delicate female hand, he heard a car door slam, the deep solid thud of heavy gauge steel built by rough, worn hands, he saw a wisp of silk dissolving into the gray air, the faint- est shades of pink and lavender, charcoal and flesh-colored pastel on gray construction board. He heard a tinkling, jin- gling sound, not breaking glass or tire chains swinging, not Santy's sleigh and eight tiny reindeer rising across the vio- let winter sky, but the sounds of a caravanserai, of camels and mules crossing deserts and mountain passes, horses and jackasses laden with gold and silver, bearing rings and bracelets to lords and ladies in ruffles and lace, silk and satin cummerbunds and ascots. He'd stepped backward or forward in time, entered or re-entered the age of prosperity, p-p-p-postmodernity, Remember, boys and girls, only five shopping days left till Christmas, Buy! Buy! Bye!

Look, there's the Salvation Army Santa, standing outside Lacy's Department Store, ringing his bell every time he farts, peeing down his pant leg, he's got a bottle of high octane dreck in his merry red coat pocket, yellow stains on his teeth, his beard, his eyes are bloodshot, jaundiced, he's so fucked up and out of his mind he doesn't even know where the hell he is, he's laughing and singing some ridiculous little tune, Happy trails to you, Rudolph the red-nosed reindeer stew, he's coughing up plehgm and talking to himself, it's alright now, Bill, we'll get through this one and then we'll head south, lie in the sun and munch on pineapples and coconuts. He's got his own dreams, see, his own vacation plans, and it doesn't have anything to do with the North Pole. It's a nice, warm place, blue skies, big smiley old father sun, fluffy white clouds drifting by, maybe he saw it in a coloring book when he was still a child, maybe somebody told him in Sunday school, yeah, yeah, the messiah, we know all about the messiah, don't we, boys and girls, we've got ten thousand messiahs sleeping over steam grates, habitating packing crates, a million more prophets and messiahs locked up in our prisons, drugs, stealing a loaf of bread, lying down on the sidewalk to sleep, to die, there's a law for every occasion. Poor old Bill's yakking his yak with a crisp new ten-spot in his red metal pot, a come-on to the Christmas crowds, a shill for the shillings. Santy's already lined his pockets with nickels, dimes and quarters, dead presidents, food stamps, IOUs, government vouchers and contributions from politicians' war chests, he's been funneling it all into a secret Swiss account, building up his retirement fund, he's so deluded with island dreams and grain alcohol he doesn't even notice the sawbuck disappear from his pot, Erde's hand shoots out, and poof, he's got himself enough for a plate of fries and a bottle of port. He was just heading in the door of the Subway Cafe when he bumped into some old bag lady snuffling and fumbling with the coin return in a phone booth.

But hey, look, what's this? This old gal looks familiar. Why, it's old Sal, Erde's long lost sweetheart. What? I didn't tell you? Yeah, sure, they got separated in the war, during the social upheaval after. He hid out for weeks, then months and years, all the time thinking about her. Was she even alive? He'd always meant to come back and find her, see if she'd survived. After it was all over he sent letters, called agencies. Nobody knew nothin'. Better if you don't ask, a sour-looking man in the Department of Human Services and Other Unimportant Stuff advised. But he could never forget old Nell. Somewhere deep in the darkest recesses of his mind he carried with him a dim image, a mental photograph, in fact, maybe it was just a picture he'd seen in a magazine, a young woman in faded denim and red bandana who fought for her cause and believed in her rights, with eyes gleaming like the sun on the sea, and the wind whipping her hair like a torn banner of freedom. And now, look, here she is, the love of your life. Boy, but she doesn't look so good these days. She's standing over a steam vent trying to get warm, maybe she's just taking a leak. She's got on about twenty layers of skirts, shirts, jackets and sweaters. She's got on sweatshirts, overcoats and dresses, two scarves, four hats, and a Japanese kimono, but she's still sniffling and snuffling and whimpering to herself, she's cold, shivering, she looks feverish, wasted. Hey, Sally! It's me, Erde! He searched her eyes for some sign of recognition, but all he saw was the dying light of submission. Look, he said, sticking the purloined Hamilton in her hand, I've gotta go now, find a job, try to make some money.

Hold on, OK? I'll come back for you, I promise.

Now what? He was penniless again, without a friend. And truth be told, his job prospects looked pretty dim. No resume, curriculum vitae. No car, phone, suit and tie. And to think, we could've bought ourselves a little drink with that double nickel you gave away, a bottle of anti-freeze for the long night ahead. Weatherman says it's gonna be the coldest night in the city's history. Is that right? Yessir, I heard it on the news today.

He was so caught up in his little meteorological concerns he wasn't watching where the hell he was going, he almost stepped off the subway platform, yeah, right there at the old Ave. F station. Turnstiles all busted up. Ticket booth's rotted and mil-be-dung, a public hazard, hangout of winos and derelicts, ex-government employees on the dole. Smells like catpiss, ratshit, shafts of light cutting down through the smoke and haze of smoldering debris. But it's a grand old palace nevertheless, gleaming walnut and mahogany, porcelain and glass fixtures, with vaulted ceilings and fading frescoes of God investing life in various kitchen appliances.

He sat on a bench, its wooden curves and grain still polished and shining in the dim light. It felt nice here, calm, quiet, a place of tranquility, contemplation, a place where he could hang out and be at peace with himself. Maybe he'd already had one too many pulls on that bottle of booze he was dreaming of. Somewhere in the back of his mind he heard a voice, sonorous and deep, resonating out of the depths of the universe, vibrating the ancient PA system, echoing in the marble vaults, Train 46 arriving on track number 9! A second later a lighted commuter car roared and rattled past with half a dozen sad and lonely and beaten-down commuter faces staring blankly into the artificial night, into the fluoresent glare reflected in their crinkled newspapers, two dollar dime store novels, the work they shoulda finished in the office an hour or two hours ago, the work they still had to do tonight, you know, beat the kid, the wife. Haven't you figured it out yet, boy? You never get that shit done. You push and you shove, you get right up to the summit, when the boss drops another stack of papers on your desk, have this in my office at 8 a.m., got it? And wham! That great big boulder comes rolling back down again, flattens out your wimpy ass, the sis of mythyphus. Here's our boy Erde, magically transformed into a working stiff, in a wrinkled suit and tie, fourth row from the back, he's bent over a laptop, he's tapping on the keyboard and muttering to himself, Right, chief, sure thing, boss, first thing in the morning, sir or ma'am. Shit, now he's gonna miss the big game on TV, in fact, he's gotta stay up the whole fucking night just to get this shit done. Ah well, better quit griping and get back to work or we'll never finish. He turns the page, stares at another column of figures, those dirty little insects crawling over the screen, each hairy, multilegged bug represents so many thousands of employees, millions of dollars. He totes them all up again, prints a number at the bottom of the page, glances up from his work just as the woman across the aisle looks up from her dreary little gothic romance, sees him perched on the seat across from her like a fucking gargoyle, naked, slimey, caked with mud, he can see the horror registering on her face, her mouth beginning to tremble, trying to form the word, to scream, Monster! And then the train was gone, hurtling into the night with its desperate cargo, leaving him alone again, in the silence of the vacuum collapsing within.

Alone and not entirely alone. There was something else, he could hear it moving around him, a liquid, trickling sound, some kind of insects, infestation. Fingernails scraped the dirty black and white parquet, the weak watery gleam of barely human eyes detached themselves from the darkness, female faces with mewling black cocoons folded under their verminous black wings, stringy, malignant male arms poked out of fluidless black sacs with tiny yellow flames flickering deep in their eye sockets, the army of the night, the secret insectoid survivors of urban blight, tax roles, welfare doles, all that worthless bureaucratic sewage and cess trickling down upon their heads, Say, Erde, can you tell us, please, are the trains running on time? And what could he say? Sorry, folks, the train ain't never coming your way? But while you're waiting, why not have a bite to eat, it's on the house. Rising on their hands and knees, they dragged themselves toward a firelit corner where the last surviving sisters of the Merciful Order of Magdalen stood over a boiling kettle, stirring the bubbling yellow scum with great wooden spoons. Cackling, laughing the hags scraped the slime and pus from their arms, stirred it into the broth—a pinch of oregano, a dash of salt, and soup's on! Care for a taste, dearie? Taking the ladle from the crone's claw, Erde raised it steaming and sulfurous to his mouth. Ahhhh! he'd never tasted anything so good in his life, he was really spooning it down. Hey, you clown! Pass it around! What a selfish cad. Behind him the lines stretched to hell and back.

Revitalized from his repast he took up his journey again, tramped through a shooting gallery of used needles, broken glass crunched underfoot. At the next corner he came across an old wino sitting on the curb. Hey, buddy, where you been? the wino said, handing him a bottle. Do I know you? Erde asked. No, the wino replied, but I know you. Pretty soon they're passing the juice back and forth, talking like old friends, yeah, you know, the usual shit, jobs and no jobs, cops and social workers and punk kids with cans of gasoline. Erde says, I don't really belong down here. Wino says, Me neither, buddy. No, Erde says, I mean it. I could've been a doctor, a lawyer. I could've even had an honest profession, an iron worker building great bridges across the world's mighty rivers, a welder putting car doors on the assembly line in Detroit. How about a teacher? That's an honorable calling, isn't it? Teach the little angels all about everything. Our fore-farters who art in heaven, how Columbus and Pocahantas got married and had a bunch of little pickaninnies who grew up free and happy as long as they did what they were told and ate their shit for breakfast. If the little dears don't like it you whip them, beat them into submission. Oh, no no no, not with your belt. I don't mean that. We don't do that anymore, do we, Erde? No, of course not. We're up on the lastest pedagogical methodology. Reason with them, lie to them, use words like hope and the future, like truth and dignity. Oh, enough, enough. Can't we have done with this madness. Are you listening to me? No, the guy next to you's already caught his train, he's on the nod, on the run, on the voyage from here to there, across the Jordan, the Lethe, the river Styx. Yes yes yes, boys and girls, we're crossing that old Mississip on a makeshift raft. What the hell, the rest of the bottle's mine. Let's glug it all down. Paint the town. You're losing it again, Erde, babbling all kinds of nonsense. They'll strap you into a straight jacket, have you sedated, convince your family and friends you're insane, maybe we're all insane, they just pick random individuals off the street to fill their prisons, their asylums, their quota systems, c'mon mac, you're coming with us. But I haven't finished my coffee yet. Yeah, but that's just another bad dream, isn't it? The product of an impoverished sleep.

You wake a coupla hours later, cold, wet, hungover. Christ, somebody drop a goddamn brick on my head? A cop

shines a flashlight down at you. Get a move on, buddy. Oh
well, lift one foot in front of the other and keep on trudging.
You and the thousands and millions of other shadows and
shades, joining the underworld parade. Say, what's going
on, anyway? I don't remember it being so goddamned
crowded down here. What'd everybody do, take the freight
elevator down a story? And does that story, that short span
across time, explain how we got from there to here? Is it
the vehicle by which we've arrived, the words in other
words our chariot? Or simply a history of our ride? Oh
Erde, this interminable debate. You've been dragging your
past behind you so long, constantly embellishing, changing
and revising until it's gotten all twisted up in your mind. Is
life only a recurring dream or nightmare dredged up from
the strata and layers of your subconscious? A fable or fairy
tale you absorbed sitting on the lap of your monkey uncle
or your ancestral ant? All the lies we had to tell just to survive, and all those who died. Who has any humanity left?
What reason do we have to go on like this, depending on
the little holidays and celebrations, birthdays, weddings
and graduations, anniversaries, communions, baptisms,
deaths, assasinations, all these events to mark our passage
through space, crawling over the face of this earth with
such determination and purpose? Is it only fear of death
that's kept us going so long? You cease, and then what?
Will things change so much? You disintegrate into that
churning flurry, our siblings of the earth, beetles and lar-
vae, microbes and bacteria, tilling the soil with their mandibles and pincers, their claws, jaws and specialized pro-
boscises, infusing and secreting acids and enzymes and
detergents, they'll have us tilled up in no time, turned into
compost, humus, ready for spring planting. And that age-
old problem of the thing called I? No more. Subsumed by
we, they, the writhing mass of existence. For lack of a bet-

ter word call it God, call it eternity. Better still, call down to the deli, order us all a pizza. We'll need our strength for the struggle ahead. To the ramparts, boys and girls. Carpe diem.

Rio, dec '86 Austin, dec '95

DALKEY ARCHIVE PAPERBACK FICTION

Dalkey Archive Press, ISU Box 4241, Normal, IL 61790–4241

fax (309) 438–7422

Visit our website at www.cas.ilstu.edu/english/dalkey/dalkey.html